D0040817

Girl

IN DEVELOPMENT

Girl IN DEVELOPMENT

JORDAN ROTER

DUTTON BOOKS

DUTTON BOOKS

A division of Penguin Young Readers Group

Published by the Penguin Group

Penguin Group (USA) Inc., 375 Hudson Street, New York, New York 10014, U.S.A.

Penguin Group (Canada), 90 Eglinton Avenue East, Suite 700, Toronto, Ontario, Canada M4P 2Y3
(a division of Pearson Penguin Canada Inc.) • Penguin Books Ltd, 80 Strand, London WC2R 0RL,
England • Penguin Ireland, 25 St Stephen's Green, Dublin 2, Ireland (a division of Penguin Books Ltd) •
Penguin Group (Australia), 250 Camberwell Road, Camberwell, Victoria 3124, Australia (a division of
Pearson Australia Group Pty Ltd) • Penguin Books India Pvt Ltd, 11 Community Centre, Panchsheel Park,
New Delhi–110 017, India • Penguin Group (NZ), Cnr Airborne and Rosedale Roads, Albany, Auckland
1310, New Zealand (a division of Pearson New Zealand Ltd) • Penguin Books (South Africa) (Pty) Ltd,
24 Sturdee Avenue, Rosebank, Johannesburg 2196, South Africa •
Penguin Books Ltd, Registered Offices: 80 Strand, London WC2R 0RL, England

Library of Congress Cataloging-in-Publication Data

Roter, Jordan.

Girl in development / by Jordan Roter.—1st ed.

p. cm.

Summary: Kate, a bookish recent high-school graduate from Massachusetts, moves in with her cousin and
uncle in California in order to undertake an internship at a Hollywood production company.

ISBN 0-525-47690-3 (alk. paper)

[1. Motion picture industry—Fiction. 2. Self-perception—Fiction. 3. Internship programs—Fiction.
4. Cousins—Fiction. 5. Hollywood (Los Angeles, Calif.)—Fiction.] I. Title.

PZ7.R7253Gir 2006

[Fic]—dc22   2005029307

Published in the United States by Dutton Books,
a division of Penguin Young Readers Group
345 Hudson Street, New York, New York 10014
www.penguin.com/youngreaders

Designed by Irene Vandervoort

Printed in USA   First Edition

1 3 5 7 9 10 8 6 4 2

To Mom and Dad, with love

ACKNOWLEDGMENTS

This book could not have been written without the imaginative foresight and generous guidance of my Fairy God-Agent, Richard Abate. Thank you for being my Captain and for believing in me from the beginning. What were you thinking?! And thank you Kate Lee, you are such a fantastic friend and future super-agent.

Countless thanks to Stephanie Lurie, the truly benevolent Dutton Queen Bee, who took a chance on me. And to the extraordinary Julie Strauss-Gabel, the greatest editor-slash-friend a girl could ask for. Eternal thanks for your hard work, your tough love, your nothing-short-of-brilliant mind, your fantastic sense of humor, and the many suspenseful meals in which you waited until the bitter end to share your editorial comments. You had me at "Oy. No."

My girls: Each of you inspires me in your own unique way. It's enough to write a book about, and in many ways, that's what this is. The following is a short list of thank yous which, if nothing else, will prove that I should never EVER try to choose bridesmaids.

My LA big sisters Amanda, Randi, and Jenny (and their wonderful families) for taking me under their native Angeleno wings when I moved here (and Jenny, the original Mayor, you really did change my life "one party at a time").

Tracy, for the innumerable laughs, the invaluable advice, and the amazing artichokes.

Lizzy for our blissful hikes; you (and your unearthly fast metabolism) amaze me every day.

Maxi, Switzy, and JB: "GTs" do not even begin to describe our adventures together. You are all unequivocally "*adorable*."

Sara, Becky, and Dani, for being the first girls to teach me the true meaning of "B.F.F."

Anita, for the therapy. Seriously.

Judy, Marisa, Emma, Heather, Jordanna F., and Sophie for all the support and love.

And to Adriana: my rock and confidante, whatever would I do without you? It all started that fateful night you came in out of the cold to hang with the (seemingly) spoiled and (definitely not naturally) blond girl in the Saab convertible. Thank you for editing my college papers, for reading every sentence I write (including these acknowledgments in which you tried to cut down your *own* section . . . SNOK!), for the endless laughs, and the unconditional love. And most of all, thank you for your friendship.

To my entire family whose love and support travel 3,000 miles coast-to-coast on a constant basis (and suffer no jet lag). Particular thanks to:

My big brother, Josh, for still being able to make me laugh harder than anyone else can.

Cousin Jill (my idol), and Cousin Laura (my muse): SCF.

And to Mom and Dad, to whom this book is dedicated. I owe you everything, but all I can offer you is my love. And this book, of course.

Girl
IN DEVELOPMENT

CHAPTER ONE

ROB: *We move to sunny L.A.*
All of show business is out there, Max.

ALVY: *No, I cannot. You keep bringing it up,*
but I don't wanna live in a city where the only cultural advantage is
that you can make a right turn on a red light. —ANNIE HALL

"Don't do anything I wouldn't do," said Betty Rose to her daughter, Samantha.

At eighteen, Samantha Rose was the spitting image of her mother at that age: pale porcelain skin, jet-black hair, and wide, dark eyes. Sam knew her mother was only half-joking. She also knew that her mother was about to cry. Right in the middle of Boston's Logan Airport.

"Mo-om, please. We're in *public*," Sam whispered.

Sam rolled her eyes and batted her eyelashes, dreading the waterworks that were about to begin. To her horror, she watched as her mother fished around her large pocketbook until she came up with a handful of crumpled tissues, which she used to loudly blow her nose and dab her eyes. Arthur Rose smiled sympathetically, and put one arm around his wife, the other around his daughter.

"Oh now, Betty," he said. "And Samantha, you can't go rolling your eyes at people in Hollywood. They'll blacklist you!"

"Ha-ha," said Sam.

"That's right, it's not flattering. What if your eyes get stuck like that, then what?" asked Betty. "And you have your sunscreen?"

Sam wiggled out from her father's embrace. She was about to say "Because they don't have sunscreen in Los Angeles?" but saw the genuinely concerned expression on her mother's face and bit her tongue. Only, she actually *bit* her tongue. Now she would have a lisp for the next eight weeks. *Craptastic.*

"We're so proud of you, honey. You're gonna knock 'em dead out there in Hollywood," said Arthur.

"You're beautiful, sweetheart, and don't let anyone tell you differently," whimpered Betty. "But please don't wear that bright red lipstick; it's so unbecoming on you. It's just so . . . *extreme.*"

Sam put her hand in the pocket of her jean jacket and pawed her crimson lipstick. She smiled.

"Did we tell you how proud we are of you? What are you doing with your tongue?" asked Betty.

"Sorry, I think I bit it. I'm fine. Look guys, I love you both, I really do, but I think we should wrap this up."

A line was forming behind them including but not limited to an impatient man in a purple T-shirt that read LOVE ME OR EAT ME.

Arthur looked at his daughter. "Now just remember to be polite to your uncle and your cousin Kate," he said. "It was very generous of Uncle Norman to fly you to Los Angeles and get you an internship out there. Don't let him down, okay?"

"And don't forget to go to the Getty—they have a wonderful Impressionist collection. You always loved the Impressionists," said Betty.

"I know, Mom, but I'm only there for eight weeks, and I'll be working almost every day." Sam had heard all this before.

"Please don't come home with any new piercings or . . . what's that thing they're doing out there now, hen tattoos?"

"*Henna* tattoos, Dad. You know, they're not even permanent!"

"Samantha . . ."

"Okay, okay. No tattoos of any kind. Got it."

Betty took her daughter's hand. Actually, she *clawed* it as if she would never hold it again. "And try to read some good books while you're out there. Don't only read scripts—they will rot your mind."

Sam stopped answering. She was more anxious than the LOVE ME OR EAT ME man, who had his eye trained on the Cinnabon stand just beyond security. Sam had never traveled alone on an airplane before and hadn't been to Los Angeles since she was six. She had no memory of that trip, just a photograph of herself smiling toothlessly and clutching her jean skirt while standing on Marilyn Monroe's star on Hollywood Boulevard.

Sam gave her parents a final hug and walked into the chaos of airport security without looking back. She knew that if she saw her mother and father staring after her, she would cry. And that was unacceptable to Sam. Never let them see you cry. Anyone. Ever. This mantra had gotten her through four excruciatingly painful years of high school, and she had a feeling she would need it now more than ever. She put on her tough "game face," but inside she was terrified; her mind and heart were racing.

Sam would miss her parents, who, for better or worse, she also considered her best friends. She would miss Northampton, the Massachusetts town where she had grown up and had spent every other summer of her life. The internship at a Hollywood production company was a high school graduation present from her Uncle Norman because her father had haphazardly told him she liked movies. Perhaps Arthur Rose had expected his brother, Norman, to send Sam some VHS tapes (the Roses still did not own a DVD player). Instead, Uncle Norman had set up an internship at Authentic Pictures, a production company owned by one of his clients. Right now, Sam was wishing she could return it for a sweater. Something soft and black with a cowl neck, perhaps?

It's not that Sam didn't like movies. She did. And like any other eighteen-year-old girl, she was intrigued by Hollywood. But Sam's true passion was for literature. She was addicted to reading the classics the way other kids were addicted to eating Pop-Tarts. She craved the sweeping social panoramas of Charles Dickens's novels, Jane Austen's restrained yet passionate romances, the sharp cynicism of J. D. Salinger, the lyric prose of Virginia Woolf, the biting and irreverent wit of Dorothy Parker.

Sam had also learned to appreciate fashion by working part-time at Fine Vintage for the last three summers and during the school year. Fine Vintage was the coolest thrift store in Northampton, and where Sam learned to pair her vintage Chanel jacket with a punk rock T-shirt, cropped pants, and a vintage pump or boot. Sam loved playing dress-up in fabulous old Halston, Armani, and Valentino dresses. It was lucky that Sam's taste was always for vintage (and that she received a generous employee discount), because her designer habit could never be supported by her parents, who were both professors at Smith.

"Can you put your jacket in the tray, please?"

Masquerading as a question, it was really a demand from the sweaty security guard with half a Chee•to stuck in his thick mustache. Sam winced. She hated being ordered around. But she did as she was told. She grabbed her belongings as the boarding of her plane was announced. This was it, no turning back now.

After boarding the plane and settling into her window seat, Sam applied several coats of red Stila lipstick followed by cherry-flavored Lip Smackers gloss from Rite Aid: designer meets ghetto. She pulled out her dog-eared copy of *Jane Eyre* and tried to read. But she was too nervous. She checked out the goods in the seat pocket like it was a gift bag at the Oscars: *In-Flight* magazine, safety card, air sickness bag.

"You can tell that *Hollywood Squares* has-been he can kiss my ass!"

Sam looked up to see a strange man yelling into his cell phone, tugging at his tie and walking down the aisle like he owned the plane. From what she could tell, he was wearing way too much hair gel and was primped within an inch of his life, right down to the loosened Hermés tie, baby blue and pink button-down, and Armani suit. She suspected his eyebrows had just been waxed. He must be the metrosexual poster boy, she thought. Ugh, eight weeks of this.

"I'm in *coach*! Can you believe that? My assistant is so fired when I get back."

Mr. Cell Phone (as Sam had come to think of him) opened the overhead compartment and shoved the contents to the back while still talking on the phone. Sam heard her bag being crushed under the weight of his compact rolling duffel. He reeked of cologne. Eau de Jerk, perhaps? Whatever it was, he must have used a fire hose to put it on.

Just then, the flight attendant announced that all electrical items must be turned off for departure. But this warning didn't seem to affect Mr. Cell Phone. Sam wondered if he would ever shut up. She worried that the plane would crash because this guy wouldn't turn off his phone, which was definitely *not* a flight-approved electrical item. She was feeling sick to her stomach. It had been a while since she'd been on a plane, and she had simply chosen to forget how nervous (not to mention nauseated) it made her. Maybe it was the overpoweringly pungent scent of Mr. Cell Phone's cologne? The plane lurched forward. *Eight weeks.* Had she made a huge mistake? Could she still get off the plane? Knowing her parents, they were still in the airport, waiting to watch her plane take off. Her sweet parents. Her lovely town of Northampton. The plane was moving and Mr. Cell Phone kept talking like it was the last phone call he was ever going to make.

Sam's stomach started doing somersaults, and she felt a bitter taste rising from the back of her throat. She reached for her air sickness bag like it was a life raft, but it was too late. Just as the wheels of the plane lifted off the ground, she vomited right on Mr. Cell Phone. And, finally, he stopped talking.

CHAPTER TWO

*The companions of our childhood always possess a certain power
over our minds which hardly any later friend can obtain.*
—MARY SHELLEY, *Frankenstein*

"And this is Marcy vomiting after her third keg stand," said Kate.

It was noon, the sun was shining over a smoggy Los Angeles, and Kate Rose was sitting by the pool at her father's house in Beverly Hills. She was wearing her favorite black-and-gold-beaded bikini, proudly showing Tatiana and Dylan the photo highlights of her freshman year at the University of Michigan.

"*Ewwww,*" squealed Tatiana.

"That's DISGUSTING! I LOVE it, K-Ro!" said Dylan.

"Puking from drinking is soooo 2003," said Tatiana. "Straight edge is totally in right now."

Tatiana slid her red kabbalah string bracelet along her wrist to avoid getting a tan line, while Dylan reapplied her sunscreen and dipped her pudgy toes in the pool.

"Oh wait, here's me trying to do a keg stand. Colby Carter was holding it for me." Kate stroked the photo as if it were Colby himself.

"I can't believe you're drinking beer now," said Tatiana. "You were always such a wino!"

"T, I'm in college—that's what I'm supposed to do. It's like in the college handbook. And a raspberry Bartles & Jaymes in a brown paper Bloomies bag does not a wino make."

"I love raspberry *anything*. DELICIOUS!" said Dylan.

"GTs, girls: Good Times," said Kate.

Kate smiled to herself. She'd missed her old friends. The threesome had known one another their whole lives. At Harvard-Westlake, the elite private school in Los Angeles, the girls had ruled the school. Together, they had everything: Kate was the brains, Tatiana was the beauty, and Dylan was the benevolent bohemian. But a lot had changed during their first year apart. Kate, accustomed to being the leader of her group (and of her high school domain), had had a disappointing freshman year of college. She had joined a sorority from which she promptly deactivated because she didn't like being told with whom she should and shouldn't be friends. She'd lost her virginity to Colby Carter—a callous young hipster—who then promptly broke up with her. Worst of all, she had gained the obligatory "freshman fifteen."

Tatiana spent the year trying to make it as an actress or—as she liked to say—pounding the pavement. She thought this terminology gave her some "street cred." But unlike most actresses in Los Angeles, Tatiana's father was Howard Ford, the famous actor. So her notion of pounding the pavement was simply appropriating his agent, manager, and publicist, and living in his mansion in Bel-Air. In the past year, she had landed several guest spots on the WB, not to mention a small role in one of her father's movies. The chatter in Hollywood was that Tatiana was the next "It" girl.

Dylan, by contrast, was less Hollywood, more rock 'n' roll. A total party girl and hopeless hypochondriac, Dylan was enthusiastic, dramatic, silly, and self-deprecating. She was now going through a Beverly Hills-meets-bohemian-chic phase after spending her freshman year at UCLA. For Dylan, this meant dying her hair brown (she had sun-kissed blond highlights in high school), putting a FREE TIBET sticker on her forest green hybrid SUV, and wearing lots of very expensive bracelets and long skirts that were made to look decidedly threadbare (Dylan had been warned that the skirts *might* spontaneously combust if they were to come within ten inches of a flame, but she liked to live on the edge).

"¡Kate-ita! Es tu padre!"

Manuela Rodriguez came running out of the house with cordless phone in hand. Manuela had been working for the Rose family for fifteen years. Truth be told, Manuela was a terrible maid. She couldn't cook and was convinced that she couldn't learn, so she refused to try. The Rose family never complained.

They'd grown to rely on Manuela for so much, and she knew everything about them. She knew when Kate was briefly experimenting with cigarettes in high school; she knew when Kate snuck out and when she had boys over. She also was the first to know when Kate's father started sleeping on the couch, and when Kate's parents finally separated three years ago. But Manuela was a vault. And she was the only one who didn't take any attitude from Kate, who respected and appreciated Manuela as an authority figure, a surrogate mother, and a friend.

Manuela had basically raised Kate. For years, Manuela picked up prepared food from Whole Foods, Gelson's, or some other gourmet market, and the two would feast at the kitchen table together while watching *Friends* reruns. Kate would complain to Manuela that she was a "latchkey kid" because her parents were never home (although as she grew up, she began to appreciate and take advantage of their absence).

"Ugh. What does *he* want?" Kate asked. In a different, more reverent voice, she looked to her old companion, took the phone from her, and graciously said, "*Gracias*, Manuela."

"*De nada, Kate-ita.*"

With an affectionate tap on Kate's head, Manuela turned back toward the house.

"Hello?"

"Hi, Kate, it's Alice. Hold on for your father."

Kate hated when her father had his assistant roll his calls to her. She knew that this was the Hollywood way, but really, how hard was it to pick up the phone and dial your own daughter?

"Thanks, Alice." Kate rolled her eyes at her friends. "I'm on hold. This is SO annoying."

"At least your father calls you!" said Dylan. "I haven't heard from my father in a month. I don't even know where he is!"

Dylan's father was a music mogul, but he was not always a mogul father. Her parents never actually married. Bill Themopoulos fell in love with Dylan's mother during a business trip to Los Angeles from New York (where he lived with his wife and two children). Dylan's mom, Natalia, was a dancer in one of his client's shows at the time, and their affair ended in baby Dylan. Bill never left his wife and family in New York, but he did stay in touch with Dylan, whom he adored. He supported them financially. "Blood money," Dylan called it. She often lamented that she had never met her half-brother and half-sister though she Googled them from time to time. But Dylan loved her father unconditionally.

"Hi, honey," said Norman.

"Nice new hold music, Norman." Kate knew her father hated it when she called him by his first name. "I actually *felt* like I was in an elevator, it was *that* boring and monotonous."

"Kate. You've been home for two days. Cut me a little slack, will you?"

"How would you know I've been home for two days? Have you seen me?"

14

"Kate, I'm sorry we've been missing each other. I just wanted to remind you to pick up your cousin at the airport today. Alice faxed over all her flight information."

"Can't we just send a car for her? It's bad enough that I have to share the guest room with her. Oh, wait, let me back up, *beep beep beep*: it's bad enough that I have to stay in the guest room at my own house, but it's downright tragic that I have to share it with my country bumpkin cousin whom I haven't seen in, like, forever!"

"Kate, we've talked about this already. According to our designer, the position of your room is the most feng shui for Molly's Pilates studio. And you are away at school for nine months of the year!"

Molly was Norman's second wife, Kate's stepmother, who was barely a decade older than Kate. Kate and her friends referred to her as Step Molly. Kate had never cared for Step Molly. Okay, she hated her with every ounce of her being. Step Molly was the typical Hollywood second wife: beautiful in that fake-boobs, zero-body-fat, Barry's Bootcamp-and-Pilates-sculpted perfect-body, expressionless-Botoxed-face (for wrinkles that didn't even exist) kind of way. As Kate saw it, Step Molly was a gold digger who had turned Kate's bedroom into a private Pilates studio the moment Kate left for college.

"Besides," Norman continued, "construction on the east wing of the house should be done in the next month or so, and then there will be plenty of room for everyone."

"Can I ask you one question, Norman?"

"Kate, I've got to jump—I've got three lines holding."

"How come no one picked *me* up at the airport when I came home?"

"Kate, I can't get into this with you now. Just take the Porsche if you want."

"Oh, great. I get to drive your midlife-crisis mobile? I'd think a big lawyer such as yourself might be able to strike a better deal with his nineteen-year-old daughter."

Kate got up from her chair and started walking around the pool. Their fighting was the most intimate their relationship ever got. And they were both really good at it. Norman often said that if Kate applied herself to her schoolwork the way she applied herself to winning their arguments, she would have gotten straight A's.

"Kate, I'm not making deals with you. I'm your father. Just please do as I ask."

"Fine. But I'm not hanging out with her."

"We'll discuss that later."

"He is so aggravating!" Kate yelled.

She threw the phone onto her chair and dove into the pool, completing an entire lap of the breaststroke under water. Coming up for air, she swam to where Tatiana and Dylan were sitting. She put her arms over the side of the pool, rested her cheek on her forearms, and sighed. Dylan popped some Pirate's Booty into Kate's mouth and gave her a sip of the watered-down remains of her Coffee Bean ice-blended drink. Tatiana put her hand on Kate's head.

"I mean, I've been home for two days. I haven't even *seen* him yet," said Kate. "You know, my father never asked me what I was going to do this summer. It wasn't even a conversation. And then I find out he's set up an internship for my cousin who he hasn't seen in, like, a *decade*! Like, she's so special? He's always saying 'Samantha gets straight A's,' 'Samantha has a part-time job,' 'Samantha reads *books*,' blah blah blah. Well, Samantha is probably a big fat dork! I mean, I had extracurricular activities in high school. I *read*. What else does he want from me?"

"At least you get to drive the Porsche, K-Ro. That car is sizzling," said Tatiana.

"And that Pilates studio is excellent! Do you think Step Molly will let us use it? Not that I've worked out in, like, years. Plus, my foot hurts. I think I have gout," sighed Dylan.

"Gout is so Middle Ages," said Tatiana.

"I can't even talk about working out. I am so pushing maximum density right now, it's ridiculous. I'm going on the Zone delivery diet tomorrow. This 'freshman fifteen' thing is killing me. They don't have spinning in Michigan. They have, like, cheese. None of my pants fit over my butt—it's depressing," said Kate.

"You know what that means?" asked Tatiana. "Time to buy shoes!"

Kate smiled. Dylan laughed heartily with her mouth wide open, her laughter quickly evolving into a coughing fit.

"Sorry, I think I have bronchitis again. So, what's the deal with your cousin? Is she, like, a total loser?" asked Dylan.

"She went to Deerfield—you know, the boarding school in Massachusetts. But she was a *day* student. Anyway, my friend Mike Hiller who's from New York, and was, you know, a boarder like all *normal* people, told me she was weird, like always alone with her nose in a book. And kind of goth, and like, thought she was too good for everyone else."

"You never know, Kate. She may be cool," said Dylan.

"Yeah, and it *may* rain tomorrow."

"All I have to say is, goth is soooo 1999," said Tatiana, looking at her Gucci watch. "Oh, girls, I gotta motor. I have a haircut at Fekkai and then I have to prepare for that audition tomorrow. Does anyone know how to get to the valley?"

"T, we've lived here our whole lives. We've really got to work on your sense of direction."

"I have a doctor's appointment, and then I promised my mom I would meet her for lunch at The Four Seasons," said Dylan.

"Oh my God, are you guys having the buffet?" asked Kate.

"Yeah, totally. It's DELICIOUS. I LOVE it! I just want to slip and slide across the whole buffet table. Is that wrong?" asked Dylan.

"It's so wrong, it's right," said Kate.

She climbed up and over the edge of the pool and retrieved her towel from her chair. As she hopped up and down with her head cocked toward her right shoulder to get the water out of her ear, Kate said, "Okay, ladies, I have a goth cousin to pick up in my daddy's Porsche . . . *hasta mas tarde*?"

Kate wrapped her towel around her waist as Tatiana stretched her slender five-foot-ten frame, gathered her red locks into a perfectly messy bun, and slipped on her white terry cloth tube dress and flip-flops. Dylan tied the drawstring of her cropped green cargo pants and shuffled into her slip-on red and white Vans. The girls walked from the pool around the side of the house, carefully avoiding the wet paint on the new east wing.

"*Ciao ciao*," the girls called to one another to the duet of car beepers, as they reached the driveway.

Dylan climbed into her hybrid ("It's like Earth Day every day in my car!"), while Tatiana slid into her white BMW convertible ("It's hot . . . white hot!").

Kate stood at the doorway, watching her friends leave as she alternated between hitting her head to get the water out of her ear and waving like it was the last time she would ever see them. They both honked as they drove down the long, winding driveway. Yasmine, the hot new sixteen-year-old rapper-ess, blasted from the speakers of Tatiana's car as she confidently peeled out, going the wrong direction. Kate smiled.

It was good to be home.

CHAPTER THREE

DOROTHY GALE: *Toto, I've got a feeling
we're not in Kansas anymore.* —THE WIZARD OF OZ

"Oh my God, it's Yasmine!"

Screams and flashbulbs erupted by the baggage claim, where Sam waited for her suitcase to appear on the carousel. Someone's bag has to be last, right? She was sure—the way her day was going—that it was going to be hers, if it arrived at all. Green, slightly ill, and embarrassed from her experience on the airplane, Sam still couldn't help but step away from the carousel for a moment to get a glimpse of the pop star. But it was to no avail—all she could see were throngs of people, cameras, and three large men who Sam assumed were Yasmine's bodyguards. It was hard to tell where Yasmine's entourage ended and where the fans and paparazzi began. The airport was suddenly a madhouse; Sam had never seen anything like it.

"Yasmine!" screamed one fan as she ran for the crowd, knocking into Sam, who dropped her carry-on bag, spilling all of its contents onto the floor. What else was going to go wrong today? When she kneeled down to gather her belongings, Sam came upon the framed picture of herself with her parents. As Sam lifted the frame, she noticed that the glass had cracked. Had Mr. Cell Phone's suitcase crushed it? Or the maniacal fan who had pushed her in her starstruck sprint? Sam didn't know, but she held on to the picture for a moment, tracing the fractured glass with her finger. The crack came directly in between her and her parents, separating them with a blurry line of chipped glass. *Perfect*, she thought. She had never felt so alone in her life.

Tired and dejected, Sam finished gathering her belongings and tried to haul her suitcase off the carousel, getting dragged along and knocking into several angry passengers in the process.

As Sam walked out of the baggage claim area through the sliding glass doors, she wondered when her cousin Kate would get there to pick her up, or if she would even remember that Sam was arriving today. Sam hadn't seen Kate since her last visit to Los Angeles when she was six and had no idea what to expect. The only thing Sam really remembered about Kate was that she wouldn't let Sam play with her Barbie Dream House, nor would she allow Sam to participate in the imaginary tea party that Kate was having with two girlfriends. When Uncle

Norman forced her to include Sam in the tea party, Kate made her play the caterer and had her wash imaginary dishes in the corner. Sam didn't really believe that she and her cousin would ever be the best of friends because they were so different, but she hoped that Kate had grown out of the bratty, selfish, and mean behavior that Sam remembered. At the very least, Sam assumed Kate would have a good heart and good intentions. She was a Rose, after all.

Beeeeeeeeeeeeeeep!

Sam was jolted out of her reverie by a pissed-off blonde in a red Porsche convertible. *No way*, she thought.

"Samantha Rose?" yelled the blonde over her blaring hip-hop music.

Sam waved back and looked around, checking to see if anyone had noticed. Everyone at the airport was staring. But then everyone looked away once they realized that neither the girl in the Porsche nor the girl with the suitcase was a celebrity.

Kate took one look at her cousin—at Sam's blunt cut, stick straight shoulder-length black hair with short bangs and her ivory skin—and thought she looked like a ghost (albeit one with a cool haircut).

"Ugh, ever heard of Mystic Tan?" Kate mumbled.

Sam looked at Kate—at her wavy highlighted blond and brunette hair, her Gucci aviator sunglasses, her flawless tan, her bright red Porsche convertible—and thought she looked like a walking (make that driving) cliché.

"Nice car. Subtle as a chain saw," said Sam under her breath.

Kate didn't make any move to get out of the car, so Sam picked up her bags and dragged them over to her.

"Hop in!" said Kate. "Just throw your stuff in the back. But hurry before the airport security gives me a ticket. I've been circling for an hour."

"Great, I mean, sorry . . . about the circling."

Kate turned up the volume on the car stereo and sang along to the radio. Sam muttered to herself as she tried to lift her bags into the faux backseat of the Porsche. Sure, just "throw it in the back."

Sam got in the car but stopped short of greeting her cousin. They were practically strangers and looked nothing alike. Sam had gone to school with girls like Kate at Deerfield and was therefore predisposed to immediately dislike and distrust them. The boarding students came from the "best" families from all over the world. Money, sex, drugs—all of it was no object to them. The day students, however (often referred to by the boarders as "day slime"), all lived within an hour of the school and commuted daily. Many of them were on scholarship and all of them stuck together, subscribing to the theory that there was safety in numbers. Sam had developed a real chip on

23

her shoulder about the spoiled rich kids who descended upon her hometown, and for the most part, she never looked past their trust funds to get to know any of them, just as they never looked beyond her "day slime" title and thrift store style to get to know her. It *was* high school, after all.

It seemed that Kate was going to be no different from the Deerfield girls Sam had detested. Kate was nineteen and driving a *Porsche convertible*, for crying out loud!

"*Mwa, mwa*," Kate mouthed as she pursed her lips and air kissed Sam. "Welcome to Los Angeles, Casper."

Kate peeled out from the curb without looking and nearly missed a collision with an oncoming car. Sam gripped her seat for dear life.

"Thanks, I think," Sam said. "Nice car. Is it, um, yours?"

Sam cringed. She suddenly decided that if it *was* Kate's, she would make her pull over and she would get on the next flight back to Northampton.

"No, it's Norman's. He got it along with Step Molly when he went through his midlife crisis, divorced my mom, forgot about me, and basically ruined my life."

"Oh. So . . . how is Aunt Jane?"

"She's in Tuscany for the summer. She saw that movie *Under the Tuscan Sun* after she and my dad got divorced, and it inspired her to go to Italy and cook. The funny thing is that my mom can't even boil an egg, so I really have no idea what she's doing over there. Yeah, our family really puts the 'FUN' in dysfunctional. You'll see." Kate wrinkled her nose, smelled under her arm, and then sniffed the air. "Something smells funky. It smells like . . . puke."

"I had a little, uh, episode on the plane. All over some guy who was sitting next to me. I suffer from acute motion sickness."

"*Ew.* That's not *cute* at all! That's just gross!" yelled Kate. "TG: Totally Gross! Well, one swim in the pool will fix you right up."

"I don't really swim."

Kate almost crashed the car (again) as she stared at Sam in disbelief while simultaneously making a precarious left onto the 405 Freeway.

"You don't *swim*?"

"Well, I mean, I *wade*. I'm just not a strong swimmer, that's all."

"So what *do* you do?"

Kate was still looking at Sam, and not at the road. Sam didn't really know how to answer her question. It wasn't loaded so much as just plain rude. Her defensive nature overpowered her increasing fear for her life.

"What do *you* do?" Sam asked.

"Well, right now, I'm wishing that I could turn off my olfactory sense."

"Nice vocab choice. I admire that. I was sure no one used more than two-syllable words in Los Angeles."

"They're few and far between, but my father spent like a million dollars on SAT tutors, so I've got that going for me."

"So, what are you doing this summer?"

"You're looking at it."

Sam wasn't exactly sure what that meant.

"You're going to be a driver?"

"No, silly. I'm just going to hang out, drive around, see my friends, you know . . . it's summertime!"

"You're not getting a summer job or anything?"

"Why would I do that?"

Sam silenced herself. She was now sure that she had absolutely nothing in common with this girl. How would she get through an entire summer with her? Forget summer, how would she get through this painful car ride? It didn't help matters that the traffic on the freeway was so congested that it looked and felt more like a parking lot. The girls sat in silence for a solid five minutes. Kate put her left leg up on the dashboard, keeping her right foot on the brake. She sighed and looked over at Sam.

"So, I bet they don't have traffic like this in Massachusetts, huh?"

"Well, around rush hour when everyone is trying to get home in their horse-driven carriages to light their oil lamps before it gets dark, it can get pretty hairy."

"Well, luckily, I see that they have a surplus of sarcasm in

Massachusetts. My kind of place. But, do they have The Coffee Bean there?"

Sam had no idea what she was talking about. She stared blankly at Kate.

"Well, as long as you don't think you're gonna hurl, you're in for quite a treat."

Kate swerved the Porsche across three lanes of traffic and exited the freeway to the cacophonous sound of horns and cars screeching to a halt.

CHAPTER FOUR

"But I don't want to go among mad people," Alice remarked.

"Oh, you can't help that," said the Cat.
"We're all mad here. I'm mad. You're mad."

"How do you know I'm mad?" said Alice.

"You must be," said the Cat, "or else you wouldn't have come here."
—LEWIS CARROLL, *Alice's Adventures in Wonderland*

The Coffee Bean was an Angelino favorite. Kate explained that she had practically been weaned on "CBIBs" (Coffee Bean Ice Blended's)—which was pretty much the truth, as her mother, Jane, never believed in breast-feeding (she thought it was "barbaric"). As the girls got in the line that snaked out the door, Sam looked back anxiously at her suitcase sitting in the open Porsche.

"It'll be fine," said Kate. "God, you are such a stress case. You're in LA now, just chill."

The girls pretended to read the opus that was The Coffee Bean drink menu, but they were really stealing glances at each other.

Kate was surprised by her cousin's appearance. Sam was certainly striking; she stood out like a pale thumb in the land of the tanned and artificial. Kate thought Sam dressed a little too "interestingly" for her taste, but she had to give it to her—she wore it well. Kate could tell that Sam was clearly high-strung, and if she didn't chill out soon, she was going to be a real bummer. But Kate was impressed with Sam's poise. Or maybe she was just snotty? Or defensive? Judgmental? Whatever she was, she definitely had an edge, and Kate had to respect a girl with some edge. *You are soooooo not in Kansas anymore*, Kate thought, happy to be back on her own turf.

Advantage: Kate.

Sam did not trust Kate as far as she could throw her. Family-shmamily—she knew Kate's kind all too well from high school, and she had never had a good experience with them. But Kate was clearly intelligent. A dangerous combination: spoiled and smart, a force with which to be reckoned. But Sam had four years of experience dealing with this kind of girl, and her skin was thick. She knew these girls thrived on attention and obsequious followers. Sam believed her own indifference was the kryptonite to Kate's superentitled powers.

Advantage: Sam.

The girls stepped up to the counter.

"Hi. May I please have a large no-sugar-added half caf/half decaf soy ice-blended mocha with whipped cream? Oh, and I'm diabetic, so could you make *sure* it's the 'no-sugar-added' kind because otherwise I will, like, have a seizure right here. It will not be pretty. I promise you that."

The young woman behind the register cracked her gum, but didn't flinch: certainly, she had heard it all before. Sam, on the other hand, had not. She was clearly not fluent in Coffee Bean-ese.

"I didn't know you were diabetic," said Sam.

Kate looked at her disapprovingly, put her finger to her lips, and shushed her. Sam was confused, by everything. Unnerved by the line of Coffee Beanos (Coffee Bean addicts, highly dangerous when not fed) behind her needing their fix, she said, "I'll have what she's having."

After Kate scrutinized the artificially sweetened assembly of her complicated beverage, the girls retreated to an outside table with their drinks. Sam looked at the people around her as if they were aliens—aliens with designer sunglasses and perfect bodies.

"What was that about? Are you really diabetic?"

"Of course not. I just don't want the extra calories. Sam, you'll see, if you want to get something done right in this town, you have to scare the crap out of people first. Otherwise, you fail, or you get fat. Either way, you're screwed."

It wasn't the most insightful thing Sam had ever heard, but she took note nonetheless. It seemed like the perfect opportunity to ask Kate what she knew about Lawrence Miller, the producer for whom she would be interning over the next eight weeks.

According to Kate, Lawrence produced big popcorn movies. She had only met him once, at one of her father's firm's Christmas parties a few years earlier. From what Kate remembered, Lawrence was often partying, usually cranky, always gay, and extremely successful.

Norman had recently told Kate that Lawrence had changed over the last few years. He stopped partying as much, but he was still as moody as ever. Lawrence had great success at an early age and continually feared it was about to end because—like most people in Hollywood—he subscribed to the old adage: "You're only as good as your last picture." Lawrence was both backstabbing and flamboyantly generous, not an unusual combination in Hollywood.

While Sam was interested in hearing more about her boss-to-be, Kate bored quickly of talking about "the business" and sucked down her Coffee Bean concoction in a matter of minutes. Quite a feat; Sam was still suffering a massive brain freeze from her first mind-blowingly delicious sip.

Once the girls resumed their drive toward the house, Sam sat quietly in the passenger seat while Kate fielded "important" calls from friends in need of boy, hair, and diet advice. She barked directions at Tatiana, who had gotten herself hopelessly lost in Studio City. She spoke to her waxer and snagged an appointment for the next day. Sam blocked out Kate's vapid conversations and cries of "NW: No Way!" and "I LOVE it!!!" and "That is SNOK: SO not okay!" Kate yelled her Beverly Hills vernacular into the hands-free earpiece connected to her cell phone (which was also a BlackBerry and a camera). The hands-free mechanism was pointless, really, as Kate spent most of her time talking while simultaneously typing e-mails to her friends *and* driving. Norman called this behavior reckless; Kate called it multitasking.

Sam was afraid she would get whiplash from gawking at all the gorgeous houses as they whizzed down the palm tree-lined streets of Beverly Hills. Each house seemed bigger than the next, each with a fleet of gardeners, each adorned with some kind of sleek, gas-guzzling vehicle. BMWs, Mercedes, Porsches, Jaguars, and Bentleys were the common denominator in these parts, and Sam had never seen so much unabashed wealth in one place.

"I think he is *sooooo* cute. Wait, but seriously, T, was he *that* cute or was it just *that* one A.M.? What? No, I don't know if you should make a right or a left because I don't know where you are or where you're going. Oh Tots, hold on a sec," said Kate. "Sam, notice we are now going north past Sunset. All the nice houses are north of Sunset."

Sam looked confused. Didn't they just pass a mile of nice houses?

"Sorry, T. Okay, break it down for me. How lost are you?"

The houses did get bigger as they went farther north, until Sam couldn't even see the houses from the road. As the gates and shrubbery became taller with each block, Sam could only imagine the elaborate abodes that lurked behind.

They arrived at a massive and modern iron gate, which opened after Kate punched a number into the intercom/keypad. Sam gasped as they drove up the driveway to an imposing gray-and-white stone house. Kate parked across three spots, threw the car into park with a flourish, got out of the car while still talking on her hands-free earpiece, and walked into the house without looking back. Sam sat in the Porsche, alone.

"Don't wait for me—I'll be fine." Sam rolled her eyes. For the first time, she actually felt sad that there was no one there to tell her how obnoxious the eye roll was.

Just then Manuela emerged from the house waving her arms with her plastic yellow dishwashing gloves still on. *"¡Bienvenidos, Samita!"*

Sam didn't speak Spanish, but she was thrilled that someone seemed happy to see her and would help her with her bags. As they entered through the front door, Sam stood in the entry foyer in shock. The interior of the house was a sea of white, beige, and several muted shades in between. Sam continued through the entry foyer into the sparsely decorated and cavernous living room. Her footsteps on the smooth, white Italian tile echoed ominously. Floor-to-ceiling windows before her revealed a large pool with a disappearing edge that seemed to spill out onto all of Los Angeles. Sam could see the entire city before her, which was just lighting up as the sun was setting. And then she saw them: they were nestled in the hills—both welcoming her and taunting her—those nine letters she had seen so many times in movies: HOLLYWOOD.

Yes, Samantha Rose had arrived.

CHAPTER FIVE

CAPTAIN: *"What we've got here is failure to communicate."*
—Cool Hand Luke

M"Manuela, have you seen my Chloe stilettos?" Kate yelled from beyond the white stone staircase.

Manuela led Sam up to the guest bedroom, past a room that Sam thought looked like a medieval torture chamber. She stopped and poked her head into it, confused.

"Pilates," explained Manuela.

Sam thought Manuela was still speaking Spanish so she just nodded and followed her toward Kate's desperate yelps emanating from down the hall. The guest room was huge— three times the size of Sam's room at home. Like the rest of the house, it lacked any kind of personality or history. Sam was amazed. She had never been in a home with so little character. In Northampton, they had framed pictures on all the walls and propped up on every flat surface, even some of Sam's old artwork from what her parents called her "blue period." This house didn't even *smell* like anything.

"I wore them my first night back, and now I can't find them and I have to go meet the girls. Manuela, can you *pleeeeaaaaaase* help me?"

Manuela put down Sam's bag and went over to Kate's shoe closet, which looked like a rack in an upscale department store: Prada, Gucci, Armani, Choo, Blahnik—the gang was all there. Her sneakers were the newest Nikes and designer Pumas. Sam tried not to stare, while Manuela took one look and plucked the preciously high heels from the menagerie of shoes.

"Ugh, you're a lifesaver! Thank you, Manuela!"

"De nada, Kate-ita."

Sam cleared her throat, as Kate hadn't yet acknowledged that she'd even entered the room.

"Oh, hi. Norman told me to make some room for you, so here's your drawer."

Kate hobbled in her stilettos over to a bureau that blended right into the wall and pulled out a single bottom drawer. Sam looked from the little drawer to her large suitcase. She had to laugh. Was she really related to this girl?

"What's so funny?" asked Kate.

"Nothing. I'm just . . . tired."

"Well, I'm going out with the girls, so I guess I'll see you tomorrow."

Sam was a little stung that Kate hadn't even asked her to

join them. Not that she would have wanted to go, of course. Sam usually chose to stay at home curled up with a good book, her journal, and a bowl of her mother's minestrone over spending time with kids her own age. She knew her parents often worried that she was too much of a loner, but being academics themselves, they encouraged her love for literature and assumed she would grow into being more sociable when she was ready.

"That's fine. I have to get ready for work—I have a big day tomorrow," Sam said.

"Oh, yeah, you start tomorrow. Break a leg. Or, whatever. I think you'll be sharing a car with Manuela. It's an old Land Cruiser from last year, I mean, it's *ancient*, but it should do the trick. This year's model is, like, so much nicer."

"I'm sure I can catch a bus or something. I don't think I should drive."

Kate let out a loud laugh.

"The bus?! Nobody takes the *bus* in Los Angeles! You're funny."

As Kate hobbled out of the guest room still shaking her head and chuckling to herself, Sam's messenger bag slipped off her shoulder and onto the beige sisal carpeting that looked like it might tear open her feet. She had to assume that whoever designed this house didn't want people to get too comfortable or stay too long. She let out a sigh and began to unpack as much as she could into her single drawer.

Sam was about to doze off when Manuela came in to offer

her dinner. As Kate had done countless times before, Sam sat in the kitchen with Manuela, gobbling gourmet food and watching TV. It wasn't Mom's minestrone, but it hit the spot nonetheless. They watched the movie *Weird Science* dubbed in Spanish. Even though Sam had never seen it before and didn't understand what the characters were saying, she got the gist of the story, and it made her think about how great it would be to create the perfect man, just as the boys in the movie created the perfect woman. But who would be Sam's perfect man? Whoever he was, wherever he was, Sam had not yet come close to meeting him. He would have to be smart, cultured, chivalrous, and inquisitive. A sense of humor would be nice. He would definitely be well read and love classic literature, but he wouldn't be pretentious and annoying about it. And maybe he'd be a rock star too, or just look like one. Now that's a movie she wanted to see (and a boy she wouldn't mind meeting). Sam finished her meal, deep in thought.

Sam had still not seen Uncle Norman or met Step Molly, but directions to her new office had been faxed over by Norman's assistant. Sam climbed between the crisp linens on her all-too-firm bed with her copy of *Jane Eyre* and was soon asleep.

CHAPTER SIX

BOB SUGAR: *It's not show friends, it's show business.*
—JERRY MAGUIRE

Sam woke up at 6 A.M., before her alarm; she was still on East Coast time. She looked over at Kate, who was passed out on her bed and still wearing all her makeup, which, twelve hours after the initial application, looked more like war paint. Kate was splayed out on top of the covers, one stilettoed foot dangled precariously over the floor, the other on the bed. She was wearing a purple crochet bra and a short jean skirt. Sam was tempted to put a mirror under her nose to see if she was still breathing, but then she figured it wasn't really her problem.

After showering and picking out her outfit—a black silk blouse with cap sleeves, loose black cotton capris, and black wedge heels (black was always Sam's color of choice)—Sam went downstairs to an empty kitchen. She flipped through the barren cabinets and settled on a bowl of organic gluten-free/wheat-free/sugar-free puffed rice cereal with nonfat soy milk. It was all she could find that somewhat resembled breakfast food. She forced herself to eat a few spoonfuls; she didn't know when she would have a chance to eat again, or where she could go to get a proper breakfast. She would have scrambled herself some eggs, but from the look of it, no one actually used the state-of-the-art Viking stove, and she certainly didn't want to be the one to christen it.

At 7:30 A.M., the Rose household was still asleep. Sam grabbed her MapQuest directions, car keys, vintage maroon purse, and headed out the door. Sam, who was a shaky driver at best, climbed into the silver Land Rover and checked the vanity mirror before starting the ignition.

"I can do this," she said.

She closed her eyes and turned the key. Spanish music blared from the radio, causing Sam to scream and leap from her seat. She quickly turned down the volume, took a breath, adjusted the seat and mirrors, slipped on her chunky black five-dollar knockoff sunglasses, and slowly pulled out of the driveway.

Authentic Pictures was located in Beverly Hills, which was about a thirty-minute commute during rush hour, a ten-minute drive any other time. Sam was giving herself an hour to be safe. She crept in rush hour traffic through Beverly Hills, past Rodeo Drive, past Saks Fifth Avenue on Wilshire Boulevard (clearly, she was not the only thing out of place in Los Angeles), past a dozen Starbucks and Coffee Beans. Her trip was punctuated by bursts of idle time at stop lights, which she used to stare into the cars stopped next to her. Rarely did she see a car with more than one person in it. Sam assumed no one had heard of car pools in Los Angeles. Almost everyone was on a cell phone, looking like they were talking to themselves because they were using their hands-free devices or speaker-phones.

The directions were perfect, and with just one or two near-accidents, Sam pulled into the parking lot behind the Authentic Pictures building. The executives parked in the structure adjacent to the office, in designated spots with name placards. The assistants and interns parked in the back. Just as Sam reapplied her lip gloss and climbed out of the Land Cruiser, an old gray Toyota pickup truck roared into the parking lot.

Jeez, where's the fire? thought Sam.

Sam could barely see the driver through the truck's dirty windshield. She watched as he turned off the engine, grabbed his papers and backpack, and jumped out of the truck like it was indeed on fire.

When the driver emerged, Sam noticed that he was cute (if a little pudgy). He had dirty-blond hair, which he had unsuccessfully attempted to spike with hair gel, and piercing blue eyes partially obstructed by wire-rimmed glasses. He was wearing khaki pants and a short-sleeved, checkered button-down with some brown shoes of the orthopedic variety. A fashionista, he was not.

"Who are you?" he asked.

"Oh, hi. Sam. Samantha Rose. I'm an intern . . . I'm supposed to. . . ."

"Oh, yeah, right. New intern. I'm Ross Gordon. Welcome to the War Room."

"Um, thanks."

Ross picked through his inordinately crowded key chain. What could he possibly need all those keys for? He took Sam in through the back door of the office, turning off the alarm and locking the door behind her. Sam cringed at the sound of the door bolting. No way out now.

The office was cold and concrete. It was a large industrial loft space with high ceilings made with exposed wooden beams and piping. Oversize framed movie posters lined the walls, and each office had a glass window, so that Lawrence could see what his employees were doing at all times, Ross explained. Like many producers in Hollywood, Lawrence was a self-proclaimed control freak. They walked past a small caged area. Sam craned her neck to see what was inside.

"Office supplies," said Ross.

He flipped on lights and charged through the empty office. They keep their office supplies in a cage? Don't feed the office supplies, Sam thought to herself with a dorky chuckle.

"What's so funny?"

"Oh, nothing. Sorry. I just, the cage. . . ."

"Yeah, I know. They should keep some of the executives in there too."

Sam laughed out loud. She followed Ross into the copy room, where he threw down his scripts and backpack.

"Just put your stuff down here. This is where you'll spend most of your time anyway."

Sam looked around. Unflattering fluorescent lighting illuminated the industrial white space. The copy room reeked of toner and monotony. Stray papers, script covers, and "brads" littered the messy and artificially bright room. Ross explained that "brads" were the little metal clips used to bind scripts. The fabric of Hollywood was basically held together by these tiny metal objects.

Ross flipped the power on for the copy machine and rested his hand on the top.

"Say hello to your new best friend," he said. He glanced at his Swatch. "Come on, we're late."

They continued to scurry around the office. Sam looked around. No one was there. How were they already late?

"The first thing to do is make the coffee. If you do nothing else when you come in, do this. This office runs on coffee. And Diet Coke. Basically, it runs on anything with lots of caffeine and no calories. Oh, and ego. Plenty of ego. But we'll get to that later."

"Can't wait."

He stopped for a moment in front of two small offices next to each other, both immaculately neat with pink iMacs on the desks.

"Quick tour: Ellen and Rebecca sit here. They're the D-girls."

"D-girls?"

"Yeah. Development girls. Hollywood is full of them," Ross explained. "For the most part, they're just cute girls who socialize a lot, read and 'develop' scripts—or at least the coverage of the scripts—talk on the phone, go to parties, and have lots of meals and drinks with other D-people, agents, and studio executives. These girls are no different. Except Ellen is about to get married, so she's just biding her time until she can quit her job and become a full-time wife and mother. She gets nothing *done*. Rebecca's on her way to doing the same thing, but she's still single. Watch out for them: I call them the D-witches. They're both homegrown."

Sam looked confused but dared not ask.

"They were both Lawrence's assistants," Ross explained. "He promoted them: homegrown. In this town, you get promoted for loyalty more often than for intelligence or talent. Right place, right time, and all that. You'll see. They'll burn."

"Burn?"

She followed Ross to another office directly across from the D-witches' offices. This one had a blue iMac on the desk. It was not as neat as the witches' offices, and there were more scripts in the bookcases. And there were actually books there too.

"This is Dan's office. He's cool. Gay. Nice guy. Smart. Good taste. But again, powerless. No one has any real power aside from Lawrence."

"What do you mean, 'power'?" It all sounded very dramatic to Sam.

"Power. You know. They can't get anything *done* without Lawrence's okay. He likes it that way—it makes him feel useful. He'll burn." Ross opened the office door, flipped on the lights, and started walking to the next office.

"And how long have you been working here?"

"Six glorious months," said Ross.

He picked up a stray brad from the floor and pointed to another office, which looked like a home gym crossed with a frat-house common room. Barbells lined the floor, and the *Sports Illustrated* swimsuit calendar was mounted on the wall. It was still open to February's scantily clad blonde, even though it was already June.

"That's Rob's office. He's a meathead, but harmless. Oddly enough, he comes the closest to getting things done. He has terrible taste, so he just tries to get everything made. Jury's still out on whether he actually knows how to read. He has a brain the size of a pea, and pecs the size of papayas."

"Do you always describe people in relation to produce?"

"Only when I'm feeling playful."

"This is playful?"

"Yeah, you should see grumpy."

Ross pointed at the little cubicles outside of the executive offices.

"Now, the assistants: Amy assists Ellen and Rebecca, the D-witches. Poor girl. She really wants to be a film editor but has been working here for two years. She's nice, but she's not going anywhere. You'll see, no one in Hollywood is *actually* doing what he or she really wants to be doing. The assistants want to be writers or to be promoted and be D-girls or D-guys, the D-girls want to be wives and mothers, the D-guys want to rule the world and get laid—not necessarily in that order—and, well, everyone wants to direct."

"I don't want to direct."

"Oh, don't worry: you will. Anyway," he continued. "Amy doesn't have to do much, as Rebecca and Ellen are completely ineffective. However, Ellen is planning her wedding, so Amy is up to her ears dealing with all the nuptials. Sucks for her. Alexandra is the assistant to Rob. She's a D-witch-in-training. She has a thing for Rob, I think, but I'll deny it if you ever tell anyone I said that. Anyway, look out for her. Dan was just promoted a year ago, so he doesn't have an assistant yet. And then, there's Matt Sullivan."

Ross walked slowly and dramatically over to the cubicle just outside of Lawrence's office. He placed his hand on top of Matt's green iMac with a thud.

"Matt Sullivan?"

"Yeah. Matt Sullivan . . . is the devil. He's Lawrence's assistant. He thinks he's the golden boy because he grew up in New York and he went to 'Haaah-vahd.' You'll see. I'm basically his bitch. He'll burn."

A door slammed. Sam's head was spinning. She couldn't remember anyone's name. She forgot who she was supposed to like and who she was supposed to dismiss, who was going to "burn" and who wasn't. She heard a male voice, clearly on a cellular phone.

"Yeah, just make sure I get the script first. Don't worry, I'll see that Lawrence gets it. No, put it to *my* attention. I can send a messenger. It's not a problem. I'll just have my intern do it."

As the deep voice neared, Sam and Ross stood frozen by Matt's cubicle. "Matt," Ross mouthed silently.

As Matt Sullivan rounded the corner with his cell phone to his ear, he nodded at the two of them. Against Sam's better judgment, her knees seemed to be giving out on her. Matt Sullivan was tall and undeniably handsome in a disheveled, I-don't-even-need-to-try-so-I-won't kind of way. He had thick brown hair, deep brown eyes, and a five-o'clock shadow on his face, even though it was only nine in the morning. He wore a blue button-down shirt that wasn't completely tucked in, a worn-in pair of brown corduroys, and sneakers. To Sam, he oozed casual confidence, charm, ambition, and, well, sex appeal.

Matt Sullivan stared at Sam as he finished his phone conversation, and as he looked at her, Sam felt like she might just be the only girl in the whole world.

"I gotta run, just got to the office. *Ciao* for now."

Without averting his gaze from Sam, Matt Sullivan flipped his cell phone closed, put it in his breast pocket, and reached his other hand out to her. Ross started to introduce the two of them, but Matt ignored him, took Sam's hand in both of his, looked her in the eye, and said, "I'm Matt Sullivan. You must be Samantha."

Sam felt like a deer in the headlights. She could barely catch her breath, let alone get any words out. This guy should be kissing babies somewhere and ruling the world. Or kissing me, she thought. But, she suspected Matt Sullivan was also the kind of guy that she had always hated. He was the guy she avoided in the halls in high school and would roll her eyes at when he talked in class. He was the guy who always had things handed to him on a silver platter, the guy who didn't take the time to get to know her—or even look in her general direction—at Deerfield. He would have dated the beautiful blonde-haired, blue-eyed, blue-blooded girl from the rich family. He would have been the captain of the football team and would have made the debate team cool if he was on it. The guys would have wanted to be his friend. The girls would have wanted to be his girlfriend. Normally, Sam would have hated everything this guy stood for, but at that moment, she just couldn't help herself.

"I vomited." *Wait, did I just say that out loud?* "On the plane. I mean, on the person sitting next to me on the plane. I suffer from acute motion sickness. There was motion . . . and . . . turbulence. I mean, we were still on the ground, but . . . it . . . was, um—"

"Turbulent?" Matt Sullivan suggested.

"Yeah. Turbulent."

"Well, the summer can only get better from there, right? Samantha, I've got to get to work, but it was nice meeting you. Ross! Buddy! You got that script coverage for me?"

"I e-mailed it to you last night."

"Great, you're a lifesaver. Thanks, buddy." Matt Sullivan slapped Ross on the back, nearly knocking him over. "You can always trust a guy who wears Dockers," he said as he retreated to his desk, leaving Sam and Ross in his wake.

CHAPTER SEVEN

It is one of the blessings of old friends
that you can afford to be stupid with them.
—RALPH WALDO EMERSON

Kate had a severe case of cotton mouth.

"Yuck," she said.

She groaned and rubbed her eyes. She looked at her hand: residual mascara and Amber Lights-colored eye shadow.

"Crap."

Closing her eyes again, she blindly reached over to her bedside table. She knocked over an unopened bottle of Evian, house keys, and her pink Prada wallet before her hand arrived at the object of her desire. She opened one eye and managed to speed dial Dylan.

On the fourth ring, the phone seemed to pick up, but then Kate heard a fall, a distant cry to hold on, and then some sleepy fumbling. Finally, Dylan's breathing could be heard in the receiver, followed by a pause, and then simply, "I know."

"Right?" asked Kate.

"I just . . . I can't even."

"I know."

"I LOVE it," said Dylan.

"You know it was a fun night when you wake up in the morning and all your makeup is still on. GTs."

Dylan started to laugh heartily, which once again evolved into a deep and thunderous cough.

"D, that doesn't sound so good." Kate picked up the bottle of Evian and started gulping it down.

"I know, K-Ro. I think I have whooping cough."

"Do people still get that?" asked Kate.

"I don't know. Maybe I have SARS?"

"Have you been on any transcontinental flights recently?"

"Does New York count?"

"No, D. New York is actually on the same continent as Los Angeles."

"Wow. That's so weird. I never thought of it that way . . . oh wait, that's Tatiana on call waiting. I'm patching her in: Tots, you're on with Dylan and Kate," said Dylan.

"D. K-Ro. Good morning, ladies," said Tatiana.

"Hey there, Mrs. Robinson," said Kate.

"Whatever, I'm nineteen—I'm hardly Mrs. Robinson. He's seventeen."

"Yeah, but T, that means he's not even legal! He's in *high school*! I mean, he's a *fetus*!" quipped Kate between gulps.

"Kate, we were in high school last year. *And nothing happened!* It's so not a big deal."

"It will be if that picture of the two of you together shows up in *Them* magazine. T, he's on the WB! Girls across America have pictures of him plastered on their walls. God, sometimes you can be so jaded," said Kate.

"Whatever, Kate. My publicist is all over it, okay?"

"Hey guys, um, could I have been any more of a klutz?" Dylan asked through a mouthful of food. "I was talking to that nice guy, and I just—"

"You fell."

"No, I didn't just fall, Kate. I was *sitting* and I *fell.* I was *sitting* and I *fell*! I didn't even know you could do that! I'm so humiliated. Ugh, and I just officially ate an entire chicken. SNOK!"

Tatiana and Kate erupted in hysterics, and Dylan couldn't help but join in.

"GTs, girls." Kate's phone beeped and she looked at her caller ID. "Ugh, hang on, it's my dad." She clicked onto the second call. "You rang?"

"Hi, Kate, I have your father for you."

"Thanks, Alice," said Kate. He never learns, she thought.

"Hi, hon, did you have fun last night?"

Kate could hear her father furiously typing as he talked to her.

"Yeah, Norman, it was a blast. What can I do for you?"

He stopped typing for a moment.

"Can't a father just call his daughter to say hello?"

"I don't know, can he?"

Kate sat up and listened intently. Her father never just called to say hello.

"Well, I am calling to say hello and also—oh wait, honey, I've got to jump, I have to take this other call." Kate rolled her eyes. "Listen, Molly and I would like to take you and Sam to dinner tonight to celebrate her arrival and first day of work. The Ivy, eight P.M.?"

"Oh, well, that is just cuh-lassic, Norman."

"Kate, don't give me a hard time on this."

"What about *my* arrival, Norman? I come home, you don't even make a point of saying hello to me, let alone have a dinner in my, you know, honor, or whatever this thing tonight is. No way. No can do, Norman. I have dinner with the girls."

"Kate, this is not a request. I ask very little of you."

"Oh, but you give so much!"

"Kate. The Ivy, eight P.M. Please don't be late."

"What's in it for me?"

"A free meal. A roof over your head. A college education."

"I need designer enchiladas at The Ivy like I need a hole in the head."

"I love you, honey. I'll see you there."

"Can't wait."

Kate lay back down as she clicked over to her friends who were in midconversation.

"And I was like, 'Ice, you're adorable!'" Dylan was saying.

"Wait a second, back up, *beep beep beep*, what?"

"Dylan met Ice Man last night. You know, that rapper-slash-model-slash-actor-slash-former-gangster. She told him he was *adorable*," Tatiana said.

"He was! He was lovely!"

"Oh, he must have loved that," said Kate.

"Guys, he's misunderstood," giggled Dylan.

"Why can't anyone just be one thing anymore?" asked Kate. "Everyone's a *slasher* these days: singer-slash-actor-slash-writer-slash-producer or model-slash-poet-slash-director-slash-yoga-clothing-line-designer or orthodontist-slash-documentarian-slash-stand-up-comic. T, please promise me that when you hit it big, you won't record an album, start a handbag line, and try to trademark the phrase 'How are you?' Just, please, fight the power. I beg you."

"I do use the phrase 'How are you?' quite often," said Tatiana.

"Cute," said Kate. "So, girls, I have bad news and I have good news: bad news is, can't do dinner tonight because, apparently, I have duties to fulfill as a tour-guiding-cousin-slash-neglected-unappreciative-daughter-slash-bratty-and-hateful-stepdaughter. Good news is, it's another beautiful day in Los Angeles, and the pool is beckoning us."

"Oh, Kate, can't do it, sorry. I have that audition at two and then I have my acting class," said Tatiana.

"Yeah, I have, like, ten voice mails I need to return for this show I'm helping to promote at House of Blues. Sorry, Kate," said Dylan.

"Oh whatever, I mean, I just thought. . . ."

Kate was sitting up again. What would she do with her day now? She knew she didn't necessarily have to be a *slasher*, but Kate was realizing that she didn't have anything to slash at all. She did have a waxing appointment, however. And maybe the weather wasn't even nice today. Oh, who was she kidding? It was nice *every* day in Los Angeles.

"So, we'll chat later?" asked Tatiana.

"*Ciao*, girls," said Dylan.

"OK, then I guess—" started Kate.

But the girls had already hung up.

"I guess I'll talk to you guys later," she said to the dial tone.

Kate looked over at her alarm clock, which she hadn't even bothered to set. It read 11:15 A.M. She groaned, let the phone drop to the floor, fell onto her pillow, and went back to sleep.

CHAPTER EIGHT

The gods had condemned Sisyphus to ceaselessly rolling a rock
to the top of a mountain, whence the stone would fall back of its own weight.
They had thought with some reason that there is no more
dreadful punishment than futile and hopeless labor.
—ALBERT CAMUS, *The Myth of Sisyphus*

All the executives rolled in by 11 A.M., and Ross took Sam around the office to introduce her to everyone. No one said much more than a hello, and most just gave a wave and pointed to their headset, as if to suggest they were on the phone and couldn't possibly tolerate the thirty-second intrusion. Ellen, D-witch #1, was on the phone with her wedding planner and frantically wagged her finger at Ross and Sam as they approached her office. She had brought her surly miniature poodle, Princess, to work that day and didn't want her to escape. Princess went ballistic and barked bloody murder, scratching at and salivating on the glass office door as soon as she saw Ross and Sam. Princess *Cujo*, was more like it.

Rebecca, D-witch #2, had a habit of ending every sentence on a high note like it was a question. So she briefly introduced herself to Sam by saying, "Hi, I'm Rebecca?" Sam wondered if she was or wasn't Rebecca. She guessed she must be. Rob was doing push-ups in his office, apparently psyching himself up for a big meeting he had later that day. Alexandra, his assistant, wouldn't let them into the office to say hi, nor would she say what the meeting was about. Ross explained that it was survival of the fittest at Authentic Pictures, so the executives were secretive and competitive: they did whatever they had to do in order to survive.

Through her rounds, Sam couldn't help stealing glimpses at Matt Sullivan. He sat right outside of Lawrence's office in his corner cubicle (which was significantly bigger than all the others), which looked like a tornado had hit it—papers and scripts were everywhere. He seemed to Sam to be the busiest person in the world. She would watch as he typed furiously, rolled calls, and talked on the phone—which was constantly ringing. He would chat with the assistants as they rolled calls with their bosses, and with the executives themselves when they dared to place their own calls, which was rare.

The Matt Sullivans of the world never paid any attention to Sam, and Sam, in turn, ignored them. So, how had this Matt Sullivan piqued her interest so quickly?

As she lifted the lid of the copy machine, Sam leaned in to sneak another peek at Matt, but this time, he looked up and their eyes met. She looked away quickly, knocking the start button on the copy machine. An unnaturally bright green light flashed directly in Sam's eyes, temporarily blinding her. When her vision was restored, she looked at Matt to see that he was still watching. He smiled and winked. She didn't know whether to wink or wave back, so she tried to do both at the same time, which looked awkward and spastic at best. She turned back to the Xerox machine. *Why me*, she kept thinking. By the time she had the courage to look over again, Matt waved her over.

It was only ten or fifteen feet from where Sam stood at the copier to where Matt Sullivan sat in his cubicle, but at that moment, it felt like a mile. Was she in trouble already? Was he really waving to her or was she seeing things? The copy machine was *really* bright, after all. What could Matt Sullivan possibly want to talk to her about? And why did she care so much? As she walked toward him, she felt like she was moving in slow motion.

"You okay?" he asked.

"Yeah, I guess. I can't speak for my corneas, though."

"How's it going—aside from the temporary blindness?"

"It's . . . going."

"Not as glamorous as you expected, huh? A Hollywood internship sounds great on paper."

"Yeah."

"Well, we should get a drink after work one night, and I'll fill you in on everything . . . oh wait, how old are you anyway?"

"Eighteen. But it's not like I've never had a drink. You

know. I've *drank* before. Like on special occasions, or if I took a sip of my mom's . . ."

What was she talking about? Sam was saved in mid-nonsensical-ramble by Matt's phone ringing again.

"I've gotta grab this, Sam. Talk to you later?"

He smiled and looked away as he picked up his next call. Great, now he thinks I'm a drunk, Sam thought to herself. And not just your plain old pitiful and dorky drunk; no, she was a drunk who couldn't seem to utter a coherent sentence, puked on strangers in airplanes, and then blinded herself with the copy machine. It just got worse and worse. But wait, hold on: did he just ask her out? Sam stared at the clock, wishing she could turn back time and start all over again.

The next task Sam was assigned was to restock the sodas in the refrigerator. Ross instructed her that the cans had to line up neatly (i.e., Diet Coke, Diet Mountain Dew, Diet Dr Pepper—each belonged in its own row). Ross told Sam to report back to the dreaded copy room when she had finished, where he had a stack of scripts that needed to be copied. The copy machine was more prone to jamming than actual copying. Sam would copy whole scripts before realizing that she had forgotten to put the copies on the three-hole-punch setting. Hollywood-1, Environment-0. Sam decided she would just put a clip on them and take them home to read, since no one else would read them in their unwieldy state.

As Sam was copying, Ross was reading "spec" scripts for

Matt, who was busy doing whatever it was he did all day. As Ross sped through one script, he explained to Sam that "specs" were available scripts that agents tried to sell by attaching producers, like Lawrence, who would then try to sell the projects to one of the studios. The whole spec market was chaotic and fast paced, and the executives tried to trump one another by using their relationships with agents and managers to get the first look at these available scripts, and then be the ones to bring them in to the studio. If they did manage to sell the script, it was their job to develop the material and get the movie made—or, in Hollywood parlance—get the movie "greenlit."

Sam heard Ellen talking to Amy outside the copy room. "Amy, today I'm cleaning out my office. Why don't you start on it for me? Princess and I have to meet the gate guy at my new house. All the old scripts on the back shelf can be recycled, but don't forget to take the brads out of them first. Just tell the new intern to do it."

When in doubt, ask the intern. Sam cringed as Amy walked into the copy room.

"Hi guys," she said.

Ross kept reading and raised his right hand. A loud noise erupted from the copy machine to protest Amy's entrance for interrupting its flow.

"Paper jam!" said Ross, without looking up.

"I know, I hate that copier. I do not envy you," she said to Sam. "And I'll envy you even less when I ask you this favor."

"That's okay."

"So, Ellen has decided to clean out her office today, which translates to me cleaning out her office today. Anyway, she has a couple piles of scripts that need recycling, but in order to be recycled . . ."

"I have to remove the brads."

"Oh, you're good. Isn't she good, Ross?"

"She's great."

Sam and Amy trudged back and forth across the office, hauling armloads of discarded scripts into the copy room. Sam tried to look as composed, cool, and confident as possible because she was walking back and forth in front of Matt Sullivan's desk. She was afraid to look at him. She was afraid he was watching her. But she was most afraid that he *wasn't* watching her.

Two hours and forty paper cuts later, Sam took the last brad out of the last script. She sighed. She sighed because she couldn't believe this was going to be her summer. She sighed because she couldn't be in more bodily pain due to the cuts on her hands and the blisters on her feet. She sighed because the whole thing was just so damn sad: three boxes filled with scripts to be recycled. Sam could only imagine how long people had toiled away and agonized over those screenplays. And now, they were garbage. Finally, she sighed because she was convinced that Matt Sullivan would never ask her out again, if he had even asked her out in the first place.

"Who restocked the fridge?" yelled Lawrence.

Sam looked up. She exchanged glances with Ross and walked out of the copy room. She had seen Lawrence that morning making a beeline for the bathroom with a copy of *Variety* in hand, but she hadn't yet been formally introduced.

"I restocked the sodas in the fridge, sir. Mr. Miller."

"Who are you?"

"Hi, sir. I'm Sam. Samantha Rose. I'm the new intern."

"Samantha, there is something you should know if you want to make it in this business. When you put sodas in the refrigerator, you put the room temperature cans *behind* the ones that are already cold. That way, *I* don't have to spend *my* time fishing in the back of the refrigerator for the coldest drink like I'm 'Coldilocks.' It's just common sense!"

Ross had slipped out of the copy room and stood next to Sam, as if he were getting in line for a firing squad.

"It's my fault, Lawrence. I forgot to tell her about the luke-warm soda rule."

"I don't care whose fault it is, I just want a cold Diet Coke! That's all I ask! I'm not asking for an Academy Award, or a boyfriend, or world peace, or even friends who just like me for me. I just want a nice cold, carbonated, caffeinated, calorie-free beverage. Is that so wrong?"

Sam and Ross stood next to each other, silent. Everyone had stopped working to watch the outburst taking place in the center of the office.

"Now, would everyone please stop making me be a jerk?"

Lawrence huffed, tilted his head up, marched to his office, and slammed the door. The rest of the office resumed their phone conversations and e-mail writing like nothing had happened. Rebecca got back on the phone with her girlfriend, with whom she had been loudly lamenting her inability to find a nice guy in Hollywood? Dan returned to his phone conversation with an agent, trying to coax him into slipping him the spec script he was going out with the following day. Rob continued his sit-ups, while Alexandra watched him moony eyed. Matt Sullivan surfed eBay while simultaneously attempting to score free DVDs from another assistant over IM. And Ellen was at her new home with Princess Cujo and the gate guy.

"Well, at least he'll nap now," Ross said. "He always naps after he has an outburst."

"This happens often?"

"Let me put it this way. It's like good weather in Los Angeles—you can pretty much count on it. You'll get used to it."

Sam didn't see that happening anytime soon. She was embarrassed. And hurt. But she returned to the copy room with her head held high, and even had a chance to read a few scripts. She had never read a script before, and while nothing could ever compare to the literature Sam was raised on, the screenplay's format challenged and fascinated her nonetheless.

Lawrence slept for most of the afternoon, and Matt Sullivan took a long lunch, as did most of the executives. After lunch,

Dan, the only Ross-approved executive, came into the copy room to apologize to Sam for not being able to talk earlier when they were first introduced. He even offered to give her some "good" scripts to read. Sam was touched; it almost made up for the crap she had dealt with for most of the day. She was exhausted and just wanted to climb into bed, but Ross told her that the interns usually did not leave until 7:30 P.M., after everyone else had left for their premieres, drinks, and dinner dates. And she was supposed to be at The Ivy for dinner with Uncle Norman, Step Molly, and Kate at eight.

CHAPTER NINE

MARGO CHANNING: *Fasten your seat belts,*
it's going to be a bumpy night! —ALL ABOUT EVE

By the time Sam finally left the office, reapplied her lip gloss in the car, and found her way to The Ivy on Robertson Boulevard, she was already late. As a rule, Sam was categorically opposed to tardiness. But even though she was running late, Sam approached the valet with hesitation. Who was this guy in a red jacket and black pants anyway? She gave him a Land Cruiser and he gave her a little pink ticket? It just didn't seem like a fair exchange. But everyone else was doing it—cars were honking and flashing their brights behind her as she contemplated the handoff of the car. *When in Los Angeles*, thought Sam. After a brief and awkward tug-of-war over the car keys with the valet, she finally relented and watched as he drove off in the SUV, leaving her clutching her little ticket stub.

Although she was fifteen minutes late, Sam was still the first of her party to arrive. The über-coifed hostess walked her over to a corner table on the outside patio. Once seated, Sam looked around the restaurant. Slater Goodwin, notorious Hollywood bad boy/actor, was at the neighboring table. He winked, and Sam looked behind her. Was he winking at her or the brick wall? Probably the brick wall. Or maybe he had something in his eye. He winked again. Sam looked down at her plate, her mind racing. Did Slater Goodwin have a tick?

Sam surveyed The Ivy, which was so intimate and cozy that it felt like it could be someone's home. The-home-that-Laura-Ashley-built-but-probably-even-she-couldn't-afford. Sam sat on a little couch with an aggressively floral pattern and an eclectically designed set of oversize pillows. The heat lamps at each table glowed, shedding an amber light onto the posh patrons. The Ivy was designed to feel cozy, but Sam couldn't help but feel incredibly uncomfortable and out of place at this prime table all alone.

Sam looked up to see Kate breeze in wearing a sleeveless beige wrap dress and leopard-print stilettos. On her way to join Sam, she stopped at three tables to say hello, including Slater's, where she air kissed him and his three appropriately hipster friends. When Sam looked at Kate's outfit, she felt conspicuously underdressed and unconsciously straightened her blouse, as if that would make it any fancier. But when she looked at Slater's crowd—in T-shirts, ripped jeans, and trucker hats—she felt overdressed.

By the time Kate got to the table, Uncle Norman and Step Molly had walked in and were making the rounds. Step Molly was just as Kate had described. Her dark hair was immaculately pulled back into a neat, low bun, and her angular features were perfect. She wore a short strapless bronze dress and matching strappy heals—decidedly overdressed for the occasion. She stood quietly behind her husband and followed his lead, her face expressionless. *So that's Botox*, Sam surmised. Step Molly's body was amazing: slim and muscular, without an ounce of body fat. Uncle Norman was also quite fit. Tan, with his hair slicked back, he wore a simple, yet elegant, black suit with a crisp, white collared shirt. Even though he was Sam's father's older brother, he looked much younger than her father, who now had a bit of a tummy, wore glasses, and was losing his hair.

Kate slipped onto the couch beside Sam, assuring her a view of everyone walking into the restaurant.

"Well, well, if it isn't the guest of honor," said Kate.

"What's that supposed to mean?" asked Sam.

"Nothing. How was your big first day of *'work'*?" Kate made a gesture with her fingers to sarcastically illustrate quotations marks.

"Do you really want to know?" asked Sam.

Before Kate could answer, Norman and Step Molly arrived

at the table. Sam tried to stand up to give her uncle a hug but was wedged in between the heat lamp, the table, and the couch, and Kate made no move to let her out on the other side. Instead, Kate looked down at her BlackBerry and started texting, pretending not to notice that Norman and Step Molly had even arrived. Norman blew both girls a kiss from across the table, pulled out a chair for Step Molly, and they sat down.

"Hello, girls," said Norman. "Samantha! I never would have recognized you. You're all grown up."

"Hi, Uncle Norman," said Sam.

After her introduction to Step Molly, Sam told Uncle Norman about her first day of work (the few positive things, at least), making sure to thank him profusely for arranging the internship and allowing her to stay with him for the summer. Even though Sam was starving, she was afraid to take a piece of bread, as no one seemed to go near the breadbasket (carbs, Sam was learning, were evil). Step Molly rubbed her nonexistent belly and asked Norman in a baby voice if she looked fat. Kate rolled her eyes. Norman replied that Molly did not, in fact, look fat, and that she looked as beautiful as ever. This was about when Kate started fielding calls from Tatiana and Dylan, until Norman finally put a ban on her cell phone use at the table.

After the reprimand, Kate didn't talk for the rest of the meal and went out of her way to order the most expensive items on the menu. She got two appetizers—the famous crab cakes and a chopped salad—and the lobster for her main course, but she barely ate any of it. As the plates were being cleared, Step Molly announced to the table in her baby voice that she was going to "the little girls' room."

"Don't fall in," said Kate under her breath.

Sam couldn't help but laugh. From what Sam could tell, Kate was right: Step Molly was a little grating and had virtually nothing to say for herself. Sam couldn't tell if Norman had heard what Kate said or not. Either way, he didn't acknowledge it.

"So, Kate. You haven't talked much. Not to us, at least. How was your day?" asked Norman.

"Oh, I'm sorry," said Kate. "I thought the purpose of this meal was to hear about Sam's day. And Sam's internship. And Sam's great 'work ethic.'"

Sam was stung and angry but remained silent.

"Now, Kate, that's enough. It's not my fault that you don't want to do anything but shop and argue."

"And that's a bad thing? I mean, isn't that what your new wife does? Oh wait, but she doesn't argue, because that might require her having an opinion or even . . . dare I say it? A brain!"

"Kate, I'm telling you. Do not push me. It wouldn't kill you to be nicer to Molly. And to me, for that matter. I didn't do anything for you to treat me like this."

"You're absolutely right, Norman. Aside from having an affair, breaking my mother's heart, and ruining our lives, you really didn't do anything at all. I am so out of here."

"Kate, you know that's not what happened!"

69

"Whatever, Norman. You say tomato, I say . . . infidelity!"

Kate grabbed her jacket and purse and ran out of the restaurant without saying good-bye to anyone. Kate was frustrated by her father's behavior, and she still didn't understand what he could possibly see in Step Molly. She and her father had had this kind of fight before, but never in front of other people. She felt stupid and petty and angry, and she knew she was sounding and acting like a child. But she hated him. She just wanted things to be the way they used to be when she was a kid.

Sam had felt Kate shaking with anger before she left. As mean as Kate could be, Sam couldn't help but feel a little sorry for her cousin. Sure, Sam and her parents had disagreements, but it was never over something like this.

"I'm sorry you had to see that, Samantha," said Norman. "Kate is having a hard time with the divorce, as you can tell."

"It's okay, Uncle Norman. I understand." But Sam didn't understand at all.

When Step Molly returned to the table, she seemed completely perplexed that there were only two people left.

"Kate wasn't feeling well," Norman explained.

Step Molly sat down and checked to see if there was any remaining food in her teeth by looking at her reflection in her knife. Norman paid the check, and they got in separate cars to return home. Sam followed Norman and Step Molly's Porsche back to the house.

All Sam wanted was to get into bed, read, and fall asleep, but when she entered the guest room, Kate was already in bed with the lights out. Sam tiptoed into the dark room so as not to disturb Kate, but she stubbed her toe and tripped over her own suitcase. She fell with a thud, biting her lip so as not to scream in agony.

"I'm not asleep," said Kate.

"Oh," said Sam. "Then, *OW!*"

"Are you okay?"

"I think so."

"Did he say anything about me after I left?" asked Kate. She didn't make a move to turn the lights on, nor did she turn over to look at Sam.

"No."

"It's not like I care anyway."

"Well, I'm sorry, Kate. It must be a hard thing to go through."

"How would you know?"

"I wouldn't. That's why I said it 'must be.'"

"Oh, right. Well, it is. Thanks."

Sam waited for a minute to make sure their conversation was over. She then blindly fished in her suitcase to find her pajamas.

"You can turn on the light if you need to," said Kate.

"I don't need it," said Sam.

"Suit yourself."

Kate turned over and pulled her covers up over her ear. As

Sam brought her pajama bottoms and tank top into the bathroom to change, she could have sworn she heard a whimper from Kate's bed. Could Kate be *crying*? It seemed that maybe Sam was not the only Rose who never let anyone see her cry.

Kate hated that she was crying. She hated that she had to hide under her covers. She didn't want Sam to see her like this. She didn't want anyone to see her like this. She missed her mom. She missed the way things used to be. She missed her old life, her old house, and her old, popular, carefree self. Kate thanked her lucky stars that she was seeing her therapist the following morning. She planned to deconstruct the entire evening.

And Sam couldn't believe that she would have to get up in just seven hours and do the whole day over again tomorrow. And the next day. And the day after that. But what made it both torturous and exciting at the same time was the knowledge that she would get to see Matt Sullivan again. Whatever would she wear?

CHAPTER TEN

WATTS: *Ray, this is 1987. Did you know that a girl can be whatever she wants to be?* —SOME KIND OF WONDERFUL

When Ashley Hatcher walked into Authentic Pictures later that week, everyone in the office was abuzz. Everyone, of course, except Ross, who muttered something indecipherable under his breath, though it was a safe bet that it was something about how Ashley would "burn." Whether he was going to burn because he was dating Susan Mandalay, who was the famous actress twenty years his senior, or because he insisted that everyone try a new diet energy drink he was obsessed with—or a combination of the two—remained unclear to Sam.

She was commissioned to go out and purchase the new hyper-caffeinated, artificially sweetened beverage called Jet, while Ashley met with Lawrence about a new project Lawrence was trying to get greenlit. With Ashley attached, it would be a sure thing.

But before Sam left, she had to get petty cash from Matt Sullivan. She took a deep breath and walked over to his cubicle. *Cool as a cucumber*, she silently repeated to herself like it was a mantra.

"Hey Sam, how're you doing?"

"I'm good. I just need to get some petty cash for the . . . Jet stuff."

"No problem. So, Ross said you went to Deerfield? I had a lot of friends from Harvard who went there. Before your time, though."

"Yeah, and I was a day student, so I probably wouldn't have known them anyway. I'm sure they were *boarders*."

No matter how much Sam liked Matt Sullivan, she couldn't disguise the chip she had always carried on her shoulder. She had momentarily stepped back into her high school armor, which she accessorized with heavy sarcasm and acute defensiveness. Matt Sullivan looked at Sam with piqued interest.

"So, where will you go next year?"

"Smith. My parents are professors there, so . . ."

"Great school. But, *all girls*?"

"What's wrong with *all girls*?"

The phone rang, and Matt put his headset back on. "I've gotta grab this call, just don't forget to bring back a receipt, okay?"

As Sam turned away with the twenty-dollar bill Matt Sullivan had given her, she thought about her decision to go to Smith. It wasn't really a decision, per se: she always knew she would go there. Maybe that was the problem. It was all so easy: her parents were professors there, so it was affordable, it was a great education, and she lived five minutes away.

But why had she never really questioned this major choice in her life? Certainly, it wasn't as if she was going to keep living at home in her childhood bedroom. She would live in the dorm with the other girls. She would have a normal college life. Or would she? Sure, she would see her parents sometimes on campus, bring her laundry home for her mom to do, have dinner with them a few nights a week. This had always seemed comforting to Sam. But at this moment, as she walked away from the boy of her dreams and climbed into her car to pick up diet energy drinks three thousand miles from home, she wondered if comfort was really what she wanted for the rest of her life.

Sam had to go to three supermarkets to find Diet Jet, finally tracking it down at Trader Joe's. When Sam arrived at the office, she couldn't help but notice Susan Mandalay waiting for her young beau in her Mercedes convertible, a can of Diet Jet in hand. Diet Jet could not possibly have been on Susan's macrobiotic diet, which Sam had read so much about. But whatever Susan was doing, it was working. She was even more beautiful in person. In gawking at the star, Sam walked directly into the front door of the building, spilling cans everywhere.

As she bent down to gather the cans, she looked over to see that Susan had gotten out of her car and was kneeling beside her, helping her retrieve the drinks.

"Happens to the best of us," she said.

"Oh, thanks. I mean, yeah," Sam stammered.

"Here, let me help you," Susan said.

And so, Sam walked into Authentic Pictures, carrying a crate of Diet Jet, assisted by Susan Mandalay. When Lawrence saw them walking in, a look of horror came across his face. He ran out to greet Susan and apologize that she had been "put to work like a mule." Susan insisted that he try the beverage, but upon opening the can, the red liquid exploded all over his white shirt. Lawrence looked at Sam as if he might strangle her, but he managed to laugh it off for Ashley's and Susan's benefit.

Next stop for Sam: the dry cleaner.

CHAPTER ELEVEN

Pause you who read this, and think for a moment
of the long chain of iron or gold, of thorns or flowers,
that would never have bound you, but for the formation of
the first link on one memorable day.

—CHARLES DICKENS, *Great Expectations*

By the time Friday rolled around, Sam was exhausted. Dan called all the assistants and Sam into his office for what she would come to learn was the Friday ritual meeting called "weekend read," during which everyone was assigned specific scripts to read over the weekend. Sam was excited to be given any kind of creative responsibility, even though Ross warned her that most of the scripts she would read would be "garbage." Sam, ever the responsible student, decided to get an early start on her reading and hunkered down in the copy room with one of her five scripts.

By 7:45 P.M., she assumed everyone had gone home for the weekend, but she didn't want to go back to Uncle Norman's house just yet. She had no weekend plans except reading. The script she had now was about kids who became possessed through their kitchen appliances. It was aptly entitled *Hell's Kitchen*.

"Ugh, pass," she said.

It was only the end of her first week, but Ross's cynicism was already rubbing off on her. Less than a week ago, Sam had been determined to remain perky, come hell or high water. But the water was rising with each passing moment, and Sam felt like she could barely keep her head above it. She knew even she could write better material than what she was reading. What was she doing here anyway? Sam couldn't bear to read another bad script, so she took her mother's advice and picked up the book she had slipped in her bag that morning. She smiled, comforted by the familiar characters and precise prose.

"*Great Expectations?*"

Matt Sullivan was leaning in the doorway of the copy room with his arms crossed over his chest. Sam was startled. She thought she was alone. She felt a wave of nausea wash over her. She was completely frozen, so she definitely couldn't blame it on her acute motion sickness. Sam had never seen Matt Sullivan come into the copy room. If he needed something, he would call out from his desk, which was all of fifteen feet away. Sam thought Matt must be very busy, but Ross had assured her it was a "power move." And Matt Sullivan never stayed this late. He always had drinks, or a dinner, or some Hollywood function to attend, or all of the above. So, why was he still there?

"Oh. Yeah. Comfort reading. I know. I'm weird," said Sam.

"No, but you're definitely different. It's nice. Not a lot of people have a brain out here."

"Tell me about it."

"I like Dickens. But I'm a Milton man myself. I wrote my thesis on *Paradise Lost*."

"Wow."

Who is this guy and where did he come from? What Sam really wanted to know was how he got to be so . . . so . . . so *Matt Sullivan*. He was staring at Sam with that piercing gaze that melted her and made her shake. He was wearing a slight variation on his customary uniform—a pair of worn-in jeans and a white button-down, wrinkled by a long day's work. His hair was messy, in an absentminded-professor-messy way. And at that moment, as he stood in the doorway looking at Sam, well, he just seemed *lovely*. It was official: Samantha Rose was sure that the world would be a better place if Matt Sullivan was her boyfriend.

"So, Samantha Rose, what are you doing tonight? My dinner canceled. How about getting that drink?"

Was he kidding? Did she hear him wrong? Was she going to be the butt of a nationwide practical joke on some twisted candid camera show? She didn't trust him. She didn't trust anyone. But Sam looked Matt Sullivan in the eye and made the executive decision that he was worth the risk.

"Um, yeah, sure. Yes, definitely."

"Cool. I know a perfect spot."

"Oh, but . . . I don't have a fake ID or anything."

Sam cringed. Was that a deal breaker? Did she just totally blow it?

Matt Sullivan laughed. "You don't need an ID in Los Angeles, Sam. Everybody lies about their age, so no one dares to ask. Plus, you're with me."

The "you're with me" part was just about the greatest thing Sam had ever heard in the history of mankind. *Sure, I'm with him*, she thought. *No biggie. I'll just be over here with Matt Sullivan! Yup, just another Friday night hanging out with a hot twenty-one-year-old man.* Sam took deep breaths and tried to stay cool . . . or be cool . . . or whatever.

In true LA form, they took two cars to their destination. Sam was shaking with anticipation from head to toe and could barely drive. She cursed herself for being such a dork. For being such a *girl*. Meanwhile, she couldn't help but feel like the *luckiest* girl in the world. He probably just wants to talk about work, she tried to calm herself. But what if this was a date after all?

They met at a little hipster bar on Fairfax. The walls were crimson stucco with oversize mirrors, so everyone could see everyone else, no matter where they were sitting. The space was lined with updated versions of traditional red velvet banquettes. Matt knew the owners of the bar and clearly reveled in being at a place where everyone knew his name.

The two sat down in a dimly lit corner of the small bar and sipped pinot noir. Sam, who hadn't had time to get lunch that day, got tipsy quickly. The pinot went straight to her head, making her giggly and temporarily easing her defensive edge.

Sam wanted to know everything about Matt Sullivan. She wanted Matt Sullivan to know everything about her. Where should they start? How could they ever catch up on the last eighteen years' worth of living? She was surprised when he described himself as a dorky kid. She assumed that cool guys like Matt Sullivan were just born that way.

Sam couldn't believe that this totally confident *man* sitting before her had ever had any insecurities. In the past, Sam would have rolled her eyes and walked away. In the present, she was smitten and paralyzed with fascination.

"And you, Sam? What's your story?"

"Oh, well, you know . . . I guess I'm 'just a small town girl living in a lonely world.'"

"Did you just quote Journey?"

"If the song fits . . ."

Matt Sullivan nodded and laughed. His professionally cocky and aloof manner gave way to reckless self-deprecation, and Sam was both surprised and charmed by it. He told her how he picked fights in high school (hot), picked up smoking cigarettes briefly in college (contrived), and how he had his heart broken by an older woman (intimidating). Okay, she was only ten months older than he was, but Sam was intrigued nonetheless. She wondered if anyone would ever talk about her the way he talked about this girl, as the proverbial "one who got away."

They talked about his own experiences with summer internships in Hollywood at different agencies, and his terrible attempt at writing a screenplay.

"At the time I was writing it, I thought it was quite profound," he said.

"Profundity is often confused with pretension," said Sam. "I mean . . ."

"No, it's okay, it's true. I'm not a writer. But I had to give it a try. It's sort of a rite of passage in Hollywood. Have you ever written?"

"Well, a little. Just short stories and stuff. I had this idea a few days ago, and I've been thinking about writing it, but I've never written a screenplay before. It's a little daunting."

"You should do it. If nothing else, it's a good exercise in humility."

God, he was smart. And for Sam, smart equaled sexy.

"What's your idea?" he asked.

Sam moved her wineglass in little circles on the table, looking down at it to avoid Matt Sullivan's gaze. Maybe she shouldn't have mentioned it?

"Well, it's stupid."

"No, tell me, I'm sure it's great."

"Okay. Did you see that John Hughes movie *Weird Science*?"

"Sure."

"So, I had this idea that I could update it and make it for teenage girls. You know, two unpopular, supersmart, and supernerdy girls, frustrated with their own supernerdiness, create the perfect guy using, like, soap-on-a-rope and dental floss, or something silly like that. And then of course everyone falls in love with this guy because he's gorgeous, and smart, and interesting, and funny, and . . . older."

There was an awkward silence. Matt Sullivan smiled. Sam looked down again, shook her head, and continued.

"But he seems to be madly in love with both girls, and so they become popular by association. All the popular girls want to be their friends so they can meet the guy, and all the boys now want to date them because they assume the perfect guy must know something they don't. The girls begin to see themselves through the perfect guy's eyes, and learn to embrace what's beautiful about who they are as intelligent and sensitive young girls. But then of course they have a petty falling-out over the guy, and then they come back together, realizing that the dorky guys who were nice to them all along are really the guys they should be with, so they start dating them, and the perfect guy fades away. And they all live happily ever after." Sam paused. "But it's not like I've really thought it out or anything."

"You know what's great about that idea, Sam? It's about people *connecting*. I like it. You should keep working on it. I think it might be tough to do with young girls—maybe not wholesome enough for that genre with the double standard and all that, unfortunately it does still exist—but you should start writing down some thoughts. I'd be happy to look at it."

The waitress returned with two fresh glasses of pinot noir, even though Sam had not finished her first one.

"This round is on me," she said.

Matt winked at the waitress, who giggled and patted his shoulder. Sam caught herself glaring.

"It was just an idea," said Sam.

"It's good. You should trust your instincts," replied Matt. "Cheers, to teenage girls."

"And perfect older men."

They raised their glasses and clinked them together. Matt Sullivan looked at her intently before, during, and after the first sip. If Sam trusted her instincts, she would have lunged across the table and into his lap. But she could not entertain such impulses right now. Her head was swimming with wine and hormones, and she was busy wishing this night, this moment, would never end.

"You're one cool girl, Samantha Rose."

Sam didn't know what to say. She was caught off guard and rendered completely speechless, so she just laughed, which unfortunately turned into a semisnort, and then she lifted her hand up, as if to say, Oh stop . . . go on. Matt Sullivan took her raised hand in his.

"You have great hands," he said. "Did you ever take piano?"

"Yeah. For like a day. But I couldn't get past 'Twinkle Twinkle, Little Star.'"

"You have to start somewhere."

"I did play the recorder for a while, though."

"That must be quite a story."

"Not really, no."

"Do you want to get out of here?"

Matt Sullivan paid the check, refusing to accept any money from Sam. He said good-bye to the bartender, the waitresses, and the owner, but he was leaving with Sam. She was sure that every woman there was jealous. Sam really liked being "the girl who gets the guy" for a change. Once outside the bar, they faced each other.

"Well, I guess I should go home," said Sam

"You probably should. But you could come to my place," he said. "It's just around the corner."

Sam didn't even know what time it was. She didn't care. But, then again, should she call Uncle Norman and tell him she would be home late? She certainly couldn't call her parents, who were three hours ahead and probably sound asleep. Would anyone notice if she came home late? Would anyone notice if she didn't come home at *all*? It was a terrifying idea and completely liberating at the same time. Sam was jolted out of her thoughts as she felt Matt Sullivan's hand take hers. She looked up at him and smiled. He squeezed her hand. *If this is life after high school,* Sam thought, *sign me up. Pronto.*

They walked to Matt's apartment, playfully bumping into each other as they went. He lived in a brown Spanish-style duplex building. His apartment had two bedrooms—one of which had been converted into a home office—hardwood floors, high ceilings, and a large kitchen with several dirty dishes in the sink. Scripts and books were littered everywhere, along with several button-down shirts almost identical to the one he was wearing.

Matt Sullivan took a book from one of his cluttered shelves, and they sat side by side on the couch in the living room. Sam's hands were clasped together and wedged between her crossed knees. The lamp was shining in her eyes, but she dared not say anything for fear of ruining the moment.

"I thought you'd like this," he said.

Sam unclasped her hands and took the old hardcover book from Matt Sullivan. It was a first edition copy of J. D. Salinger's *Franny and Zooey*, one of Sam's favorites.

"Wow! This is beautiful!" said Sam.

"*You're* beautiful," he said. "You know, Sam, I wanted to kiss you the moment I saw you."

Sam nearly choked. Matt Sullivan gently patted her back until she stopped coughing. No, it was not Sam's most graceful moment. But she had not seen this coming. Not at all.

"You did? Really?"

"Yeah. You're hot! Do you realize how hot you are?"

Sam turned away from him and could feel her face turning bright red. This was too much. This was not real. Then she felt his hand on her cheek. She turned to look at him. Sam felt like Matt Sullivan was really looking at her, the way no one had ever looked at her before. And then it happened: he leaned in, and he kissed her. To Sam, it was the most perfect kiss in the world. It was sweet and slow, it was gentle, and it was real. His mouth and his tongue tasted like red wine and experience.

It was nothing like Sam's first kiss when she was fourteen and Tom Hastings fluttered his tongue in her mouth like a snake with raging epilepsy. Tom referred to kissing as "playing tonsil hockey," and after their kiss, Sam understood why. But this was a whole new ball game. Every slight move Matt Sullivan made was gentle, deliberate, and confident. His hand rested on the side of her neck, his thumb wrapping around her ear. The world stood still. Time stood still. Sam worried about nothing. Not her lip gloss, not her parents, not her heart.

They kissed for what could have been thirty minutes or thirty days. Their lips fit together like a flawless game of Tetris, every block falling effortlessly into place. They would pause once in a while, and she would press her lips to his forehead, and his nose, and his chin, and she would put her arms around his neck, and pull him closer to her. He stood up and took her hand. And then, slowly, they started moving, swaying. It wasn't clear who initiated it. There was no music playing, but it didn't matter. Sam tilted her head back, and she smiled up at him. He smiled back and put his hand through her hair. She put her head on his shoulder, and they continued their silent dance. It was just a simple box step, but to Sam, they might as well have been the most perfect dancers who had ever lived.

When she lifted her head off his shoulder, he lifted her arm above her head, slowly twirled her out and away from him, and then reeled her back in toward him. She looked over her shoulder, planting a kiss on his lips. He twirled her again so that she was facing him, and the two resumed their dance.

"So, is this how you sweep all the girls off their feet?" she asked.

"No, Sam. Just you."

He pulled her into him so that his arms were around her, holding her tightly. What did she do to be this lucky? Sam figured Matt Sullivan could have anyone he wanted. And he wanted her. Just her.

"Do you want to . . ." Matt started to say as he motioned toward his bedroom.

Sam, panicked, pulled away from him. Her heart sank into her vintage pumps. Was he just after one thing? Were his "expectations" greater than she was comfortable meeting?

"Matt, I'm not going to . . . you know . . . ."

"Sam, I wasn't asking you to . . . 'you know,'" he said. "Do you want to stay over? I'll be a gentleman, I promise."

"So, it's just, like, a sleepover?"

"Sure."

They both slept in their clothes that night. Matt Sullivan held Sam in his arms, and she was positive she would not sleep a wink. She was afraid to move, even though she was sure her cheek had fallen asleep on his chest, and that her head weighed a million pounds, which might severely and permanently injure him. She tried to contain her laughter when he snored a few times, and twitched his head like a horse shaking off its reins. She stared at the clock. She stared at the ceiling. She stared at Matt Sullivan.

Can you fall in love in one night? Samantha Rose wanted to know. Because she thought that, maybe, she had.

CHAPTER TWELVE

By the time you swear you're his
Shivering and sighing
And he swears his passion is
Infinite, undying—
Lady, make a note of this:
One of you is lying.
—Dorothy Parker

Sam must have eventually dozed off, because she awoke to NPR on Matt Sullivan's alarm clock. She nuzzled her cheek against his chest and smiled with anticipation. What would they do today? Would they walk to the farmers' market hand in hand, read the paper, and kiss in between bites of organic flaxseed blueberry pancakes? Would they drive out to Malibu, huddle on the beach, eat fish tacos, make fun of surfer dudes, and talk about their future together?

Sam watched Matt Sullivan's arm with wonder as he reached it over her to turn off his alarm. He looked at her as he rubbed his eyes.

"Hi," he said.

"Hi."

"What time is it?"

"Nine-fifteen."

"Did you sleep okay?" he asked.

"Yeah, you?"

"Like a baby."

He pulled Sam to him and yawned. She wondered if her breath smelled terrible, and whether or not she was supposed to go brush her teeth, and generally how all this worked. After all, Sam had never woken up with a boy before. And she really had to pee, but she dared not get up. She snuggled her head into his chest. He was only twenty-one, but he had a man's chest (or what she assumed was a man's chest). Sam wanted to rest her head on it forever.

"Listen, Sam, I gotta go soon."

Matt Sullivan took his arms back and ran his hands through his hair. Sam was stunned, and lifted her head so that he could extricate himself from their embrace. No pancakes? No fish tacos?

"Oh, yeah. Sure. That's cool," she said.

It was so *not* cool.

"I have my S.A. at ten," he said.

"S.A.?"

"Yeah, spiritual advisor."

"You have a spiritual advisor?"

"I only see her twice a month or so. I know it sounds weird, but it's actually really helpful. My therapist referred me to her."

"You have a therapist?"

"And an accountant. A trainer. A lawyer. And an acupuncturist."

"Wow. You have . . . a staff."

"Yeah, I guess I do."

"So what do you do with your S.A.?"

"Well, she chants."

"You chant?"

This was getting weird. Instinctively, Sam pulled the covers up to her neck, even though she was fully dressed. She looked around her and realized that he had nothing on the walls in his bedroom, nor did he have a duvet cover on his comforter. In fact, aside from his queen-size bed, the only other piece of furniture in his bedroom was a dark wood bedside table, which held his alarm clock. Matt pulled the sheets back and got out of bed, stretching his arms over his head.

"No, she chants," he said.

"Oh." As if that made it any better. "So what does she tell you?"

"Basically, she tells me that if I keep working hard, stay directed and focused, and don't let anything get in my way, I'm going to be really huge."

"Huge?"

"Hugely successful."

He walked to the door of the bedroom. Sam took this as her cue to get out of bed. Where were her shoes? Did she leave them in the living room? She quickly looked around the barren bedroom but didn't see them anywhere.

"Are you okay to get home?" he asked. "You remember where your car is, right?"

"Oh, yes, sure. I don't really know where my shoes are, though."

"They're probably in the living room."

They stood awkwardly in his bedroom for a moment. Sam broke the silence.

"So I'm just going to go."

"Listen, Sam, I'm sorry I have to leave so early. I really had a great time last night."

"I did too."

Sam's heart melted. One kind word from him, and she was putty in his hands. It was so unlike her.

He led her out of his bedroom, into the living room, past his couch and the copy of *Franny and Zooey* on the coffee table. And there, in the middle of the room, were Sam's vintage pumps. She must have kicked them off mid box step. She wondered if there would ever be an encore. She slipped her shoes on silently as he went to the door and opened it for her.

"You can borrow the book if you want," he said.

"Oh, thanks." Sam felt as if she were on some demented game show and this was her parting gift. She carefully placed the book in her bag.

"I want to see you again, Sam," he said. "This week."

"Well . . ." Sam started to say the obvious.

"I mean, outside of the office. Maybe Wednesday night?"

"Yeah, sure. I can do Wednesday."

"Oh wait, no, I don't think I can do Wednesday. Let me check my calendar, and we'll figure it out, okay? So, I'll call you," he said.

"Okay!" Sam couldn't think of anything else to say. She just did not seem humanly capable of being cool at that moment.

They stood in the open doorway. He was going to call her. But *where* would he call her? Did he have her cell phone number? Did he have the house phone number at Uncle Norman's? Should she ask?

"Listen, Sam. I'd really appreciate it if we could keep this between us. I mean, no one at work needs to know about this, right?"

So, did that mean the billboard on Sunset Boulevard she had ordered announcing they spent the night together would have to go? Sam was both annoyed and hurt by his comment, but she covered it up.

"No, of course. I mean, *of course not.*"

Then, Matt Sullivan leaned toward her. Sam closed her eyes and went to kiss him on the mouth, but he must have been trying to kiss her on the cheek, as she ended up grazing the corner of his mouth with her puckered lips.

"Well, have a great weekend!" she said, as cheerfully as she could muster.

"You too, Sam. See you Monday."

She still loved hearing him say her name. And then there was that smile of his combined with his should-be-patented disheveled look that made her stomach drop into her shoes. She heard the door close and lock behind her. So was he going to call her or just see her on Monday? Would she actually be able to physically *live* until Monday without seeing him or speaking to him? Could she really wait the forty-eight long hours until she would see him again at the office? She walked downstairs to the entrance of the building in a daze. As she reached for the front door, it swung open, hitting her in the head and knocking her down.

"I'm so sorry! Are you okay?"

Sam was splayed out on the Spanish tile floor. She put her hand on her throbbing head. Didn't she know that voice from somewhere? She looked up.

"Sam?"

"Ross?"

"What are you—" they both asked at the same time.

Ross kneeled down beside her and helped Sam to her feet. He looked Sam up and down. Could he tell that she was still wearing the clothes she had been wearing at work the previous day, and that Sam was sporting a tragic case of bed head?

"I had to bring Matt some scripts he forgot at the office," he said.

"I, um . . . I have a friend who lives in this building. An old

95

friend. I mean, she's not *old* per se; she's young . . . at heart. She's young at heart. She's ninety. She's a friend. I was visiting her."

"Uh-huh."

"Yeah, I like old people. I feel we can learn a lot from them. Because . . . they've been on this earth much longer than we have. So they know more. Even though they forget sometimes. But I mean, I forget things sometimes too, and I'm eighteen! I mean, don't you? Forget things?"

"I have a photographic memory, so no."

"Oh, wow, really? Wow, well, that's . . . something."

"Sam, are you okay?"

"Yeah. Sure, yes! I am fine, Ross. But I have to go, so I'm just going to . . . I'll see you on Monday, okay?"

Sam went out the front door and walked toward Fairfax, cursing herself all the way. What a disaster. Could things get *any* worse? As she approached the Land Cruiser, she noticed something on the windshield. She grabbed it from the wipers and looked at it closely. A parking ticket. Her first. She groaned. *Perfect*, she thought. And now she would have to do the "drive of shame" back to Uncle Norman's house and do damage control before he spoke to her parents. If he had even noticed her absence at all. And if he hadn't noticed, she was sure Kate would have. She hopped in the car and started thinking about how she would explain herself.

But first, Sam would have to actually find her way back to the house.

CHAPTER THIRTEEN

ALLISON: *Why are you being so nice to me?*

CLAIRE: *Because you're letting me.* —THE BREAKFAST CLUB

Kate was picking at her bland Zone Delivery breakfast: a decidedly slimy egg-white omelet with asparagus. Wasn't asparagus supposed to make your pee smell? Yuck. She eyed Manuela's corn muffin.

Kate heard the front door open quietly, and then the unmistakably clumsy pitter-patter of the tiptoe of shame. Kate knew it well. Manuela knew it too, and looked up. Kate put her finger to her lips and scurried quietly to the doorway of the kitchen with a mischievous grin. *Miss Perfect isn't so perfect after all*, she thought.

Sam was cringing as she carefully tiptoed barefoot, shoes in hand, through the entry foyer past the kitchen. The stairs to her room were in sight; she was in the home stretch, when . . .

"Good morning, Sunshine!" said Kate.

"Oh, hi," said Sam.

"You don't have to tiptoe, Cuz. They're already gone."

"Oh. Did they—"

"Did they notice that a certain little someone didn't come home last night? Hmmm . . . let me think about that for a minute. . . ." Kate rubbed her fingertips on her temples and shut her eyes tightly. "I'm trying to remember. Hold on, I think it's coming to me. . . ."

"Come on, Kate, seriously."

"Nope, I just lost it." She opened her eyes and shrugged. "Sorry, Cuz, I simply can't remember."

Sam walked toward Kate as if she might just throw down and punch her. She was exhausted and not in the mood for this.

"Okay, what's it going to take for you to remember?"

"Details, dear cousin, details."

"There's nothing to tell."

"See, I would bet that there is. Come on, Cuz. Spill it. Who is he?"

Sam knew Kate was not to be trusted, but she was dying to tell someone, *anyone*, about her evening with Matt Sullivan. Who was she kidding? She wanted to scream it from the expensively tiled Beverly Hills rooftops! But she couldn't. And she still didn't know what Uncle Norman knew of her whereabouts. Sam didn't know whether to cry or to scream. She must have looked like she was a girl on the verge of a nervous breakdown because Kate gently put her hand on Sam's arm.

"Sam. Don't freak out. Listen, I was kidding around. Norman left early to play golf, and Step Molly is at Barry's Bootcamp 'working that ass,' or what there is of one. Just chill. You can have some breakfast with Manuela and me. I mean, if you want."

"I should go upstairs and change."

"Oh, come on, Massachusetts. Join us. Hell, you can even eat my omelet, although I wouldn't wish it upon my worst enemy."

They both paused. Was Sam Kate's worst enemy?

"Just tell me, Kate. Does he know?" Sam asked.

"Norman? I told him you were still asleep—jet-lagged and all that. You'll see, he doesn't really care. Come on, I won't bite."

Sam dropped her bag and shoes at the bottom of the stairs, and walked with Kate into the kitchen. Kate didn't have to cover for her with Norman, and she had. Sam might have been delirious from lack of sleep, but she was starting to think that maybe, just maybe, Kate wasn't so bad after all.

"Look what the cat dragged in, Manuela," said Kate.

Yup, Sam was definitely just delirious from lack of sleep. She glared at Kate.

"Hi, Manuela," said Sam.

"*Buenos días, Samita.*"

"Don't worry Sam, Manuela won't say anything. She's cool."

Sam sat between Manuela and Kate, and Kate pushed her egg-white omelet toward Sam, who looked at it suspiciously. She had never had just egg whites before. And it was in a special super-non-degradable plastic delivery container that was definitely not environmentally sound. It looked like it was food for an astronaut.

"I don't really have to eat this, do I?"

"Nah. I couldn't stomach it either. Wanna get some real breakfast?"

Sam looked at her cousin appreciatively, but she was still hesitant and trying to remain cool.

"Yeah, sure. Why not?"

Sam pushed herself out from the table, and as she headed upstairs from the breakfast nook, Kate called out, "Oh, and your parents called!"

Sam paused on the stairs, taking in the information.

"Okay, thanks."

Sam closed the door of the guest room and dialed her home number. She felt like she was calling another world. She had been away from home for barely a week, but it seemed like forever. Her heart melted when she heard her father's voice answer the phone.

"Hello?"

"Hi, Dad."

"Samantha! Now that you're a Hollywood hotshot, you forget to call your dear old parents?"

"Is that Sam?" Sam heard her mother yell from another room.

"Yes, dear. Pick up."

"Hold on, don't say anything yet. I'm picking up! Hello?"

"Hi, Mom."

"Hi, honey, how's it going? Norman told us you look beautiful and that he took you to The Ivy and that you're doing well at work. Have you gone to the Getty yet?"

Sam loved her mom, but sometimes, she was a bit much, especially on zero sleep.

"No, Mom, I haven't gotten to the Getty yet. I've only been here a few days. I promise I'll go."

"She'll go, Betty, she'll go," said Arthur.

"Just as long as you go, Sam, it's important to stay cultured."

"I know, Mom. How are you guys?"

"We're fine, Samantha. Same old, same old," said Arthur.

"We miss you," said Betty.

"I miss you too. It's weird out here. But I think I'm having fun."

"You think? Will you call us when you know for sure?" asked Arthur.

"Ha-ha, Dad. I'm going for breakfast with Kate now."

"Oh that's nice, honey. Have you made lots of friends?" asked Betty.

"Some."

"Betty, I think she wants to get off the phone," said Arthur.

"But I haven't heard anything about work, or—"

"I'll call you later next week when there's more to tell, okay?"

"We miss you," said Betty again.

"I miss you too. I love you."

"Love you too, honey. Have fun," said Arthur.

Sam hung up the phone and fell back briefly onto her unslept-in bed, forcing herself to get up before she started to doze off. She took a quick cold "body shower" (no washing of the hair) and retired her day-old clothes for her loose black culottes and a sleeveless black and brown vintage blouse. After throwing her hair into a short ponytail, and using several bobby pins to fasten the stray short hairs, Sam met Kate in the entry foyer.

"Culottes," said Kate. "Wow. Interesting choice. I haven't seen culottes since 1991. Briefly replaced by the skort, a good culotte is hard to find. What's the top, Gucci?"

"Just something I found at a vintage store in Northampton. Three bucks."

"How thrifty. I could never pull that off. Good for *you*."

"Good for *me*."

"Let's rock."

The girls walked outside and got into Kate's convertible. Kate took a deep breath when she put the top down, as if she herself was shedding a superfluous layer of skin, before screeching out of the driveway. Sam held on to the door handles for dear life and kept kicking the floor on the passenger side with her foot, as if there was actually a brake there.

"What's that thumping?" asked Kate.

Sam put her hand on her leg to stop it from moving.

"I don't know what you're talking about."

"Sam, I think we need to discuss your chill factor. Right now you're on like zero chill. It's just not going to do."

"Kate, can I be honest with you?"

"Honesty? That's so East Coast—I love it!"

"I think you're a really terrible driver."

"See, Sam, I disagree. I'm not a terrible driver, I'm just impulsive."

"That's a euphemism if I ever heard one."

Kate cut off a car as she changed lanes and roared into the parking lot at Fred Segal, the famously fabulous Angeleno department store. She pulled in next to two girls who were also in a convertible, applying lipstick and admiring themselves in their vanity mirrors.

"Ugh. That's Gynger with a *y* and just Ginger. Same name, different spelling, and they were always best friends. They went to my high school. Gynger with a *y* hooked up with my boyfriend junior year and she still thinks I don't know."

"So she's a bytch with *y*?" asked Sam.

"Totally."

"Is that Kate? Kate Rose!" screamed the redhead in the driver's seat.

"Oh my god, Gynger! Hi! You look fantastic! Did you lose weight?"

"Well, yeah, actually I did. How are you?"

"I think she was talking to me," said just Ginger.

"Well, you both look great," said Kate. "This is my cousin, Sam. She's visiting from out of town and is just dying to see Fred Segal, so we gotta run, but so great seeing you. We should do lunch sometime. Bye!"

Before the Gingers could reply, Kate pulled Sam toward the café section of the department store.

"Hi . . . bye," said Sam over her shoulder.

The girls passed through an outside area where trendy Angelinos sat on stools sipping various types of coffee beverages and designer juices. Kate kept her sunglasses on—as if she was a celebrity who just couldn't bear to be recognized—as they walked inside the dimly lit and bustling restaurant in the store, scoring a prime corner table. She ordered another egg-white omelet, hold the asparagus, but she still ended up eating most of Sam's pancakes. Kate posited that calories didn't count when eating off of someone else's plate, especially if it was the plate of a family member. This was news to Sam, who never really thought much about calories.

"I hate you! We are over!" yelled a superthin blonde in an orange baby-T, jean shorts, and flip-flops. She was in tears, had mascara running down her cheeks, and was sprinting from the store through the restaurant, out toward the parking lot.

"I didn't mean it! I'm sorry!" yelled a handsome and equally superthin hipster guy in Elvis-style gold glasses, who was running after her.

Everyone in the restaurant watched the brief spectacle, and then immediately returned to their meals.

"Wow! What was that about?" asked Sam.

"The girl is Bliss Goldstein. The guy is Zen Hughes. They've been dating on and off since high school. They have a notoriously turbulent relationship."

"Bliss and Zen? You'd think, with those names . . ."

"I know. The irony kills me. So, you're not going to tell me about last night with Doe, are you?"

"Doe?"

"Well, you won't tell me his name and I've got to call him something, so he's *John Doe. Duh.* Doe."

"Oh, Doe. No. I'm telling you, there's nothing to tell."

"That's cool. I have ways of making you talk." Kate twirled her fork at Sam, as if she were hypnotizing her. Sam twirled her fork back at Kate who continued talking. "You don't have a lot of friends, do you?"

Sam stopped smiling. This was a sore subject for her. It was true. She didn't have many friends, unless she counted the fictional characters she loved reading about in her favorite novels.

"I'm sorry. I didn't mean it like that. I just mean that you're not very open. You don't trust me. It's cool, though. I get it. Hey, I wasn't dying to like you either."

"Yeah, well . . ." Sam trailed off. "I didn't really like high school. It sounds lame, but my parents are my best friends.

They're smart. They get me. I always felt like kids my own age never did."

"Huh."

"What's that?"

"What's what?"

"That. The 'huh.' What does that mean?"

"Sammy, honestly, I'm sure your parents are great and all, but it just sounds to me like you have a serious case of Stockholm syndrome."

"What?"

"You know, that's when if you're a prisoner you start to get attached to your captors."

"I never thought of it like that."

"I used to be a daddy's girl. But somewhere along the way, Norman lost interest in me. My therapist says that's why I like guys who don't pay attention to me. I'm repeating the relationship with my father."

"That's weird."

"What kind of boys do you like?"

Sam smiled despite herself. Her stomach turned a bit. She shrugged her shoulders and hugged her arms to her chest as she imagined Matt Sullivan, and their first kiss the night before.

"Okay, you have to spill it! You totally love Doe . . . I am *dying*!"

"Seriously Kate, I don't know. He's just a guy I met. It's not a big deal. I'll probably never see him again."

"You're impossible."

"Does everyone have a therapist out here?" asked Sam.

"Pretty much. I love mine. I have her on speed dial. But I also have my favorite take-out restaurants on speed dial, so what does that say?"

"Food is love?"

"Well, if food is love, then right now I am madly and passionately full of love. Let's go spend some money."

Sam looked hesitantly at Kate.

"Don't worry, it's on Norman."

"Oh, I couldn't," said Sam.

"Sure you could."

The girls walked from brightly lit room to even more brightly lit room, blasted by the trendiest rap and techno music while they browsed the most sought after and overpriced threads all in aggressively small sizes. *No three-dollar blouses here*, thought Sam. The saleswomen—who all looked like models—lingered at the registers, aloof and bored. Each female shopper was hipper and thinner than the next, and several had their significant other in tow, who was dutifully seated on the white leather couch outside the dressing rooms.

Every time Sam saw a guy in the store who was even remotely the same physical type as Matt, her heart sank and she would do an immediate double take. But Matt Sullivan himself was nowhere in sight. Kate, on the other hand, ran into a dozen more people she knew—from ballet class when she was eight, summer teen tours, high school, college—she knew everyone from somewhere. She would introduce Sam to all of them, and once out of their earshot, she always gave Sam their life story, or as she called it, their "411."

"You're the mayor!" said Sam.

Kate laughed. She put down Norman's credit card and insisted on buying Sam some designer jeans like the ones she had, two sexy tops that Sam would never have bought on her own, a pair of stilettos, and a black bikini.

"How do you feel about hitting the beach?" asked Kate.

"Oh, okay. But I need to get my sunblock. I left it at the house."

"Sam, I hate to tell you, but I guess you didn't get the memo, so here goes: tan is in. This white porcelain skin business you have going on is cool and retro and all, but it's summer in California, and it's about time you got your tan on."

The girls hopped back in the car and headed west toward the beach. As they listened to the radio and roared along the 10 freeway, Sam looked up at the blue sky and closed her eyes. She wondered how Matt Sullivan's appointment with his "S.A." went, and what he was doing all day. She thought about how tenderly he had held her, and how their kisses were unlike any other she had ever had. Not that she had had many. In addition to Tom (the fluttering-tongued king of tonsil hockey), she had kissed her best guy friend, Adam Scott, when she was fifteen. He professed his love for her right after, and she freaked out, proclaiming that she didn't think of him in that way. Their friendship had never been the same after that. And neither was Sam. They drifted apart senior year, and he didn't even sign her yearbook at graduation. Sam was still regretful and confused about it.

But this was entirely different. Matt Sullivan was the guy who was never supposed to notice her. He was smart, he was handsome, and oddly enough, he was nice. Wasn't he? Sam cringed as she remembered the run-in with Ross that morning. Her head throbbed. She wasn't sure if it was from the door hitting her on the head, or the glass of wine she had imbibed the previous evening.

"Hangover setting in?" yelled Kate over the music and the wind.

"Nah. I walked into a door."

"Smooth."

"Thanks."

The girls drove through a short tunnel, and when they emerged, it was beach and ocean as far as the eye could see. Sam took a deep breath of the salty sea air. Nothing was under her control, everything was new and exciting and terrifying at the same time. In theory, she should have been having a massive anxiety attack, but this was the new Sam, and the new Sam was happy in spite of herself.

They pulled into the gated parking lot of Kate's exclusive beach club. A valet ran over to take the car from the girls.

"Good afternoon, Miss Rose," he said.

"Well, good afternoon to you too. Could you do me a little favor, and please keep the car close?" said Kate.

She handed the valet a ten-dollar bill and tossed him the keys. Sam followed Kate through the tall white gates, past the pool filled with screaming kids, across the light gray deck crowded with club members in lounge chairs, and into the locker room, which was designed in blond wood and white tile. Kate led Sam to a locker and stripped absentmindedly, changing into one of her new bikinis. Sam, a little more modest, took her new bikini with her into the bathroom stall and changed there. When she returned to their locker, a maid was cleaning up with her cart of extra towels, soaps, shampoos, and conditioners in tow.

"*Pssst!*"

Kate was partially hidden behind her locker door. She waved Sam over to her. Perplexed by Kate's erratic behavior, Sam looked around to see from whom or what she might be hiding.

"You have to distract that woman," said Kate.

"What? Why?"

"Just ask her a question or something. Go. Now!"

With all her clothes in hand, her new bikini on, and a large white beach towel wrapped around her waist, Sam approached the woman wearing a gray and white uniform.

"Hi, um, I'm new here, and I was just wondering if you could please point me in the direction of the pool?"

Out of the corner of her eye, Sam could see Kate nearing the cart, motioning for her to continue.

"*No hablo Englis, niña.*"

"Um, okay. *Agua.* Big . . . *agua?* Where? *Donde agua* for . . ." Sam mimed the breaststroke.

"*¡La piscina! Alli!*" The woman pointed toward the pool deck as Kate furtively slipped several little bottles of shampoo and conditioner into her beach bag.

"*¡Muchas gracias!*" said Kate.

"Thanks," said Sam.

Kate grabbed Sam and ran toward the door. Sam followed her out of the locker room, and back into the blinding sunlight. Sam was shocked at her cousin's behavior and afraid they would get in trouble.

"I like your work!" Kate said.

"I can't believe you just stole that stuff, Kate. Why would you do that?"

"Whoa there, Miss Thing. I did not steal. I have never stolen anything in my life. I don't believe in it."

"So, what would you call what you just did then?"

"Sam, there is a very fine line between stealing and 'complementary.' That was me taking advantage of a complementary situation. Why pay for something when you can get it for free? Sammy, you are in the gift bag capital of the world, enjoy it! Besides, Norman pays enough to belong here. And this shampoo is fabulous."

Sam wondered if she should be worried that Kate's elaborate explanations were starting to make sense to her. She followed Kate past the noisy pool area toward the Roses' cabana on the beach, where a guy dressed in white was already setting up their beach chairs. Kate gave him ten dollars and plopped down with a sigh, because sometimes, it was just that hard being Kate Rose.

Sam was amazed at how easy it all seemed for Kate. Like, how did she know how or when to tip people? Sam's parents always took care of that stuff when they traveled, which was rare. But it was all new to Sam. And it seemed like everyone got tips in Los Angeles.

Kate opened up her canvas beach bag and took out her gooey orange suntan lotion, SPF 4. She slathered it on and passed it to Sam.

"For that San Tropez tan?" she offered.

As if it were some illegal substance, Sam held it suspiciously, inspecting the greasy tube, smelling the lotion, and then, with a "when in LA" shrug, she carefully applied the lube to her smooth white skin. It actually felt good and smelled sweet. Slippery, but sweet.

Just as Kate reached for the lotion again, her cell phone rang.

"Hi, Tots. I'm at the beach club. Yeah, GTs: Good times. What? No, Robertson is west of La Cienega. Well, I don't know if you go left or right to go west because I don't know where you are. You don't know where you are? Why don't you ask someone? It's shocking, T, really. Remind me to get you a sense of direction for your birthday. Hey *Magellan*, we still on for tonight? Great, can't wait . . . we'll figure out all the deets later. Bye, babe. Good luck."

Kate put her cell phone back into her bag. She smiled at Sam and settled into her chair, concentrating on the sun, as if that would make her tan faster, or deeper. Sam suddenly felt like a fool. She should have known Kate was not to be trusted. Kate didn't even tell Tatiana that Sam was there. Sam wanted to yell "I'm right here!" and "I don't need you!" and "I kissed a really cute boy last night!" But she didn't. She felt like a fraud in her new bikini and greasy lotion. She could feel her skin burning. She imagined that she looked like the poster child for peer pressure. She wanted to just get up and leave. She should have known better than to think Kate would include her in her life, with her friends. She just wanted to go home and read a good book on her own.

"So, do you want to come out with the girls and me tonight?" Kate asked.

"Yeah, sure."

"You just wait, Sammy. We're going to change your life . . . one party at a time."

And then it happened. Sam closed her eyes, settled into her own chair, and upped her chill factor.

CHAPTER FOURTEEN

Sam and Kate left the beach around five, singing along to disco music and shimmying in their car seats. Men would honk at them at stop lights. Women would look them up and down from their rearview mirrors. It was so much fun that Sam didn't think about Matt Sullivan for three whole minutes.

In midshimmy, Sam paused to look at Kate, who was wholeheartedly hitting the steering wheel and screaming along to the music in the wrong key with the wrong lyrics. Kate was an enigma to Sam. She was highly entertaining, smart, and completely different from her. For these reasons, Sam was intrigued with and pleasantly surprised by her cousin. This did not mean, however, that she trusted her yet. Kate would have to earn that. Sam was still skeptical about Kate's motives for being nice.

And Kate was surprised by her increasing affection for her cousin. Sure, Sam could be defensive and annoyingly distrustful at times, but it was nice to have a playmate, especially one who was so totally different from herself. Not to mention the fact that her childhood playmates all seemed to have jobs and important things to do, while for the first time ever, Kate . . . didn't. If she did nothing else this summer, at least she knew she had taken her East Coast cousin under her native Angeleno wing.

Sam was wary about the outfit Kate suggested for Sam to wear to dinner: new white designer jeans and a sexy yellow silk halter top. Sam insisted on wearing her own vintage black crocodile shoes, even though Kate (who wore the same size) had offered to let Sam borrow whatever she wanted.

And Kate, after pointing out that 99 percent of Sam's clothes were black, asked Sam if she could borrow her black crochet top. When Sam admitted that the top was from a large chain store in Massachusetts that also sold lawn mowers, Kate paused thoughtfully for a moment, and then said, "*Excellent.*"

Sam caught a glimpse of herself in the full-length mirror on the back of the bathroom door. She was a little sunburned, but Kate assured her it would turn into a tan the next day. Dressed in white and yellow with a little sun-kissed (and just-been-kissed) glow, Sam almost didn't recognize herself. She made sure Kate was still in the other room, and then she struck the same pose for the mirror that Kate had been doing earlier at

Fred Segal. Sam pursed her glossed lips, put her right hand on her hip, and stared. It was almost an out-of-body experience, and she was reveling in it.

The girls descended the staircase from the guest room they shared. Norman was downstairs in the living room, reading the newspaper. He folded over one side so he could get a look at them.

"Wow!" he said. "You girls look great! Sam, you're starting to look like a regular Beverly Hills babe. Where are you off to this evening?"

"We're going to dinner with the girls," replied Kate.

"Sounds like fun. Home by two, right?"

"Are you kidding?" asked Kate.

"No, I think you girls should be home at a reasonable hour."

"I haven't had a curfew since junior year of high school!"

"Well, I just think that since Sam is here—"

"Oh, since Sam is here, now you're going to decide to be a parent? Afraid she's going to tell your little brother that you're an absentee father? Too little, too late, Norman."

"We'll be home by two, Uncle Norman," said Sam. "Come on, Kate, let's just go. See you later, Uncle Norman."

Sam grabbed Kate, who stood with her feet firmly planted and poised for an argument.

"Whatever," said Kate.

"Have fun, girls!" said Norman.

Kate rolled her eyes but allowed Sam to pull her toward the

front door. The taxi was waiting for them outside, and Kate's mood had noticeably switched from her earlier excited and silly demeanor. Now she was fuming.

Once in the taxi and heading toward Hollywood—to the fancy new sushi restaurant Shi—Kate didn't talk much. Sam didn't really know how to comfort her cousin, or if Kate even wanted her to. They had made so much progress that day, and Sam worried that their new relationship had all been ruined by one bad run-in with Uncle Norman. There was no denying that it was Sam's fault that Kate had to be home earlier than usual. Sam felt sorry about that. But she also thought Kate was over-reacting. Sam boldly decided to go where no cousin had gone before. She leaned forward to the driver.

"Excuse me? Would you please turn the radio station to 98.7, and turn it up?"

Kate stared straight ahead. "I Will Survive" came over the radio, and Sam looked at Kate.

"What?" Kate snapped.

"You can't let him get to you."

"It's easy for you to say, your parents are perfect. And they care."

"They're not perfect. But they do care. So does Uncle Norman, he just has a weird way of showing it. And you don't really make it easy for him."

Kate looked at Sam. Sam didn't know if Kate was going to get angry with her and tell the taxi driver to turn around and drop her off at home, or if she would respond to Sam's tough love. Kate hung her head like a scolded dog, then looked up at Sam with a half smile. She bumped her shoulder against Sam's to the beat of the music. Sam swayed with her, and the girls continued the movement without speaking until they arrived at the restaurant.

Dylan was already sitting at their table when Kate and Sam arrived at Shi. Her left arm was in an embroidered silk sling, but that didn't inhibit her from using that arm to peel the edamame, which were already on the table. Their table was adjacent to a little stone fountain in the cobblestone garden of the restaurant, illuminated only by square paper Japanese lanterns. As Sam and Kate walked toward the table, Sam could see a crowd of people waiting for their tables at the bar. The inside of the restaurant was modern and dimly lit, with waiters scurrying throughout at lightning speed.

"Hi, hot stuff! What's with the fancy sling?" asked Kate.

"Hi, K-Ro!" said Dylan. "I think I have carpal tunnel syndrome! It's a nightmare! But I'm fine!"

"Sorry, babe. I thought you had gout."

"That was last week."

"Oh. Dylan, this is my cousin Sam."

"Wow! You don't look like you're from Massachusetts!"

"Um, thanks?"

"I mean, you look great. I mean, you look like you fit right in."

"Sam, Dylan has perfected the art of the faux pas."

"It's true, Sam," admitted Dylan. "I have."

"We've had her foot surgically removed from her mouth on more than one occasion," said Kate.

"It's not pretty," said Dylan.

"Where's Tatiana?" asked Kate.

"You know her, always late."

Kate and Dylan sat down facing out toward the patio, while Sam sat in the one chair facing the latticed back wall.

"Oh, yeah. I see the Massachusetts now," said Dylan.

"What do you mean?" asked Sam.

"That chair, it's the LA dining equivalent to 'sleeping in the wet spot,'" explained Kate.

"You can't see everyone walk in. Star gawking. That's half the fun of dining out," said Dylan.

"It's okay, Sam. You're taking one for the team, we appreciate it."

"Oh. Well, then, you're welcome, I guess," she said.

Sam looked over her shoulder self-consciously as flashbulbs went off outside.

"What's that?" asked Sam.

"Paparazzi wait outside the hot restaurants for shots of celebrities arriving and leaving," said Kate.

They heard yells from outside:

"Tatiana, over here."

"Give us a look over the shoulder, Tatiana."

"Tatiana, where's your father?"

"And there's our girl," said Kate.

Kate waved as Tatiana walked into the restaurant wearing a sexy but simple "LBD" (little black dress) and black stilettos, while everyone else whispered, turned, and stared. Tatiana was so beautiful that it seemed as if she was eternally followed by a professional lighting designer who never failed to cast her in the perfect glow. Kate tried to explain to Sam that one of the many bizarre yet endearing things about Tatiana was that she never realized how truly exquisite she was, both inside and out. Aesthetically, she was perfect, and she was fun, smart, caring, and a fiercely loyal friend. But she spent more time noticing her nonexistent physical flaws than realizing how wonderful she truly was. Many people assumed that Tatiana was conceited and snobby because she tended to be quiet when she first met anyone. And while "shy" is usually a Hollywood euphemism for bitchy and aloof, Tatiana was truly shy and guarded when meeting new people. Kate said it was because Tatiana knew most people were interested in her for the wrong reasons (the hazard of growing up in the Hollywood spotlight).

"*Holler!*" said Tatiana with a giggle. "I am starving! Why am I so hungry?"

"Um, did you eat today?" asked Kate.

"I had my protein bar."

"And she wonders why she's hungry?" said Dylan.

Tatiana blew kisses to everyone.

"You must be Sam. I've heard so much about you."

Sam had never seen Tatiana act, but everyone knew that Tatiana was a fixture on the Hollywood scene. Sam had seen pictures of her the few times she cared to look at gossip magazines, and in highlights of the Lakers game on the news (Tatiana and her father were avid fans, *or so they said*).

"It's nice to meet you," Sam said.

"Kate, you look gorgeous," said Tatiana. "I love that top! Chanel?"

Kate looked at Sam and winked.

"Oh, I don't remember."

"Well, it's *excellent*," said Tatiana.

"Here Tots, have some edamame. They're so DELICIOUS, I just want to stuff them down my pants!" said Dylan.

"Thanks for the visual, D, truly," said Tatiana.

"Okay, let's get our food on. Where is that waiter?" asked Kate.

After the girls rattled off dishes that Sam had never heard of, the tiny plates of raw fish concoctions arrived at the table so quickly and so often, it was dizzying. In between mouthfuls of sushi, Dylan complained about her stomach being upset (she was sure she had developed an ulcer over the past forty minutes), Tatiana was convinced she looked fat in her dress, and Kate acted like a den mother giving them both tough love, but love nonetheless.

The girls were virtual samurais with their chopsticks, as they were born and raised on Japanese food. At Harvard-Westlake, they were known for cutting class to get a quick sushi fix at the most expensive Japanese restaurant in Beverly Hills. Sam, on the other hand, was still an amateur sushi eater and chopsticks handler. She got so frustrated trying to get a bite of her seaweed salad into her mouth, that she actually started stabbing at the seaweed with her chopsticks, piercing it, and eating it weed by weed.

"Interesting technique," Kate commented.

"Do they even have chopsticks in Massachusetts?" asked Dylan. Kate gave her a look. "I'm just kidding?" she asked Kate.

Kate let it pass. She knew that while smart in many ways, Dylan could be shockingly ditzy. Sometimes, she used it to her advantage to catch people off guard. Other times, she was just plain clueless. And while she had traveled all over Europe extensively and frequently went to New York to visit her father, she had never seen any of the United States in between the two coasts.

"Do we have a chopstick virgin here?" asked Tatiana, pointing her own at Sam.

"Didn't your mother ever tell you it's rude to point?" asked Kate.

"Wait! Are you a virgin, Sam?" asked Tatiana.

"I've used chopsticks before, I'm just not that experienced with them."

"No, but I mean, are you a *virgin* virgin? Like, have you had sex?" Tatiana clarified.

"You don't have to answer that," said Kate. "Girls, Sam keeps everything close to the vest. Tread lightly, would you?"

Sam put her chopsticks down. She was on the spot. All eyes were on her, and inquiring minds wanted to know. Sam let her curiosity get the best of her.

"Are *you all* virgins?"

"Oh God, no!" replied Tatiana.

"Tatiana grew up on film sets," said Kate.

"There's a lot of time to kill," explained Tatiana.

"Are you a virgin, Dylan?" asked Sam.

"Well . . ."

"Here we go," said Kate.

"That's still up for debate," said Dylan.

"I say either you did or you didn't," said Tatiana.

"But it was just for a second, and it was a mistake."

"Yeah, right," said Tatiana. "It's always a mistake."

"I say, I'm still a virgin," announced Dylan. Loudly.

A balding man in an ill-fitting suit at the next table looked over at Dylan lasciviously.

"Um, inside voices please," said Kate to Dylan. She often had to remind Dylan to keep her voice down. Dylan believed she "projected," but really she was just loud.

"But we are outside," she said. "And this seaweed salad is DELICIOUS. I just want to rub it all over my entire body!"

"Seaweed wraps are so 2002. Come on, Sam, sharing is caring," said Tatiana.

Sam took a moment to think about it. What the hell, why not?

"Yes, I'm a virgin," Sam announced.

The balding man looked up again. His jaw dropped and his chopsticks fell to the ground. In retrieving them from under the table, he hit his head, knocking his table and spilling his sake all over his male dining companion, who was chuckling until he was drenched in alcohol.

"A toast!" said Kate. "To my cousin the virgin, may your deflowering be a much less traumatizing experience than my own!"

Sam raised her glass, although she didn't really understand to what she was toasting.

"What happened?"

"Well, Sam, I'll tell you the Cliffs Notes version."

"I'm going to the bathroom," interrupted Tatiana. "Sorry, Kate, I've heard this story already. A thousand times. Anybody want to come with me? *Pleeeeaaaaase?*"

"Okay, okay, I'll come with you," said Dylan. "I swear you have a bladder the size of a soybean. Anyway, that fountain is making me have to pee like a racehorse."

"Thanks for the support, girls," said Kate.

"Oh, Kate, you know I'd kick that guy's ass if I ever saw him," said Tatiana.

"I know you would, Tots. And for that, I thank you whole-heartedly."

Tatiana blew a kiss to Kate as the girls got up from the table and made their way to the bathroom.

"So," Kate began. "It was rush week at Michigan, and I was kind of miserable being away at school, and not sure I was into the whole sorority thing. Which, I know now, I definitely wasn't. I used to go to the library to avoid dealing with other pledges and the sorority sisters, and I kept seeing this guy there who would stare at me from behind all the books on his desk. So, I finally went over one day and introduced myself. His name was Colby Carter. At first, he was incredibly romantic, and he was smart and funny and sexy in a tortured-grungy-hipster-with-a-trust-fund kind of way. That was before I realized that he wasn't as smart as he was pretentious, and he wasn't as funny as he was just plain mean. But at the time, I was sure that he was 'the one,' so we went away to this little romantic hotel to, you know, have 'the sex.' The setting was just how I had always imagined it should be. But I was so nervous, I had actually forgotten to eat all day. And I *never* forget to eat. After it was over—"

"Was it painful, Kate?"

"Uh, yeah?! *And* I did gymnastics and went horseback riding as a kid, so you'd think it would make it a little less excruciating, but *nooo*! Pain-FULL! If I were you, Sammy, I would take a monster Xanax before you lose yours. I wish I had. But I digress."

"Sorry."

"No problem whatsoever. So!" Kate took a deep breath and continued. "It was painful and it was completely unromantic, even in front of a beautiful blazing fire—so, naturally I felt relieved when it was finally done with, and I tore into the minibar to get something to eat. I grabbed a big chocolate chip cookie, took a bite, and curled up next to him. And that's when he said it."

"Well, what did he say?"

"He said, 'So you're going to get fat now?'"

"No!" said Sam.

"Yeah, not so nice. We broke up shortly thereafter."

"I'm sorry to hear that, Kate. Are you okay?"

"Yeah. I'm fine. Look, it's no big deal. I mean, I had some issues with food to begin with, so it didn't *help*. But, there are other fish in the sea, more of the sex to be had, and all that, blah blah blah."

"Have you slept with anyone since?"

"No. But I did manage to open every single food item and beverage in the minibar, which as you know, they mark up to an embarrassing degree. And he was paying the bill. Revenge was almost as sweet and delicious as that ten-dollar Pepperidge Farm cookie I ate."

"Wow. My parents never let me eat from the minibar when we travel."

"Sam, there are two types of people in this world: those who take from the minibar with no hesitation, and those who won't touch it no matter how hungry they are. It's how you separate the gluttons from the prudes."

"So, what are you?"

"Depends on the day."

Tatiana and Dylan reemerged from inside of the restaurant and returned to the table.

"K-Ro, are you going to get fat now?" asked Dylan.

"Cute," said Kate.

Dylan gave her a hug. Kate smiled.

"Love ya. Mean it," said Kate.

"So Sam, are you going to tell us about your little slumber party last night? Come on, who's Doe?" asked Tatiana.

"T!" said Kate.

Sam was horrified. She looked over at Kate. Thank God she hadn't given her any details.

"What's a Doe?" asked Dylan.

"Doe. John Doe," said Kate. "Sorry, Sammy, I was excited for you! I couldn't help it. But I don't know anything, so I didn't say anything."

"It's true, she didn't tell me anything," said Tatiana.

"John Doe? That name sounds so familiar. Did he go to high school with us?" asked Dylan.

All three girls looked at Dylan.

"What?!" Dylan asked.

"John Doe is a name used for someone whose identity is unknown. Come on, D, didn't you see the *CSI* episode I was on?" asked Tatiana.

"I must have missed that one."

"I really don't want to talk about it, okay? Can we just drop it?"

"Sorry, Sammy," said Kate. "Girls, icks-nay on the oe-Day."

While Sam was initially hurt that Kate had obviously been talking behind her back, it was hard for Sam to stay mad at her for long. Kate and her friends were the cool girls with whom Sam would never have been friends in high school, and here she was, holding her own, even breaking bread with them (or in this case, breaking sashimi with them). And she was actually having fun.

After a long debate over whether green tea had more or less caffeine than coffee (it has less), and whether green tea ice cream was less fattening than regular ice cream (it's not), the waiter arrived with another dessert of Japanese mochi balls.

"Um, we didn't order that," said Kate.

"It's from the gentleman at the next table."

The balding guy raised his glass, and the girls erupted into hysterics.

"I LOVE mochi balls! They're *delicious*! Thank you," Dylan said.

"G.T.A.A.: Good Times All Around, girls," said Kate.

They raised their glasses again and toasted to mean boys, minibars, mochi balls, and the mysterious John Doe.

CHAPTER FIFTEEN

MAX CALIFORNIA: *If you dance with the devil, the devil don't change. The devil changes you.* —8MM

*I*t was Monday morning at Authentic Pictures, and whether it was because of the June gloom (the rare time of year when the weather is not perfect in Los Angeles), the beginning of a new work week, or the fact that Sam hadn't spoken to Matt Sullivan or Ross since Saturday morning, the overall mood in the office was tense at best.

When Sam arrived at 8:45 A.M. (with Kate's special Coffee Bean concoction in hand—Kate had been delighted to write down the details of her deliciously elaborate beverage for Sam), Ross was already in the office, and Sam could smell coffee brewing. Sam threw her bag and armload of scripts in the copy room. She had barely managed to read them all the day before while sitting by the pool with Kate. Sam never had so much trouble concentrating as she did that day. Reading was always easy for her, an escape and a treat. But whether it was because the scripts she was reading were terrible, or because she was unable to stop thinking about Matt Sullivan and their evening together (and what she would wear on Monday and how he might act toward her and how she would react to the way he acted, etc.), it took her forever to read the few scripts she had left. She tried to come up with every Matt-Sullivan-scenario conceivable so that she would be prepared for anything. The old Sam expected the worst: he was just another shallow-trust-fund-kid-slash-Hollywood-sleezeball, and the whole night meant nothing to him. The new Sam was excited about the potential for love and romance, and desperately hoped he would ask her out again. But neither the old Sam nor the new Sam could figure out how Ross would behave? Would he confront her? Would he confront Matt Sullivan? She froze as he entered the copy room.

"Hey," he said.

"Hi."

"How was your weekend?"

"Good. Fine. Thanks. How was yours?"

"Fair."

The two stood still in the middle of the room as if it was a face-off, each waiting for the other to mention what happened on Saturday morning.

"Monday morning we have a staff meeting. The interns go too. You may have to talk about what you read," he said.

Staff meeting? Talking? Sam was not big into public speaking. That was the only criticism she ever got from her teachers. She rarely voiced her opinion in class. One on one with the teacher, she spoke eloquently and made cogent points about whatever material she was reading. She was a straight-A student, after all—with the exception of that darn B she got in biology freshman year. Thankfully, Sam never claimed to be a scientist—no, she was literati, through and through.

As she copied the development status reports for the meeting (these listed the status of all the projects in development and production at Authentic Pictures), she could hear the office waking up, but as far as she could see, Matt Sullivan had not arrived yet. She smoothed her jean skirt self-consciously. She had painstakingly picked it out from Kate's closet that morning. Sam's own suitcase remained half-unpacked and barely touched in the corner of the guest room.

The phone rang by Ross's computer. When he picked it up, Sam could tell it was Matt calling the copy room from his desk simply by Ross's suddenly even more-downtrodden-than-usual demeanor. Matt Sullivan seemed to have that effect on Ross. He listened briefly and hung up the phone.

"Lawrence told Rebecca to tell Matt to tell us that it's time for the staff meeting," he announced.

Sam took a deep breath, grabbed her stack of weekend read scripts, and followed Ross into the conference room. Like the other offices at Authentic, the conference room wall facing the center of the office was all glass. Inside it was a long rectangular polished brown wood table with black swivel chairs. Ross led Sam past the table to the back of the room where there was a floor cabinet with an angled ledge on top.

"We sit here," he said.

Ross sat down on the ledge. He crossed his right leg over his left, attempting (and simultaneously failing) to make it look comfortable and inviting. Sam looked from the cushy swivel chairs surrounding the table to the precarious ledge where she was expected to sit, and then down at her jean skirt. She was the first to admit this was a bad outfit for this situation, but how was she supposed to know she would be sitting on a ledge? Even worse, how could she have known that she would be sitting on a ledge in a jean skirt and *speaking in front of everyone*, including (and especially) Matt Sullivan! She knew she was just an intern, but Sam wanted to rise up and say that she deserved to sit in a chair. She was a person too! And right now, she was a person in a very short jean skirt! But, instead, she hopped up next to Ross, crossed her legs, and tugged her skirt down as far as it would go.

Ellen was already sitting at the table filling Dan in on her wedding plans and showing him pictures of elaborate cakes. Her blond hair was pulled back into a slick ponytail which accentuated the perpetual pout on her face. Dan, polite as always, feigned interest. Sam could see Rob through the glass as he rolled into the office with his gym bag over his shoulder and his sunglasses still on. Alexandra lit up when she saw him, and followed him into his office, nearly stepping on his heels in the process. Amy walked into the conference room, took a seat at the end of the table near Sam and Ross, and said hello.

Before Sam could greet Amy, she saw him out of the corner of her eye: Matt Sullivan was walking in from the kitchen with Rebecca. They both had coffees in hand, and they were laughing as they moved toward the conference room. Sam had to remind herself to breathe as she watched Matt reach over the wall of his cubicle, pick up a bunch of scripts, and lean into Lawrence's office to tell him the meeting was starting.

Lawrence entered and fell into his chair at the head of the table. With Rebecca on one side of him and Ellen on his other side, they sat smiling like his doting minions. Matt Sullivan sat next to Rebecca, raising an eyebrow and nodding over to Sam and Ross. Rob entered, followed by Alexandra, who was wearing a light purple sweater, a shapeless brown skirt, and chunky black heels with a big silver buckle. Alexandra's hair was blown meticulously straight, her bangs held back with a purple headband (according to Ross, she had been trying to grow them out ever since she overheard Rob saying he didn't like girls with bangs).

"All right, who saw what this weekend?" asked Lawrence.

The Monday morning staff meeting began by talking about what movies everyone had seen over the weekend. Lawrence hadn't seen anything, as he had been submerged in a mud bath at a spa in the desert for most of the weekend. Rebecca and Ellen gushed about the leading man in some romantic comedy, and how "cute" the blond ingénue was. Rob said he liked the action movie that had been the number one movie at the box office that weekend. Alexandra agreed with Rob (big surprise). Dan had seen several independent films (no one else had heard of them). Sam thought they sounded interesting and took note.

Everyone had read specs over the weekend, but some of the executives had also read "samples." Samples were scripts that were used as examples of a writer's work in case someone was needed to rewrite an existing project, or to develop an idea originated by an executive.

When it was Matt Sullivan's turn to talk, he spoke eloquently and intelligently about the stack of scripts he had read. He had notes in front of him and talked about why and why not each script would make a good film. As Sam focused more closely on Matt's notes, she could have sworn that the writing resembled Ross's chicken scrawl. Ross was squirming, huffing, and puffing throughout Matt's speech. Sam looked at him with a furrowed brow.

"Sorry," he said.

Everyone was listening intently to Matt Sullivan. He had a way of commanding attention with charm—not fear, the way Lawrence did. He had confidence and a sense of humility that textured everything he said and did. In leaning forward to get a closer look at him, Sam forgot all about her discomfort and precarious position on the ledge. She looked at his hands as he gestured. She must have been staring, because Ross leaned over to her and whispered, "If you dance with the devil, the devil don't change. The devil changes you."

Sam looked at Ross like he was crazy. He nodded back at her, winking. What was he talking about? Did he know that she and Matt Sullivan had danced in his apartment on Friday night? How could Matt be the devil? Who's changing? And was Matt Sullivan reading from Ross's notes?

"And the thing that I liked most about this script," Matt continued, "was that it was really about *people connecting*."

Wait a second. Didn't Matt Sullivan say that very same thing to Sam when she told him her idea on Friday night? Did he say that phrase about every project? Was Matt Sullivan just an utter and complete phony? Sam was confused, not to mention paranoid about what Ross knew, and in leaning forward to find out if Matt was indeed using Ross's notes, her foot slipped off the bottom of the cabinet. Unable to uncross her legs in time, Sam fell onto the floor behind the conference table with a loud thud. Everyone stood up and looked down at Sam. She scrambled to recover, pulling herself up one hand at a time.

"I'm fine!" she said.

Sam attempted to gather herself, and Ross helped her back up onto the ledge.

"So, Sam, did you have any thoughts about the scripts you read?" Lawrence asked.

All eyes turned toward Sam again, and the chairs squeaked in unison as everyone switched their focus toward the back of the room.

"Well, um, on the whole, I was pretty disappointed. But, I had never even read a script before last week."

"What did you think of *Hell's Kitchen*?" asked Lawrence.

"To be honest, I really didn't like it," Sam began. "The whole premise, that these kids become possessed through their kitchen appliances, it just didn't make sense. I mean, who wants to see a kid be afraid of a whisk? And the characters all sounded alike. They weren't unique or interesting, so I didn't really care what happened to them."

The room fell silent. Ross kicked her. Sam glared at him, but he said nothing. She took this as her cue to continue.

"Everything about this script felt generic to me. Take Dickens, for example: his characters are timeless and endlessly entertaining because they are each so fully realized, unique, and bizarre. I guess what I'm saying is, I wouldn't pay money to see this movie."

Sam looked at Matt Sullivan, who was looking at Lawrence. Lawrence looked furious.

"Well, if our resident film critic has finished, I think this meeting can be adjourned," said Lawrence.

Lawrence raced out of the conference room. Everyone gathered their belongings and silently walked out after him. Sam could feel that something was wrong. Ross remained seated next to her, shaking his head.

"What?!"

"Sam, Lawrence bought that script last week. Didn't you read the trades?"

No, in fact Sam had *not* read the trades. All the executives received them, but she hadn't had the chance to look at any. The trades (*The Hollywood Reporter* and *Variety*) were the daily newspapers for the film industry. They announced what projects were sold, who was starring, producing, writing—anything and everything about the business of entertainment.

"Why didn't you tell me?" asked Sam.

"How was I supposed to know you were going to commit professional hari-kari?"

"Great, now I look like an idiot."

"Hey, Sam, I'm really sorry. I thought you knew. Seriously."

Sam grabbed her scripts, hopped off the ledge, and walked out of the conference room. What a terrible start to the week.

"Sam."

Matt Sullivan's voice came from behind the wall of his cubicle. He had his headset on and pressed mute as Sam put her hand on the wall and leaned in to him.

"I don't like that project either. I thought what you said was dead-on. Don't worry about it, okay?"

As he patted her hand, and winked at her, Sam couldn't help but smile. She kept her hand on the wall. She was paralyzed.

"It's really good to see you. I'm sorry I didn't call. I didn't realize until after you left that I didn't have your number."

"I thought so! I mean, I thought . . . I mean . . . were you supposed to call? I totally forgot."

"Let's talk later about your idea. I was serious when I said you should write it."

Talk later? Was Matt Sullivan asking her out again? Sam felt short of breath and couldn't respond. Matt looked past Sam at Ross, who was standing behind her.

"Hey buddy," Matt said.

"Hey."

"You got a little something on your shirt over there."

Matt Sullivan pointed at an ink stain that was growing in Ross's breast pocket. Ross grabbed the leaking pen out of his pocket, and, ink all over his hands, he retreated to the bathroom.

"Talk to me if you have any problems with him. He's a little . . . you know. And I have 'Great Expectations' for you," said Matt.

Okay, it was a little cheesy, but Sam couldn't help herself: she loved a guy with a good literary reference.

Matt Sullivan returned to his phone call, and as best she could move her now-leaden legs, Sam went back toward the copy room. She was in such a daze from the morning's events that she didn't even notice that Rob had followed her. As she turned around, he literally bumped right into her. Rob and Sam stood awkwardly close to one another in the doorway of the copy room. Apparently, Rob was a "close talker," one who had no sense of personal space. His face was about a quarter of an inch from Sam's, and it didn't help that he had terrible breath.

"Hey, Sam," said Rob. "I know we met last week, but I just wanted to tell you, I thought what you said in the meeting this morning was really smart."

"Oh, thanks."

She took a step back. If this guy were green, she thought, he might as well be at a casting call for *The Hulk.*

"Listen, um, you talked about another writer, some guy who is good with characters?"

"Yes, Charles Dickens, he's one of my favorite authors."

"Yeah, well, I've been trying to find a good writer to rewrite this project we have, and I thought I'd really like to read him. You know, I like to think 'outside the box,' as we say here in Hollywood. So, I was just wondering if you know where this guy Dickens is represented."

"Represented?"

"Yes, what agency represents him?"

"Um, Dickens has been dead for a really long time. He wrote books. In the nineteenth century."

"Oh, okay. So he's unavailable?"

"You could say that."

"All right, well cool, thanks anyway."

Rob walked out of the copy room and around the corner to

his office. As Sam watched him go, she realized that Alexandra had seen the whole exchange and was glaring at her. Sam didn't really understand why. Maybe her headband was too tight.

Ross entered the copy room, his shirt soaked. The blue ink stain that he had tried to get out with water had spread, staining the majority of his shirt as well as his hands. It was truly a sad sight to see. Sam shook her head and tried her best not to laugh.

"Oh, Ross," said Sam.

"I know. Just don't. I'm fine."

Ross sat down at the wobbly table, which he used as his desk, and started reading a script, his wet shirt clinging to him. Amy walked in carrying a large white cardboard box.

"You are so not glad to see me right now," she said.

"I'm not?" asked Sam.

"Wedding invitations. Must stuff. And stamp."

"GTs."

"What?"

"GTs: good times. It's just, my cousin Kate is big on abbreviations. She says that all the time. I thought it was appropriately sarcastic for the occasion."

"Yeah, right. Serious GTs. Ellen wants them to go out today. There are about two hundred fifty of them. Do you think you can do it?"

"I think I can handle it."

Sam spent the rest of the day in the conference room stuffing wedding envelopes. In addition to the sheer monotony of it all, there was an RSVP card and envelope (that also had to be stamped). And then there was the pink bow, which had to be tied *just so*, and the sprinkle of pink glitter ("Just a sprinkle!" warned Ellen, as if that made it all much more tasteful).

Just as Sam was licking the last envelope with her cotton mouth and swollen and paper-cut tongue, Rebecca stuck her head into the conference room.

"Sam, right?"

"Right."

"Listen, I need you to—oh, I'm sorry, I didn't even ask, how *are* you? That was a nasty spill you took this morning—are you okay?"

"Well, I actually could use—"

"I fall all the time, and as my grandma always used to say, 'It'll be healed twice before you're once married'?" Rebecca's overly cheerful demeanor subsided for a moment as she eyed Ellen's pink wedding invitations. "Anyway, I'm still not married? Which is fine? Because I have a career? And, what would Lawrence do without me? Um, Sam, I have some important calls to make, because I'm a vice president? But Lawrence asked Matt to ask Amy to ask Ellen to ask me to ask you to pick up some Starburst for him at the supermarket, thanks?"

Rebecca ran off before Sam could protest. Now Sam would have to find her way back to the supermarket while Rebecca sulked in her office making her important calls, ending every sentence like it was a question, and praying for her prince to come.

CHAPTER SIXTEEN

TESS MCGILL: *I have a head for business and a bod for sin.*
—WORKING GIRL

*T*he next day, Sam was walking past Matt Sullivan's desk when he looked up to catch her staring at him—again. It was lunchtime on Tuesday, and Lawrence was napping while Matt had uncharacteristically decided to work through lunch. The office was empty and quiet. Even Ross had run out to get something to eat.

"Sam, could you get me some staples from the office supplies cage?" Matt asked.

Sam smiled at him and walked to the back of the office. The cage was notoriously disorganized, so as she searched for staples, boxes were falling out of nowhere and it seemed to be raining paper clips.

"Let me give you a hand."

Matt Sullivan walked into the cage just as a teetering col-

144

umn of boxes of letterhead and script covers almost fell onto Sam. He reached over her, grazing her right arm, and caught them just in time.

"Thanks. Nice catch," she said.

"Are you okay?"

"Yeah. Who would have thought letterhead could be so dangerous?"

Matt Sullivan and Sam stood just inches apart, facing each other. The office was so quiet she could hear the hum of the fluorescent lights. She could hear him breathing. She could feel him breathing. She could smell his cologne (or maybe it was the detergent he used, Sam hadn't had much experience differentiating between the two). Whatever he was wearing smelled comforting, familiar, intoxicating. Matt Sullivan leaned closer to her. Was he going to kiss her *here*? What if someone saw? Should they talk first? Should she say something? Sam subscribed to the theory of when in doubt, talk.

"How was your spiritual advisor?"

"Great."

"What did she advise you?"

"To take advantage of every opportunity that presents itself."

"That doesn't sound very spiritual—"

"*Shhh.*"

He put his arms on Sam's shoulders and gently moved both of them behind the stacks of boxes. He put his hands on her face, and then he kissed her. They kissed, just as they had the first night. Except now, they were in the office. In the cage. This was *dangerous*. And Sam was a good girl. Wasn't she? What was this guy doing to her? Whatever it was, she liked it. But she worried, was she as good a kisser as the older woman who had broken Matt Sullivan's heart? Was the older woman blonde and beautiful and experienced? Could he tell Sam hadn't done this kind of thing much? Sam shut her eyes tighter and tried to just focus on enjoying the moment and silencing her own thoughts.

They kissed passionately behind precariously stacked boxes of Xerox toner, recycled paper, personalized buck slips, and indelible markers. But Sam was no longer in the office supplies cage. No, she had been transported to a much better place where there was a lifetime supply of passion instead of Post-it notes. It was a place where she was not only noticed, but she was also desired. It was a place where the good girl *does* get the guy in the end. This was what she had been waiting for over the last eighteen years. This was what she thought about late on Saturday nights when she read Henry James novels and wondered who would ever make her feel the way the characters in the book felt. Until now she had buried those feelings, choosing to focus on her schoolwork and her future.

"Matt!" Lawrence called from his office.

Matt Sullivan pulled away, put his hand on Sam's cheek, and smiled at her. He kissed her once more on the lips, turned around, grabbed a box of staples, and walked out of the cage as suddenly as he had entered.

"Coming!" he called.

Sam fell back against the wall of the cage, put her hand to her lips, and smiled. She leaned forward to make sure no one was around, and then she silently jumped up and down in place, arms squeezed by her sides and her hands in fists.

"Sam?"

Sam froze in midjump with a huge grin on her face and saw Ross standing in the doorway of the cage with a brown paper bag in his hand. He had come in through the back door of the office.

"Oh, hi," said Sam.

Attempting to look nonchalant, Sam leaned on a stack of boxes, which immediately toppled over, taking her with them. Ross removed some of the boxes that had fallen on top of her and pulled Sam up. She brushed herself off.

"Happens all the time," she said. "I'm fine."

"I brought you a sandwich. You know, just in case you didn't have lunch yet."

"Oh. Thanks."

"Sam, are you okay? What were you so happy about?"

"Oh. I um . . . I thought we were out of Post-it notes, but it turns out we're totally not! YAY!"

"Uh-huh."

Ross looked at her like she was crazy. Sam grabbed a box of Post-it notes, took her sandwich from him, and walked out of the cage back to the copy room.

Sam and Matt met in the office supplies cage during lunchtime every day that week. They had developed an unspoken ritual. She would walk past his desk just after all the executives had left for lunch. He would ask her if she could get something from the cage. Then he would meet her there. Sometimes they would talk briefly as they had the first day, but most of the time, they would just start making out. Sam started watching the clock, waiting for lunchtime to come. And after lunchtime, she would think about how many hours ago it had been lunchtime, and then how many hours until the next lunchtime.

But when Friday rolled around, Matt Sullivan left the office without saying good-bye. She stayed late in the copy room, attempting to do her weekend read, but she was secretly hoping that Matt would call or return to the office to get her, and that they might have an impromptu evening just as they had the week before. But no such luck. Sam finally left Authentic Pictures at 9 P.M. that night, alone.

Surprisingly, Kate was home when she got there. She was in her pajamas, eating fro-yo, watching Court TV, and reading Matt Sullivan's first edition copy of *Franny and Zooey* alone in the media room. She muted the TV when Sam entered.

"Cuz! Where ya been all my life?"

"Working late."

"Cool. Hope you don't mind I borrowed your book."

"Just be careful. It's not mine. It's a first edition."

"Yeah, well, this family makes mine actually look functional. It's totally depressing."

"Yeah, Salinger isn't really a 'feel good' writer."

"Wait, but didn't he write *Pretty Woman*? I'm kidding!"

"Good one. Look at you, cracking dorky literati jokes. Speaking of dorky, why are *you* home on a Friday night?"

Sam collapsed on the couch next to Kate, who dipped her spoon in her fro-yo and fed her cousin the bite. Sam made a face. She wasn't accustomed to fro-yo.

"Dylan is working at a concert, and Tatiana has a photo shoot tomorrow, so she's getting her beauty sleep . . . as if she needs it. I didn't really feel like going out anyway. I'm so bored. Sammy, do you ever feel like your life has no purpose at all? Oh wait, but I did get fabulous new mascara today. So I've got that going for me. What do you hear from Doe?"

"Nothing much. I don't really know what's going on."

"Well, the love doctor is in. And I'm listening."

"And you're telling."

"I'm really sorry about that, Sammy. I won't say anything to anyone. I promise. 'What happens in Vegas, stays in Vegas.'"

"But we're not in Vegas."

"You know what I mean!"

"I'm just really surprised that he hasn't called or, like, asked me out on a proper date or something. I mean, I don't know if this is normal or not."

"Normal is as normal does, Sammy."

"What does that mean?"

"I don't know. But the point is, that what makes me feel better when I haven't heard from the guy I like is just to know where he is and what he's doing. You know, to find out what he would rather be doing instead of hanging out with me. Do you remember where he lives?"

"Kind of. Why?"

"Duh? It's a lovely evening for a Doe drive-by."

"But, isn't that, like, stalking?"

"I prefer to think of it as 'micromanaging.' Because we care, Sammy. They may not care. But we do. A drive-by is definitely in order. Let's go."

Kate, still in her pajamas with her plastic fro-yo spoon in her mouth, grabbed her keys and her bag, stepped barefoot into her UGG slippers, and walked out of the media room. Sam stayed seated. This did not sound like a good idea. Kate stuck her head back in the doorway.

"You coming or what?"

Sam knew there was no saying no to Kate when she was fixated on something. So Sam peeled herself off the couch and followed Kate out to the car. The top was still down. Kate hopped in.

"Come on, Sammy. Don't worry, I'll put the top up. He won't see us. I've done this a million times. I'm a pro."

They drove toward Matt Sullivan's house, chatting and listening to music along the way. Sam could tell something was on Kate's mind.

"So, these drive-bys you've done a million times, they wouldn't happen to have been Colby Carter drive-bys, would they?"

"He never put blinds up in his apartment in Michigan. He was begging for it."

"I would never have pegged you for a voyeur."

"Call me what you wish, Sammy. I just like to know where everyone I care about is at all times. Is that so wrong? But speaking of Colby, which we were doing, word on the street is that he's in town."

"What street would that be, Kate? Rodeo Drive?"

"Cute, Sammy."

"So, are you going to see him?"

"My shrink tells me I shouldn't see him unless I know I can behave in a way that represents the best version of myself."

"What does that mean?"

"Do you think that if I knew, I would still be doing drive-bys? Sometimes I feel like my therapist is speaking in code."

After going up and down several wrong streets, Sam and Kate pulled up in front of Matt Sullivan's apartment. Sam was nervous. What if he saw them? What if he was there with someone else? She shuddered at the thought. Kate slowed down. Matt Sullivan's apartment was dark.

"That's it," said Sam. "The second floor, on the right."

"I guess he's out, Sammy."

"Maybe he's asleep already?"

"Way to keep the dream alive."

"I don't think this is very healthy, Kate."

"Oh, it's not. However, rest assured that the drive-by is significantly healthier than the stakeout."

"What's the difference?"

"Well, Sammy, we just drove by. We *slowed down*, but did not actually *stop*. Had we actually stopped the car and waited, that would be a stakeout, and that would be totally, like, 'boiling-his-bunny' creepy."

"Boiling his bunny?"

"Yeah. Glenn Close in the movie *Fatal Attraction* gets, like, totally obsessed with Michael Douglas, so when he doesn't call her back, she boils his kid's bunny. Totally psycho."

"That's just gross."

"Yeah, I know. Are you hungry?"

"Starving."

"Me too."

The girls drove away from Matt Sullivan's apartment, and went to the famous In-N-Out Burger drive-through, where Kate convinced Sam to get the low-carb burger wrapped in a lettuce leaf. It was the best burger Sam had ever tasted, even without the bun. But even a great burger couldn't stop Sam from wondering just where Matt Sullivan was that night, and why, after their week of secret rendezvous he wouldn't have said good-bye or made an out-of-the-cage plan with her?

CHAPTER SEVENTEEN

While arranging my hair, I looked at my face in the glass,
and felt it was no longer plain: there was hope in its aspect,
and life in its colour; and my eyes seemed as if they had beheld
the fount of fruition, and borrowed beams from the lustrous ripple.
—CHARLOTTE BRONTË, *Jane Eyre*

With no word from Matt Sullivan (aka Doe) on Saturday, Sam took Kate up on her invitation to go with her, Dylan, and Tatiana to a party at a house in the Hollywood Hills sponsored by Jet.

Dylan and Tatiana picked up Kate and Sam at Uncle Norman's house. Kate slid in first, and then Sam moved in with half her butt cheek still out the door. She barely managed to close it, but after several attempts, they were on their way.

"How's Doe, Sammy?" asked Tatiana.

"I wouldn't really know."

Kate put her arm around Sam and squeezed her. She looked over at Dylan, who was furiously texting with her left arm. She was wearing the same embroidered silk sling she had been wearing the previous week, but tonight, it was on her right arm.

"You're not texting Alan, are you? And I thought the carpal tunnel was in the other arm?" asked Kate.

Dylan pulled her phone to her chest so Kate couldn't see the screen. "I don't know what you're talking about."

"She's texting him!" yelled Tatiana.

"Give me the phone, Dylan," said Kate.

"Kate. I am not texting Alan. I'm over him. I told you."

"Who's Alan?" asked Sam.

"He's just a lame wanna-be indie rocker," Tatiana explained.

"He's very talented!" yelled Dylan.

"Inside voices," said Kate.

"He's Dylan's most recent obsession. She needs some replacement therapy. The moment we find a new guy for her to crush on, she'll be over him," said Tatiana.

"I resent that," said Dylan.

"You resemble that!" said Tatiana. *"Holler!"*

"He invades my soul," whispered Dylan.

"I know he does, honey. Now give me the phone," coaxed Kate.

While Dylan reluctantly relinquished her cell phone, the taxi weaved up through the winding Hollywood Hills. Sam, again suffering from acute motion sickness, was focusing on being someplace stationary and not vomiting, while the other three girls laughed, bickered, told each other how pretty they looked, and talked on their cell phones.

When they arrived at the house, three large security guards

carrying clipboards—which contained the list of names of guests approved to come inside—were stationed at the foot of the wide, white marble staircase. Next to them stood a well-coiffed and superpetite twenty-something woman. One of the giant guards had to lean down to her height so that she could whisper something in his ear as the girls approached. He then cleared a path for the girls through the impatiently waiting crowd and lifted the red velvet rope so that they could enter without breaking their stride.

"Kate! Tatiana! Girls . . . hi!" she yelled in a raspy voice.

"Sam, this is Sarah, PR maven extraordinaire," said Kate.

"Oh, please," said Sarah. "You guys look *gorge*! Go inside, it's hopping. I'll be in in a minute."

She air kissed them all and ushered them inside. As they walked up the stairs, Sam looked back at the crowd still waiting to get in.

"What's a PR maven?" Sam asked.

"She organizes parties and events," Kate replied. "She's out, like, every night. You think I'm the mayor? It's her *job* to know everyone."

"Sounds exhausting," said Sam.

As they arrived at the pool deck, the music got louder, but everyone momentarily stopped trying to yell over it in order to catch a glimpse of the fresh meat arriving. Guys elbowed their buddies, and girls looked them up and down, evaluating their competition.

After saying hello to some people and simply nodding to others, the girls made a beeline for the outdoor dance floor, tossing their purses and jackets on a nearby chair. Sam tentatively tried to find her groove. She wished she could dance like Kate and Tatiana, who had all their seductive moves down and caused quite a stir when they rubbed up against each other on occasion. She would even have liked to dance like Dylan, who was more of a goofy dancer, performing the "running man" move in the middle of the dance floor, and shimmying from side to side while removing her silk sling from her arm and waving it over her head. Dylan seemed to have such a great time when she danced and had told Sam that she was always the one who ended up dancing with a guy, while the other guys drooled from a distance watching Tatiana and Kate. In fact, a very handsome and impeccably dressed guy started dancing with Dylan. She was giggling and hamming up her silly dance moves, while Kate and Tatiana continued to dance together, as sexy and aloof as ever. Caught between silly and sexy, Sam excused herself to go to the bathroom.

As Sam walked through the living room filled with partygoers, she spotted Dan across the room. Sam had developed a great deal of respect for Dan at work and was happy to see him. He was smart and well read and never seemed to let the petty office politics of Authentic Pictures get to him. Dan saw Sam approaching and waved to her. She smiled and walked over to him, giving him a big hug.

"Hello, dahling!" said Dan. "Samantha, this is my partner, Nick. Nick, this is Samantha, the intern extraordinaire I was telling you about."

"The teen literati wunderkind from Massachusetts?"

"Wunderkind?!" Sam asked.

"Wunderkind by day, diva by night . . . I think a little turn is in order!"

Sam spun slowly, punctuating it with a curtsey to Dan and Nick, who applauded.

"Samantha, Dan loves you. And he's a tough customer. I should know."

"It's true, Sam. It's great having you at the office. You're a breath of fresh air."

Sam was blushing.

"Thank you, Dan. That means a lot to me."

Sam knew that she and Dan had hit it off, but she didn't realize how highly he thought of her. And she respected his opinion. Sam was happy to be appreciated, to run into friends at a random Hollywood party, and to feel pretty and smart three thousand miles from her comfort zone. Sam said her good-byes and continued in search of a bathroom until she was stopped abruptly by what felt like two large rocks.

"Oh, excuse me," Sam said.

Sam looked up to see she had just bumped straight into Susan Mandalay (and her breast implants). Susan looked as coifed and tan as ever in jeans and a tight red wrap top, guzzling her ever-present can of Diet Jet. They were standing in the narrow hallway outside the bathroom.

"Oh, hi," said Sam. "We met, I mean, you helped me bring cans . . . I work at Authentic Pictures."

Susan looked at her for a moment before erupting into a squeal.

"Of course! How *are* you? I didn't even recognize you! You look fabulous!"

"Hey, babe."

Ashley Hatcher walked up behind Susan, putting his hand protectively around her waist.

"Oh, Ashley, you remember . . ."

"Sam," Sam said.

"Remember, honey, from Authentic Pictures? When Lawrence spilled the Diet Jet all over his shirt?"

"Oh, dude! That's right! That was awesome! The look on his face was friggin' priceless! I did that to all my friends for the rest of the day just to mess with them!"

"Well, I didn't really mean to—"

"Great seeing you, Sam."

As the A-list couple walked out of the party, Kate, Tatiana, and Dylan—who had been watching the exchange from the dance floor—walked quickly through the living room to Sam, who was still standing outside the bathroom.

"Um, Cuz, were you just talking to Susan Mandalay and Ashley Hatcher?"

"Yeah," said Sam. "I met them at Authentic."

"Your cousin is SO in the know. I LOVE her," yelled Dylan.

"Inside voices," Kate said to Dylan.

"And I LOVE Greg!" yelled Dylan.

"Who's Greg?" asked Tatiana.

"*Duh!* The guy I was dancing with?"

Tatiana and Kate looked at each other and rolled their eyes.

"Dylan, he's a great dancer, he's a great dresser, his hair is clearly frosted, and he was wearing brown eyeliner . . . do the math, would you?"

Both Dylan and Sam were stumped.

"Wake up and smell the sexual orientation," said Tatiana. "He's gay!"

"Maybe he's just metrosexual?" asked Dylan.

"I'm bored," said Kate. "I've totally lost my sparkle. Anyone else want to go?"

After Kate said good-bye to several people she knew, the girls left the party. On the ride home, Kate realized she wasn't just losing her sparkle that night. She felt as if she might be losing her sparkle in general. As she watched her cousin blossoming and developing her own sparkle, she felt proud of and happy for her, but she couldn't help feeling a bit envious.

Perhaps Kate was just having a midsummer crisis? She assumed that when she came back for the summer from college, everything would be just like it had been when she was in high school. But everything had changed. Everyone had changed. Except her. She decided she would leave a message on her therapist's voice mail when she got home so that she would remember to talk about all this with her in their session on Monday.

CHAPTER EIGHTEEN

*A*fter that Monday morning's staff meeting, during which Matt Sullivan didn't even glance at Sam, she began to watch the clock again and wondered if Matt would meet her in the cage at lunchtime, even though he hadn't even said good-bye when he left on Friday. But at 1 P.M., Matt Sullivan was nowhere to be found. He was not as his desk, not in the kitchen, and he certainly wasn't in the cage. Sam went to the cage and pretended to be looking for something, but she ended up just sitting on a box of letterhead, alone, waiting. *Pathetic*, she thought. This was not her. She couldn't let this guy get to her like this. What was it about him she was so attracted to, anyway?

She decided she would have to say something to Matt Sullivan when he got back to the office. Or write him a note. Or an e-mail. Something! Anything! But she didn't. She couldn't. She was confused. She was hurt. She felt stupid, and naive, and vulnerable. And then, she just got pissed off.

She went into Dan's office and asked him to give her some more substantive, creative, and challenging work to do. He gave her some spec scripts to read and some new drafts of projects in development to do notes on. Sam was happy to have some real work to concentrate on, and to put Matt Sullivan out of her mind. She loved thinking analytically, and she was good at it. Both Dan and Ross told her that her script coverage and notes were improving with each passing day.

But, no matter how many projects Sam took on, it was difficult to stop thinking about Matt Sullivan altogether. After all, every time she looked up from her work, there he was. Sam would catch Matt looking at her once in a while, and he would abruptly look away.

Every day that week, Sam stayed in the office during lunch. Sure, she stayed in the office to keep working on all the extra projects she had taken on, but in the back of her mind, she hoped that maybe Matt Sullivan would show up in the cage. But Matt went out for lunch every day.

That Friday, Amy entered the copy room wearing her ever-present apologetic expression.

"Sam," said Amy. "I don't really know why he couldn't ask you himself, but Rebecca just told me that Matt asked her to ask me to ask you to clean out and organize the office supplies cage. I can give you a hand when the girls go to lunch if you want."

If the cage was cleaned out, there would be no place for Sam and Matt to hide. That was *their* place. How could he be asking her to change it? To ruin it? To, in effect, truly end their affair . . . or whatever it was.

"You think the cage is disorganized? It seems totally accessible to me."

"Sam, come on. You know the cage is a frigging disaster. No one can find anything! Lawrence has been asking Matt to deal with it for months."

Sam worried, was she entering "boiling-his-bunny" territory? She had never thought about someone, anyone, so much in her entire life. She was even annoying herself! But none of it added up for her. Was he embarrassed to be seen with her? Did he find someone else?

Sam looked at Matt Sullivan over her shoulder as she walked to the back of the office toward the cage. She was sure he could see her, but he didn't look up and didn't acknowledge her. Sam sighed upon entering the cage. If only she could box up some of the moments she had spent in here with him: she would pack them carefully in bubble wrap and seal them with duct tape so that they would be safely preserved and she would have them forever.

But maybe this was his plan? She would have to work through lunch and he would come to the cage, and in the utter chaos of reorganizing, they could surely find someplace still hidden to have a moment together. But she had been there the last four days, and he hadn't come near it. What could Sam say or do?

Matt Sullivan never came to the cage that day. Instead, lunchtime came and went, as it had every day that week, and Sam sat alone, sorting through staple removers, yellow notepads, large ring binders, mechanical pencils, and neon highlighters. She tried to keep the columns of boxes stacked so she and Matt would have something to hide behind if he ever changed his mind, but it turned out that half the boxes were empty anyway, and she knew she had to get rid of them. By the end of the day, Sam was covered with dust and dirt, and her back and arms were killing her from all the lifting, bending, and sorting she had done. It was corny for Sam to admit even to herself, but what truly ached the most was her heart.

And then it hit her like a box of blank VHS tapes. Of course! Why hadn't she thought about this before? Since Sam was not the kind of girl to "booty call" Matt late at night, or dress supersexy to get his attention, she would have to rely on something entirely different: her brains. He went to Harvard, after all, so wouldn't he want to be with a girl who wasn't just "hot"? Wouldn't he want to be with someone who challenged him intellectually and creatively? Isn't that why he was attracted to her in the first place?

Sam decided to start developing her movie idea about high

school girls who create their perfect man. She thought that if she wrote something that was smart and funny and poignant, Matt Sullivan would be impressed and realize just what he was missing. He would see she wasn't just any girl. She was special, and he would have to recognize that. After all, he had said as much on more than one occasion.

After the Friday weekend read meeting, Sam asked Dan how someone might go about explaining and developing a movie idea. He suggested writing a "treatment" and gave her some samples to read. A treatment, Dan explained, was basically an elaborate yet concise synopsis of the screenplay. Sam decided she would read the samples over the weekend, and then sit down to map out her idea.

That night, as Sam and Kate sat in their pajamas on the beige Ultrasuede couch in Uncle Norman's screening room, Sam relented and told Kate more about Doe. She didn't tell her that they were working together, but she did say that they would meet at lunch to make out.

"That is so hot, Sammy! Talk about a power lunch!"

"Yeah, but I think he doesn't want to meet anymore."

"What gives you that idea?"

"Um, he stopped showing up?"

"Oh. Yeah. That's definitely a sign. Well, maybe he's just afraid of how much he likes you?"

"You don't really believe that, do you?"

"Not really. I was trying to make you feel better."

"Gee, thanks. I feel better already."

Sam grabbed a handful of low-fat microwave popcorn, and took a sip of her CBIB. Kate bit off the end of a long Red Vine, and pointed one of the seven remote controls at the flat screen.

"Why are we watching this again?" she asked.

"It's called *Weird Science*. I've only seen it in Spanish, and it gave me an idea for a screenplay, so I wanted to watch it again. In a language I understand, I mean."

"Sammy, you are so Hollywood! So, you're a writer now? Wait, but what you really want to do is direct, right?"

"Ha-ha."

"Isn't basing your movie on another movie, like, totally derivative?"

"Yeah, but what isn't these days?"

"SNOK."

"Totally SNOK."

The girls giggled and pulled the light brown chenille blanket evenly over their legs. Kate dimmed the lights with a different remote, and they curled up to watch the film while Sam took notes. After the movie, Kate turned the lights back on and looked squarely at Sam.

"That was really good! Who knew they were so funny in the eighties? So, how will you make your version different? I mean, who's your perfect man?"

"Well, I don't know. He would be a combination of men, I guess."

"Anyone I know?" asked Kate.

"I don't think it would be anyone *I* know! The only thing I can think of is a combination of my favorite male characters from my favorite novels."

"Snore."

"Kate! Seriously! Think about it: the boys in the movie created their perfect woman by cutting out different female body parts from swimsuit magazines and stuff, right? Well, the girls in my movie would take different attributes from their favorite literary characters, because a person is the sum of his or her parts, and those are not just body parts."

"That's so beautiful, Sammy. I think I'm going to cry."

"Kate!"

"I'm kidding. But it is a little dorky."

"But that's the point: they're dorky girls who have the imagination and the knowledge to literally construct a strong, smart, romantic, creative, well-read Renaissance man. Or, Renaissance boy. Whatever."

"Well, I did really like Hugh Grant's character in *Sense and Sensibility*."

"That's because Edward Ferrars was a man of his word. He would also have the passionate intensity of Brontë's Heathcliff, tempered by the moral integrity of Atticus Finch, and the bravery of . . . of . . . Beowolf!"

Once Sam had started, she couldn't stop. She went through all her favorite novels in her mind, dissecting each male protagonist while Kate listened.

"Hey, Sammy, it's like a checklist! So, how many of these qualities does Doe have?"

Sam shrugged. She really couldn't say anymore. She was beginning to feel like maybe she didn't know Matt Sullivan at all.

CHAPTER NINETEEN

Over the next week, Sam focused her energy on the treatment and work at Authentic, and tried not to look at, talk to, or think about Matt Sullivan. But as Sam worked on her treatment, as she wrote about young girls creating their perfect man, she couldn't help but imagine Matt in her mind's eye. In essence, the treatment became, for Sam, a kind of love letter to him. And if anyone would get it, would understand what she was saying, she hoped it would be him. Because she felt that, regardless of his erratic behavior, he understood her in a way no other boy ever had, and he saw something in her that she had never seen in herself: inside the cage and out.

But something else happened as Sam continued writing. She found that she truly enjoyed it. She always had such reverence for her favorite authors, and she had been content to immerse herself in the stories they told. She never would have thought she would have the courage or the creativity to tell her own story. But she fell in love with telling this story in particular, and not only the part that was wrapped up in the Matt Sullivan of it all. She loved creating a new world, and making these characters in her head live and breathe on their own. She would think about her favorite authors and the characters she loved and loved to hate. Writing the treatment allowed her to marry her knowledge and passion for literature with her new-found script development skills.

While Sam idealized Matt Sullivan on the page, part of her continued to hate him in real life. She simply didn't understand why he was being such a jerk. What had changed? Did she do or say something wrong? She would catch him looking at her sometimes, but they hadn't had a real conversation in over a week. Sam had mastered the Xerox machine, had written good script coverage for Dan, had reorganized and cleaned up the copy room (as well as the cage), and had made some good points in the Monday morning staff meeting without falling on the ground in the middle of it. Sam had even switched up her Coffee Bean order, making a few key alterations to Kate's order, making it her own.

While Sam was starting to feel fulfilled and challenged both intellectually and socially, Kate was spending more and more time at home looking through her old Harvard-Westlake yearbooks, and reading some of the books that Sam had brought with her. Kate even came up with more good ideas for Sam's treatment. Kate had been such a good cousin-slash-friend that she easily convinced Sam to accompany her to a photography opening, despite Sam's bursting workload.

"I never would have pegged you for a Wilmer Von Gulag fan," said Sam.

"Yeah, well, you know I'm nothing if not full of surprises," said Kate.

"I feel like you're not telling me something."

"What gives you that impression?"

"First of all, you've never expressed any interest in German minimalist photography. Second of all, you're wearing your shirt—or, my shirt—backward."

"Oh. See, this is why I hesitate to wear this hipster clothing. It's so experimental, I never know how to put it on."

"It's not revolutionary, Kate, it's just off the shoulder."

"*You're* off the shoulder."

"What does that mean?"

"I don't know."

Kate shrugged, checked her smoky eye makeup in the mirror once again, and headed downstairs to her car. It was warm outside, so Kate insisted on driving her convertible "topless."

The small art gallery was in the design Mecca that is the art/furniture district in West Hollywood. After circling the block once without finding a parking space, Kate parked in a red zone directly across the street from the gallery. Before turning off the ignition, she checked her makeup, reapplied her lip gloss, and smiled at Sam.

"Kate, won't we get a ticket if we park here?"

"I don't feel like circling again. It's making me dizzy. I think I'm catching your proclivity for acute motion sickness."

"You can't 'catch' motion sickness, Kate."

"Okay, well, then I guess it just runs in the family."

"Kate . . ."

"Come on, Sammy. Let's go see some ART! You love art . . . you should be excited!"

Sam looked at Kate suspiciously but followed her out of the car nonetheless. With a deft backhanded click of her car key, Kate locked the topless car.

Standing outside the gallery were throngs of hipsters in all black. They were drinking Red Stripe from the bottle and red wine from clear plastic cups. For the first time, Sam saw Kate was actually out of her element. Kate was doing her best to look like a hipster, dressed in Sam's clothes.

"Isn't this fun?!" asked Kate.

But Kate didn't look like she was having fun. She seemed nervous. Sam knew something was up. They walked into the stark gallery space, which was balmy at best (okay, it was broiling). The lighting was painfully bright, and the walls were institution white. There were very few photos on the wall, and everyone spoke in hushed voices. The crowd was a sea of goatees, navy Dickies pants, baby doll dresses over jeans, and painstakingly messy attire. Hipsters walked around with their eyes squinted, their hands rubbing their chins, and with decidedly pensive expressions on their faces.

Kate stopped in front of the first grainy black-and-white photo, which showed a leaking container of laundry detergent in a dark alley.

"I don't get it," said Kate. She looked around. "Oh. My. God."

"What?"

"There he is."

"Who?"

"Colby."

"Losing-your-virginity-are-you-going-to-get-fat-now-Colby?"

"The one and only. Oh, Sammy, don't look!"

"Are you okay, Kate?"

"Sure, of course. I am totally over him." Kate's ankles started shaking in her high stilettos.

"Yeah, Kate, I can *totally* tell."

"Cuz, is he looking at me?"

"Um, I don't think so."

"I think I saw him look at me."

"I don't think so."

"How about now?"

"Nope."

"Now?"

"No. Kate, I think we should go. You're shaking!"

"Oh, please. Sammy, this is all a power play. I'm not leaving. He'll come over. Trust me."

And then it happened, every hipster inch of Colby Carter looked over and seemed to be staring at Kate.

"Okay, now he's staring, Kate."

"See, Sammy. It's all about playing it cool."

"You're still shaking."

"Shhhh."

"Kate, he's coming over."

"Okay. How do I look?"

"Excellent."

"Really?"

Colby Carter approached the girls with his perpetual mock-shy snicker and his deceptively unassuming swagger. He walked with his head down while still managing to retain eye contact with Kate. She knew that look. That was how he used to look at her in the library before they met. It was that damn creepy/sexy semistare of his.

"Kate Rose," he said.

"Well, well. Colby Carter. As I live and breathe. What a surprise."

He leaned in to kiss her. Kate thrust her cheek toward him.

"Surprise? You know Gulag is my favorite photographer."

"Who, Wilmer? *Willy?* Please. I had no idea. So, Colby, what are you doing this summer?"

"You know, making art. Starting a band. Writing a novel. You?"

"Same. Pretty much."

"I just bought one of his photos."

"Oh, really. How . . . splendid! I was thinking of buying one too."

"Oh, yeah? Which one?"

"Um . . . that one."

Kate blindly pointed at the photograph behind her.

"Wow," said Colby. "That's pretty aggressive."

Sam pulled on Kate's sleeve. Kate tugged her sleeve away from Sam and adjusted it accordingly.

"You think? I think it's just . . . darling," said Kate.

"Darling?" he asked.

Sam pinched Kate's arm. Hard.

"Ow! What is your *damage*?!" Kate asked Sam.

Sam coughed, tilted her head toward the wall, and through clenched teeth, she managed to say, "Look. At. The. Photograph."

"How bad?" whispered Kate.

"Bad," said Sam.

Kate turned around slowly to look at the photograph in question. It was even worse than she could have imagined: Kate Rose had just told Colby Carter that she was thinking about purchasing a close-up black-and-white photograph of . . . a giant vagina. In her wildest dreams, this was not how Kate would have imagined her run-in with Colby to play out.

"Is that what I think it is?" whispered Kate.

"I'm afraid so," replied Sam.

Kate took a breath, tried to gather herself, and turned back to face Colby Carter.

"Listen, Colby, this was really . . . fun. But we have a dinner we have to go to. Nice seeing you."

The girls left Colby Carter as he admired the giant vagina.

"Oh. My. God," said Kate.

"Are you okay?"

"No, Sammy, I do believe I am going to be in therapy for the rest of my life."

As Sam escorted Kate out of the gallery, they ran into Gynger with a *y* and just Ginger, who were on their way into the gallery.

"Kate Rose! Are you leaving already?"

"Yeah. It's really hot in there and there's a giant vagina on the wall. Not my thing."

After the disastrous gallery experience, neither Sam nor Kate felt much like going out. They went home, where Sam worked on her treatment before falling fast asleep with her pen still in her hand. Kate curled up and tried to sleep while listening to the familiar sounds of "All I Want Is You" endlessly repeating on her iPod.

CHAPTER TWENTY

Some people go to priests; others to poetry; I to my friends.
—VIRGINIA WOOLF

The next morning, Kate managed to pull Sam away from her writing again, just long enough to take her on her first Los Angeles hike. Kate, Tatiana, and Dylan used to hike all the time when they were in high school. Kate, who was a creature of habit, liked to hike in Runyon Canyon, which was in Hollywood. Something Kate had always loved about Los Angeles—but didn't fully appreciate until she lived in Michigan for a year—was that she could go for a long hike and feel like she was a million miles from civilization, even though the view was of the sprawling city. But the hike that the girls did up Runyon was more a walk on a paved road (which happened to be on a slight incline) than it was a real hike. Certainly, no rock climbing would be required. Dylan liked hikes in Malibu better than Runyon because she said that it smelled less like dog poo there. Tatiana liked doing Pilates with a trainer at her fancy health club better than doing anything outdoors because she was always sure she would get lost. Which she always did.

But Tatiana and Dylan had agreed to meet Kate for a hike on Saturday morning. They had both been so busy the previous week that the girls hadn't seen one another in days. And everyone knew better than to cancel last minute on Kate Rose. When they met at the bottom of the hill, Kate was in her chocolate brown velour sweat suit with one of Sam's punk rock hip belts over her pants. It was a little much for a hike, but Kate liked to be prepared. Plus, being the "mayor," as Sam called her, Kate was sure to run into people she knew. Dylan was wearing an oversize "The Elbows" T-shirt (her new favorite band) and cut-off Harvard-Westlake sweatpants. Tatiana was in all black: stretch pants and sports bra top, with a baseball cap and sunglasses. Sam had borrowed Kate's loose black yoga pants, which she paired with her own worn-in sneakers and vintage T-shirt. She put her shoulder-length hair in a short ponytail.

Kate regaled the girls with her story from the gallery opening the previous evening. She entitled it "Colby and the Giant Vagina." Sam was learning that this was how Kate dealt with most disappointments in her life: she made them into humorous and self-deprecating stories, stories that she told repeatedly, editing and adjusting them a bit each time, trying them out in different ways on different audiences. Sam listened to the different versions, and it made her think about the way she was telling her own story in the treatment, and how important it was to revise, rewrite, and experiment with it. Kate never told a story the same way twice.

Tatiana reiterated that Colby wasn't worth Kate's time and that she wanted to kick his ass. Sam didn't say anything, but as she listened, she realized how silly Kate's obsessiveness sounded. Was she as obsessive about Matt Sullivan as Kate was about Colby Carter? Dylan was uncharacteristically quiet and seemed to lag behind the girls as they walked briskly up the canyon. Kate noticed Dylan trailing behind and looked over her shoulder, annoyed.

"Come *on*, D!" said Kate.

"You guys go ahead," said Dylan.

"We can slow down," said Sam, who wouldn't have minded the rest herself.

Just then, two women wearing Tevas who looked about fifty passed them, chatting up a storm, and not at all out of breath.

"Okay, girls, we've just been lapped by senior citizens. And I'm totally losing my heart rate. Let's go!"

"K-Ro, you're a slave driver, you know that?" said Tatiana.

"That's why you love me," said Kate.

"Are you sure we're going the right direction?" asked Tatiana.

"You guys, I'm just going to go down," said Dylan.

"What? What are you talking about? I haven't seen you all week!" said Kate.

"I know, I just . . ." Dylan looked at the girls, and the hill that loomed ahead of them. She began to hyperventilate. "My asthma," she said.

"D, you don't have asthma," said Tatiana.

"I (*wheeze*) guess (*wheeze*) I do."

"Okay, calm down, Dylan. Just take deep breaths," said Sam.

Kate went into action. She waved her arms at a bare-chested guy with his t-shirt dangling from his shorts and a cheerful black Labrador retriever in tow. He jogged in place as he took off his earphones. Dylan was breathing faster and deeper by the second.

"Hi. I'm so sorry to bother you, but would you happen to have a paper bag of some sort?" asked Kate.

"I just have this copy of *Variety* I was going to use for my dog. . . ."

"I'll give you ten bucks for whatever you have."

The guy shrugged his shoulders and made the trade with Kate.

"Who knows origami?" asked Kate.

"I can knit," said Tatiana.

"T, we need a paper bag kind of thing, but thanks for playing."

"I can try," said Sam.

Sam tried to construct some semblance of a bag using the copy of *Variety*, and passed it to Dylan, who was breathing quickly and making lots of dramatic noise as she held the trade paper to her face. The girls continued up the hill with Dylan breathing into the folded copy of *Variety*.

"I think I just got a paper cut on my cheek!" complained Dylan.

"Maybe that will take your mind off the asthma!" said Kate.

Eventually Dylan's breathing went back to normal (or whatever was normal for Dylan). As the girls reached a plateau at the top, they sat down on a long wooden bench and looked out onto Los Angeles. It was a clear day and they could see all the way out to the ocean to the west, and to snowcapped mountains to the east. Sam was amazed. Where else can you have all this in one place? It might not be Northampton, but there was no denying it: Los Angeles was a beautiful city.

Kate breathed in deeply and sighed. "Okay, girls, tap the bench and let's head down."

Sam was confused, so Tatiana tried to explain the essential "bench tap" ritual to her.

"Sammy, it's one of Kate's little OCD-isms. You have to tap the bench at the top of the hike. Just do it. We all do," said Tatiana.

Sam did as she was told, and Kate smiled approvingly. Tatiana tapped the bench too, and then made a face as she looked at the residual dirt on her hand. She wiped it on her pants.

"Yuck," she said. "Only for you, Kate."

"*Mwa!*" said Kate. "D, you haven't tapped the bench. Come on, we haven't got all day."

Dylan looked pretty pitiful still breathing into her crumpled copy of *Variety*.

"Nah," said Dylan.

She turned around and slowly started walking down the hill. Sam and Tatiana looked at each other in fear. Kate looked perplexed.

"What do you mean 'Nah'?" asked Kate.

"I mean 'Nah.' That's what I mean. What? I don't want to tap the stupid bench."

"Listen, *Custer*, it's not like it's a choice. It's just . . . I mean, you *have* to do it! You *have* to tap the bench! That's what we do! That's what we always do—"

"No, that's what *you* always do—"

"D, just please tap the bench already so we can leave," Tatiana pleaded.

"Why? Will Kate's head just explode if I don't tap the damn bench?"

"No, my head will not *explode*, Dylan, but don't you understand? This is all part of the hike . . . this is what we do! If you don't tap the bench, the hike doesn't count! It's like the jokes were never made . . . the stories were never told . . . the calories were never burned . . . it's like . . . it never happened."

"Why?" asked Dylan.

"D! Just tap the bench!" yelled Tatiana.

"Fine," said Dylan.

She walked up to the bench and tapped it not just once, not just twice, but three times. Satisfied, she grinned at Kate.

"There. Now we took three hikes," said Dylan.

Kate looked and felt like her head actually *was* going to explode.

"What the hell was that?!" asked Kate.

"What?"

"You know you're only supposed to tap it once! You don't go and tap it three times!"

"Well, maybe *you* don't, but *I* do. It's my 'thing.'"

"It's your '*thing*'?"

"Yeah."

"What do you mean, it's your 'thing'? How can it be your 'thing,' D? It's *my* 'thing'! The whole 'thing' is my 'thing' . . . the bench-tapping thing! My 'thing'!"

"Calm down, Kate. It's just a bench," said Sam.

"No, no, it's not just a bench, Sammy! It's my thing! It's the one thing I have left, okay? Give me *one* thing! That's all I want. Sammy, you have your internship and your treatment and your weird secretive Doe obsession. T, you've got your acting and your photo shoots and everything. D, you have your various ailments and your music stuff . . . see, you guys all have your 'things.' I have nothing. I can't stand it! I've never not had a 'thing.' Any 'thing'!"

Kate sat down on the pavement, putting her elbows on her knees and her head in her hands.

"SNOK," she said quietly.

As the tears started rolling down Kate's cheek and off her nose, the girls congregated around her. Kate just couldn't play tough one more minute. She was usually the caretaker and leader of the group, but here she was, "thing-less" for the first time in her life.

"And my shrink says that I'm drowning in a sea of narcissism," said Kate.

"I'm sorry, K-Ro . . . I didn't mean to upset you . . . if it makes you feel any better, I think I swam in that sea when I was in Greece last summer and there was a *serious* undertow. I almost drowned too."

Kate, Sam, and Tatiana looked at each other and started laughing hysterically.

"What?" asked Dylan.

"Nothing, D. Apology accepted," said Kate.

"What did I say?!" asked Dylan.

"Group hug!" said Tatiana.

Kate stood up, put her arms around her cousin and her friends, and smiled as she determined to find a new "thing" before the summer was over.

CHAPTER TWENTY-ONE

LLOYD DOBLER: *Joe. Joe. She's written sixty-five songs . . . sixty-five. They're all about you. They're all about pain.*

JOE: *So what's up?* —SAY ANYTHING

The next week, Sam put the finishing touches on her treatment. She had gone back to some of her favorite novels and pieced together what she considered her perfect man and, in turn, perfect for her two young female protagonists.

So when Matt Sullivan arrived in the office Thursday morning, she was ready for him. Sam was wearing one of the new pairs of designer jeans that Kate had bought for her and a fabulously trendy T-shirt of Kate's that she'd borrowed. She had brought in the first-edition copy of *Franny and Zooey* that Matt Sullivan had lent to her the night they spent together. She hoped that maybe the sight of it would remind him how much fun they had had that night, and how much he liked her.

Lawrence was in a meeting when Sam approached Matt

Sullivan's cubicle. He was typing on his computer while simultaneously reading a script. Okay, she might have hated him, but she still loved to watch him multitask. She knocked on the wall of his cubicle like it was actually a door, and he looked up at her. How she wanted to hurdle that wall and curl up beside him. Damn him!

"Hey, Sam," he said. "What's up?"

"Hi. Um, a couple things . . ."

"Did you change your hair?"

"No, I just . . . no, I didn't. Why?"

"You just look nice, that's all."

Sam didn't know what to say. Did the tighter jeans make her hair look better?

"Thank you. I think. Listen, Matt, I wanted to thank you for letting me borrow your book. It's one of my favorites."

She carefully placed the book on top of his overflowing in-box.

"Oh, yeah. No problem. I forgot I lent it to you. Thanks."

"And also . . . I wanted to talk to you about that idea I had—"

"Oh . . . *Weird Science* for girls, right?"

"Yes. Well, I wrote it. I mean, I wrote a treatment . . . of it . . . and now it's more Jane Austen than John Hughes. But anyway, I was wondering if you might, you know, take a look at it."

"Yeah, sure."

"Okay. Well, should I just give it to you or—"

"Why don't you e-mail it to me? As you can see, I'm not the most organized person in the world."

"Oh, okay. Sure."

Maybe he wouldn't like it. What had Sam done? This was a terrible idea.

"I bet it's great," he said. "I'll read it this weekend. I'm looking forward to it."

Sam smiled. Everything was going according to her plan. But just as she turned to walk away, Matt Sullivan continued.

"Hey, Sam, can we talk?"

"Um, yes. Sure."

Okay, this was not part of the plan.

"I mean, now," Matt clarified.

"Oh, yeah. I thought you meant . . . never mind."

"Let's go into the conference room."

Although the cage hadn't been totally private since Sam had reorganized, the conference room had never been private. It was all glass. Everyone could see them in there. Sam glanced toward the copy room. Ross was hard at work at his computer, and it looked like she wasn't needed for any copying or envelope stuffing. Was this the moment she had been waiting for? Was he going to apologize for his weird behavior and ask her out? Sam tried desperately to remain calm, cool, and collected. *Easy-breezy*, she said to herself silently.

Matt Sullivan peered into Lawrence's office to make sure he was engrossed in his meeting. Matt forwarded his phone lines to voice mail, took off his headset, stepped away from his cubicle, and, putting his hand lightly on the small of Sam's back, led her into the conference room. He closed the door behind them. Sam could feel the beads of sweat accumulating on the tip of her nose. This always happened when she was truly anxious, and it annoyed her to no end. Why did she have to wear her nerves like a badge? A beaded badge, nonetheless. She used her cardigan sleeve to rub her nose.

They sat down across from each other at the wide table. Sam self-consciously covered her hands with her sleeves and rubbed the hyperpolished table with her forearms, even though it was spotless. Matt Sullivan looked over his shoulder out at the Authentic office. Then he looked at her.

"Listen, Sam, I've been thinking about everything that has been happening with us. So I talked with my trainer and my spiritual advisor about it, but they both said it was more in my therapist's domain. My therapist said that I've been unfair to you."

He needs a therapist to tell him that?

"I guess it probably shouldn't have happened. Us, I mean," Matt said. "I mean, you've been totally cool. I'm just not really in the right emotional space to be . . . I want you to know I feel *really* guilty about all this. I mean, it's been eating me up inside. Do you know what that's like? But I just want you to know that it's nothing you did, you've been really cool, and you're doing a great job here."

"Thanks. I mean, I'm fine."

She didn't mean a word of it. There was that lump in Sam's throat again. She couldn't really swallow. She was doing a great *job*? What?! Guilt? What happened to her being "really hot"? What had changed? Why was he breaking up with her? Wait, no, he couldn't break up with her because they were never "together." But how could he say it shouldn't have happened? How could he want to take back some of the most exciting moments of Sam's life?

"Okay, good. I am so relieved! See, I knew you would be cool about this!" he said.

Sam half-expected him to high-five her at that moment—which would have just been too much for Sam to handle. *Really.* But Lawrence's door slammed, and Sam watched as he stormed out of his office, walked straight into Rebecca's office, and slammed the door behind him. She was on the phone but quickly hung up as he entered. She seemed to listen patiently while Lawrence vented about something, writhing with discontent on the couch in her office. They both looked over toward Sam at the same time.

"Sam, I should get back to work," Matt said. "I'm glad we talked. So we're cool, right?"

"Yeah," she said.

She had no idea what they were "cool" about.

"I feel so much better!" said Matt.

He stood up, hurried out of the conference room, and went

back to his desk. Sam remained seated, stunned. What had just happened?

Sam didn't have time to dwell on whatever it was because as she headed back to the copy room, she almost bumped into Rebecca and Lawrence as they were leaving Rebecca's office. Lawrence huffed and went out the back door of the office. Rebecca went into Ellen's office and slammed the door. It seemed to Sam that no one ever just walked into another person's office at Authentic Pictures. A door slam signified drama and conflict, and what better place for that than a Hollywood production company?

Over the past few weeks, Sam had learned that if she just stayed out of sight and kept a low profile, she would be okay—except this time, the tornado found her. Like something out of a bad horror movie, Sam looked up to see Ellen and Rebecca staring at her from the copy-room doorway. Ross, who was completely immersed in his work and made it a practice to ignore the D-witches, barely looked up from his computer.

"Sam, can we talk to you?" Ellen asked.

"Do you mind if we steal your girlfriend?" Rebecca asked Ross.

"Huh?"

"Sam, do you mind?" asked Rebecca.

The D-witches led her back to the conference room, where they sat her down and looked at her sternly.

"Sam," Rebecca began, "you're doing a really good job and

everything—I mean, aside from the lukewarm soda situation and the Diet Jet incident which were, like, really *really* bad— but this is what we like to call in Hollywood 'constructive criticism'?"

Wasn't that a term used everywhere?

"The thing is," said Ellen, "Lawrence is very particular, so you really have to pay attention to every little detail. And right now, he's really upset."

"What did I do wrong?"

"Starburst, Sam, Starburst?" Rebecca said.

"But I bought the Starburst! I brought back the receipt and the change and—"

"I know, Sam, it's just that you bought regular Starburst. Lawrence likes the Starburst *jelly beans*," said Ellen.

"What's the difference?"

The girls looked at each other and laughed.

"Sam?!" said Rebecca. "The Starburst jelly beans are more like, um, *jelly beans*?!"

"It's an entirely different consistency," qualified Ellen.

"Lawrence doesn't like regular Starburst? He's really upset?" said Rebecca.

"I'm sorry, I didn't know." Sam wracked her brain; had Rebecca told her and it had slipped her mind? "I can go out and get more."

"He says that he can't trust you with these things anymore," said Ellen. "This is just for you to know for the future."

"But otherwise, you're doing so great?" said Rebecca. "Are you having the greatest summer?"

"Well, I—"

"Oh, and Sam," said Ellen. "Please watch the levels of the Coffee-Mate nonfat nondairy calorie-free no-sugar vanilla-flavored coffee creamer. Lawrence can't drink his coffee without it."

"Oh, and Sam," added Rebecca. "Lawrence said you brought him a Diet Mountain Dew the other day with five ice cubes? He only likes it with four?"

Sam nodded. The D-witches both cocked their heads, smiled falsely, got up in unison, and walked out of the conference room to their respective offices. Sam stayed seated for a minute. She was afraid she might start to cry. *Never let them see you cry*, she thought. When she gathered herself, Sam went back to the copy room. Ross looked over at her as she walked in.

"You okay?" he asked.

Sam didn't answer. She took one look at Ross, and the tears came rushing to her eyes.

"Whoa, wait. Hold on," he said.

Clearly, Ross didn't know quite how to deal with Sam like this. Neither did Sam. Like her cousin, Sam was not accustomed to crying in front of anyone.

"I'm fine," she said between sobs.

Ross grabbed a box of tissues and thrust it at her. She took three tissues from the box, blew her nose, and dabbed her eyes, hoping that the eyeliner that Kate had showed her how to apply was not running down her cheeks. But she could already see mascara and Kate's eye shadow on the tissue.

"Starburst," she sobbed.

"Oh, they got you on the Starburst, did they? They got me on that too when I first started here. You can't let them beat you down, Sam. They're just bitter and jealous because they're not eighteen and smart and beautiful with their entire lives ahead of them."

"Yeah, right."

"I'm serious! Do you know how *cool* you are?"

"Why does everyone keep *saying* that?"

"Sam, seriously. You're great . . . I mean, you're doing great. Just keep on doing what you're doing."

"I'm not. I'm a wreck. But thank you. How do you deal with all this stupid stuff?"

"It's all part of some twisted Hollywood rite of passage. Everyone goes through it. I love movies. Always have. I just wade through the crap so I can eventually do what I want to do. Make the movies I want to make. You can do it too. You're stronger than they are."

"I don't even know what's happening to me. This is all so stupid. I feel like I'm becoming this other person. And I promised my mom I would go to the Getty."

The floodgates opened at the thought of her parents and what they would think of what she was becoming, and what they would think of the D-witches and how they treated her.

"Hey, I'll go to the Getty with you," Ross volunteered. "I haven't been there in a while. Let's go on Sunday. You could come have a family dinner at my parents' house after. Well, my house. I still live there. It's not Beverly Hills, but my dad barbecues a mean burger."

"Thanks, Ross. I'd love that. You're a good friend."

"Nah, I'm a hack like the rest of them."

Sam elbowed him as they stood in the middle of the copy room. And then, in an impulsive and highly uncoordinated maneuver while still holding the box of tissues, Ross gave Sam a hug. At first, Sam was taken aback, but then she settled into his embrace. It was actually just what she needed.

"Ahem."

Sam dropped her arms and turned toward the coughing sound to see Matt Sullivan standing in the doorway. She was horrified.

"Am I interrupting something?"

"No, of course not, we were just—"

"Hugging?" he asked.

"Yeah, but, he was . . . I was . . . ," stammered Sam.

"The witches are torturing her," said Ross.

"Uh-huh," said Matt. "Listen, Ross, we just got this spec in. I need copies and coverage ASAP."

Matt Sullivan threw the script on Ross's desk and turned around. Matt was always tough on Ross, but Sam couldn't tell

195

if he was mad at her too. Did he think there was something going on between her and Ross? Should she go explain? Did she even care anymore? Sadly, she knew she still did.

But just as Matt Sullivan walked out of the copy room, Amy walked in with a pleading look in her eyes.

"Can one of you do a coffee run for Ellen and Rebecca?" she asked. "I'm sorry, I would go, but now Rebecca has me cleaning out her office because she does whatever Ellen does. Can one of you go for me please?"

"Why don't you go, Sam?" Ross offered. "You could use some fresh air. I'll make the copies."

Amy breathed a sigh of relief.

"Thanks, Sam, I really appreciate it. They both get large nonfat decaf lattes, and just please make sure they're nonfat and not caffeinated—they're both on major diets, and they can't have caffeine after three P.M. or else they're up all night."

"Okay."

Sam grabbed her car keys and bag. She looked at Ross, who had already started the copies.

"Hey, Ross, thanks."

"Make me proud," he said.

Sam didn't really know what he meant by that until she stepped up to the counter to order the coffees for the witches. And then, suddenly, she understood.

CHAPTER TWENTY-TWO

Honest people don't hide their deeds.
—EMILY BRONTË, *Wuthering Heights*

"You got them FULL-FAT lattes! Samantha Rose! I had no idea you had it in you. You are EVIL! I'm so proud," said Kate.

"And an extra shot of regular caffeinated espresso in each," said Sam.

It was Friday, just twenty-four hours after the Starburst D-Witch debacle. Kate had met Sam at a little deli around the corner from Authentic for a quick lunch, Sam's first one out of the office since she had started her internship. She knew that Matt Sullivan had a lunch that day, and she didn't have much hope left of having another lunchtime rendezvous. The girls were both having salads, and Sam was on day three of Kate's no-carb diet. Misery loves company, and all that.

"I cannot believe you! Tell me you spit in it too?"

"Nah, that's just gross. I'd rather see Ellen struggle to fit into her wedding dress."

"That's right. Save your saliva for Doe. Have you seen him?"

"Yeah. I think it's pretty safe to say he's lost interest. But I have one more trick up my sleeve."

"Well, maybe if you told me something about him, I could give you some advice!"

"Because your love life is such a success story?" asked Sam. She immediately corrected herself upon seeing Kate's reaction. "Sorry, K-Ro, that wasn't nice."

Sam checked her watch for the twelfth time in five minutes. Kate caught her.

"Chill factor, Sam. And we were doing so well. . . ."

"Kate, some of us actually have to work!" Sam said. She saw the hurt look on Kate's face. "Sorry, I didn't mean that. I'm just stressed out. I should get back."

"That's okay, Cuz. I'm just looking for that dare-to-be-great 'thing.' And when I find it, there'll be no stopping me."

"I have no doubt. Do you want to see the torture chamber? I mean, the office?"

"Oh well, I have some really important meetings, and um, I have that press conference I should attend . . . yes, of course! I'd love to see it. I want to see the D-witches in the flesh."

"Just, Kate . . . best behavior, okay? I have to work with these people."

"*Moi?* I am always on good behavior!"

As the girls walked the half block from the deli to Authentic Pictures, Kate complained that she was getting blisters from her shoes.

"Didn't you get the memo, Sammy? Nobody walks in LA. Are we there yet?"

Sam tensed up. Maybe she shouldn't be bringing her cousin to work. Was that terribly unprofessional? Especially in light of all the trouble she had gotten into recently, maybe it wasn't Sam's best idea. But, as she suspected, all the executives were still out to lunch when they arrived at the office. Ross was in his usual spot—hard at work on script coverage for Matt Sullivan.

"Ross, this is my cousin, Kate."

"Charmed," said Kate.

Kate looked him up and down, and Ross glared at her.

"I'm sure," he said.

"Be nice," Sam hissed to Kate.

"I am," Kate hissed back. "Chill factor," she said in a singsong voice.

"So, this is the copy room," Sam said, opening her arms grandly. "Ross and I call it our office. Do you like it?"

"Yes, I do. It's just . . . outstanding! But who do we talk to about the lighting? I mean, really, Cuz. I'm afraid you might photosynthesize in here."

"It's too late, I think I already have," replied Sam.

"Well, I'm wilting. Ross, it was a pleasure. Please take care of our girl, would you?"

"She does all right on her own."

Ross winked at Sam. She giggled. Kate watched Ross staring at her cousin.

"Okay then! I'm going to let you two get back to '*work*,'" she said, gesturing quotation marks with her fingers. "Sammy, do you want to walk me out?"

As they walked through the office, Kate grabbed Sam's arm.

"Okay, he *loooooooves* you," she said. "You realize that, don't you?"

"What are you talking about? You're insane."

"Um, no, it's pretty clear. He's madly, passionately, completely in love with you."

"Please, Kate. He's so not. He's my buddy. He's my only real friend in this place, so please don't freak me out, okay?"

"If you say so," said Kate. "Oh my God, wait . . . is he Doe? Because if he is, he is definitely still into you."

"No, Kate, he is not Doe. Would you please just give it up?"

As Sam and Kate approached the front of the building, the door flung open, flooding the entryway with sunlight. Partially blinded, Sam could barely make out the figure coming toward them. As Sam's eyes adjusted, she realized that the blurry figure was none other than Matt Sullivan with his car keys in his mouth, a script in his hand, and his phone held precariously between his ear and his shoulder. Both girls stopped in their tracks.

"Okay, who is *that*? And why don't I know him?" asked Kate.

"No one. Matt Sullivan. He's just an assistant. He's on the phone, so we probably shouldn't—"

But it was too late. Matt Sullivan had just flipped his phone closed and dropped his keys from his mouth into his hand. Kate was staring at him. And he was staring right back at her.

"Introduce me, introduce me," Kate whispered.

"Matt, this is my cousin, Kate. Kate, Matt."

"*Enchanté*," said Kate.

"Nice to meet you, Kate," he said.

He averted his gaze from Kate just long enough to look at Sam suspiciously. She knew he must have been wondering what Kate was doing there, and what, if anything, she knew about Sam and Matt's relationship (or whatever it could be called).

"And what do you do at this fine establishment, Matt . . . Sullivan, is it?" asked Kate.

"I work for Lawrence."

"My father is Lawrence's attorney! Yeah, good 'ole Norm, that's my dad. That's daddy!" said Kate.

"And you, Kate, what do you do?"

"I'm currently taking the summer off from my rigorous academic schedule. I'm looking for a dare-to-be-great situation."

"Well, best of luck with that, Kate. I should get back to work. Maybe I'll see you around?"

"Oh, I am sure of it."

"See ya, Sam."

Matt Sullivan walked past the girls and into the office.

"Cuz, he is so cute!" said Kate. "Why didn't you tell me about him?"

Kate grabbed Sam's hand and did a minijump in her kitten heels. Sam didn't know how to respond. She just wanted to drop it, but how could she?

"I should really get back to work."

"Will you do me a favor? Will you just give him my number please?"

"Kate . . ."

"*Pleeeeeeaaaaase*, Cuz, *pleeeeeeaaaaase*. I really like him, and you know I haven't really liked anyone since Colby. My shrink tells me to use my 'observing ego' and my ego just observed a *really* hot guy, so please be supportive, would you?"

"Okay, I will," said Sam.

"Really?"

"Yes, I said I'll do it."

"Give him my cell phone number, okay?"

"Okay, I will."

"Thank you so much," Kate gushed. "I'm so excited! I totally heart Matt Sullivan! Yay!"

Kate skipped out the front door, already speed dialing

Tatiana to tell her she'd met a cute boy. Sam went back to the copy room and carefully wrote down Kate's cell phone number on a sheet of Authentic Pictures letterhead. She folded it up and carried it around the office with her for the rest of the afternoon like it was an albatross around her neck. She couldn't bring herself to talk to Matt Sullivan again. She didn't know what he was thinking after seeing her and Ross in midhug in the copy room the previous afternoon. She didn't know if she should still e-mail him her treatment, as he had asked before he saw her and Ross together, and she certainly didn't know how or if she should give him Kate's cell phone number. How could she?

After the weekend read meeting in Dan's office, Sam returned to the copy room, where she clutched Kate's number and stared at the clock on the wall above the copy machine. Would she lie to Kate and tell her she gave the number to Matt Sullivan? Tell Kate that she forgot to give it to him, that she forgot her cell phone number altogether? That he left early before she had the chance to give it to him?

"Sam, for you. Line two," said Ross.

"For me?" No one called Sam at work. "Hello?"

"Did you give it to him yet?" asked Kate.

So much for the "I forgot" excuse.

"Oh, hi. No, not yet."

"What are you waiting for?"

"Kate, I'm working. I just haven't had a minute. I will. I promise, okay?"

Sam crossed her fingers behind her back even though Kate couldn't possibly see her. Sam knew it was immature, but she hated lying, and she hated breaking promises even more.

"Okay, GTs all around, Cuz. I trust you. Don't forget about the *Magazine* party tomorrow night."

"Okay, I'll see you later."

"Don't let me down, Cuz. Be my friend here."

"I know. I won't. I mean, I will."

"Love ya!"

"Bye," Sam said to the dial tone.

She took the piece of paper with Kate's cell phone number out of her pocket and studied her own meticulous handwriting. She looked over to Matt Sullivan's cubicle, where she could barely see the top of his head, but she knew he was there. She just couldn't do it. She ripped the paper up into eight pieces and threw it in the recycling bin. Then she sat down at Ross's computer, logged on to her e-mail account, and took a deep breath as she e-mailed her treatment to Matt Sullivan.

CHAPTER TWENTY-THREE

"So did he say when he was going to call?" asked Kate.

It was the following evening, and Kate was doing Sam's makeup in their bathroom at Uncle Norman's house.

"Um, no, he was really busy, so I just put it in his in-box. He gave me the thumbs-up sign. Ow!"

"Sorry. Stray eyebrow hair. Compelled to tweeze it. He gave you a 'thumbs-up'? What is that? Does that mean he's going to call or not?"

Kate put the tweezers down and started rubbing iridescent pink liquid blush into Sam's cheeks.

"Kate! I don't know! I gave it to him like you asked. What's the big deal? He's just a dumb guy!"

"He's not dumb, Sammy. He went to Harvard. He's hot *and*

smart. My friend Amber is a junior there. She said he was a total heartbreaker. Though in Hollywood, heartbreaker is usually just a euphemism for flake."

Kate painstakingly applied black liquid eyeliner to Sam's eyes. Sam squinted at Kate.

"What? I do my research," Kate said. "Now, look down. Good. Now, look left. Look right. Left. Right, left, right . . ."

"Kate!"

"Calm down! Jeez, I was just kidding around. What's up your butt the last few days, anyway? Close your eyes. Seriously."

"Nothing. I'm just tired. It's been a long week. That's all. Seriously."

"What do you hear from Doe?"

"Kate! Can we please just drop it?!"

"So touchy!"

Kate spun Sam around so she could see herself in the mirror. But Sam wasn't in the mood for another makeover. She felt so uncomfortable in her own skin at this point that having different makeup on her face felt like just another layer of lies. She was lying to her cousin, who had also become her best friend and who had taken her under her wing, introduced her to her friends, and involved her in her life. She was lying to Ross, and worst of all, she was lying to herself.

Sam was dressed in one of Kate's slinky black dresses. Kate insisted Sam wear her stilettos, which were higher and more precarious than any heel Sam had ever worn. Kate emerged from the closet wearing jeans and the silk halter she had bought for Sam at Fred Segal.

As the phone rang, indicating that someone was at the front gate, the girls grabbed their handbags, and Kate headed down the stairs. Sam looked in the mirror, struck a halfhearted pose, and sighed. The out-of-body experience was getting old. She flipped off the lights and carefully walked downstairs in her borrowed stilettos.

Kate opened the front door to see a white stretch Hummer waiting outside. Dylan rolled down the car's darkly tinted window, and she and Tatiana stuck their heads out.

"Oh my God! Does it get any cheesier?" shrieked Kate.

"I know—I LOVE it!" said Dylan. "But we're going to get in serious trouble with the environment people. Do you know how much gas these things use?"

"Arriving in a Prius is so 2004," said Tatiana.

As Kate climbed into the monstrous mobile, Sam looked dubiously at the girls giggling inside.

"Hop in, Sammy, we're going to be late," said Tatiana. "Tardiness is so eighties."

Sam had never been in a Hummer before (let alone one that had been stretched). For Kate, Tatiana, and Dylan, it was the prom all over again. Sam didn't go to her prom. And now, if this was any indication of what it was like, she was truly glad she hadn't. Tatiana was wearing a tight purple crepe dress, matching purple stilettos, and a silver scarf around her neck.

Her signature long red ringlets had been blown straight, and her makeup was done to perfection so that she had the "dewy" look. Tatiana complained that she would have to walk down the press line, pose for the cameras, and answer silly questions like "How does it feel to be the forty-sixth hottest ingénue?"

"What am I supposed to say?" she asked. "Better than forty-seventh? Not as good as forty-fifth? It's a real honor? Ugh."

Kate had explained to Sam that while Tatiana knew to take these things with a grain of salt, she felt a little insecure and nervous nonetheless. Just a week earlier, Tatiana had found herself on a fashion "Don't" list and was still horrified about it.

Dylan was as enthusiastic (and injured) as ever. Her embroidered silk sling was gone, but she now carried an antique black carved cane. Apparently, she did not have carpal tunnel syndrome, nor did she have an ulcer, gout, SARS, or the whooping cough, as she had suspected. Now, however, she was sure that she had broken her ankle, possibly and probably due to an early onset of osteoporosis. At least she was a hypochondriac with style, and she had an uncanny ability to accessorize no matter what the ailment was. She complemented her black cane with flowing white pants and a black silk tank top with black sandals.

Tatiana was busy trying to make sandwiches consisting of heaping teaspoons of beluga caviar and sour cream on toast (with no crust, of course), but the Hummer—originally designed for combat, not car pool—was not the smoothest of rides. In combining the über-expensive ingredients, most fell onto the red carpet of the vehicle. Tatiana sampled her caviar concoction and sighed after her first delicious bite.

"Isn't it amazing that, like, ninety-nine percent of the world doesn't know what caviar is, and we enjoy it so much?" asked Tatiana.

"Oh, come on, Tots!" said Dylan. "Everyone knows what caviar is!"

"Okay, D, you think people in, like, Tasmania know what beluga caviar is?"

"What's Tasmania?"

"My point exactly."

Kate looked over at Sam, who was rolling her eyes. Sam couldn't believe the shallow conversations that were going on around her and couldn't remember why she had agreed to go to this event in the first place.

"Enough, girls," said Kate. "You're freaking out the Massachussian."

The *Magazine* party was set up on an entire block in Chinatown in downtown LA, which, in traffic, was a good forty-five bumpy minutes from Beverly Hills. By the time they pulled up to the party, Sam was once again suffering from acute motion sickness. She was sure she looked green. She certainly felt like it.

Between the photographers, PR people, and guests trying to get in the party, it was chaos. Kate and Dylan got out first and walked straight into the party, avoiding the red carpet/press line by going in through a side door. Tatiana stepped out next.

"Oh, Sam, can you hold this, please?"

Before Sam could answer, Tatiana thrust her silver mesh purse into Sam's lap and exited the Hummer. From inside the vehicle, Sam could see the blinding flashbulbs and hear the overlapping yells. *How do people live like this?* she thought. She didn't see where Kate and Dylan had gone, and she was carrying Tatiana's purse, so she decided to follow her. Sam stood at the entrance of the red carpet while Tatiana walked slowly down it toward the end, stopping for pictures and to answer questions.

"Excuse me!" A PR woman with a clipboard and headset said as she bumped into Sam. "Are you a number?"

"I'm sorry, what?"

"A number? One of the hundred hottest ingénues? What number are you?"

"I'm not a number. I'm just a friend of Tatiana Ford's."

"Oh. You shouldn't be here. You need to go through the back. This is for numbers only." She turned to her colleague on the other side of her. "These struggling actresses will stop at nothing to get their pictures taken. It's pitiful."

Sam heard her nasty comment and looked down at her feet. Which, by the way, were killing her due to Kate's ten-feet-high stilettos. She glimpsed Tatiana way up ahead along the press line, confidently flirting with an entertainment news show anchor. She certainly didn't seem nervous to Sam, who backed out of the press line and entered through the side entrance.

The theme of the party was a Chinese carnival. Waiters dressed in colorful dragon costumes served dim sum on cocktail napkins that were printed with the pictures of different actresses from the magazine list. Instead of her name accompanying her picture, each actress's number on the list appeared across her image like a stamp of approval. Sam had never seen anything like it. She was hungry, but she was carrying her bag, her jacket, and Tatiana's bag in her hands and didn't have any way to get the damn dumpling into her mouth, short of asking one of the dragons to feed her. And she certainly was in no mood for that.

"What number is she? She's hot."

Sam turned around and saw a short guy in a gray suit with a visible duck sauce stain on the lapel. He and his doppelganger friend were eating egg rolls and staring at Sam lasciviously. As far as she could tell, the only thing that really differentiated them from each other was that one was wearing a blue tie, the other a yellow tie. Both jammed their egg rolls into their mouths to free their hands so they could furiously flip through the magazine (copies of which were everywhere), while looking at Sam as if it were a drunken game of Memory.

"Ask her, dude," said Blue Tie.

"No way, dude, you ask her," replied Yellow Tie.

"Roshambo for who asks her?"

Sam, perplexed, was watching the whole thing. They stuck out their hands. Blue Tie won with his "rock" prevailing over Yellow Tie's "scissor."

"Two out of three?" asked Yellow Tie.

"I'm not on the list!" Sam interrupted. "I'm not an actress! Okay?"

As she walked away from them, she heard Yellow Tie say, "What's her problem?"

"She's probably just bitter," said Blue Tie. "Oh, wait, who's that redhead? She's definitely on the list. I've seen her before. What number is she?"

Sam turned around to see Tatiana entering the party. As always, heads turned, and at this party, pages turned as well, as men tried to figure out just where she fell on the list.

"Found her," said Yellow Tie. "Number forty-six."

Sam watched the two Ties approach Tatiana.

"Dude, talk to her," said Blue Tie. "This is your shot."

"You talk to her, dude."

Yellow Tie pushed Blue Tie forward so that he was standing right in front of Tatiana, who had just noticed Sam and was on her way to her.

"Hey, didn't I see you in that movie with the snakes?" asked Blue Tie.

"I never did a movie with snakes."

"Was it lizards then?" asked Yellow Tie.

"I have never worked with any reptiles to my knowledge, no."

"Well, we think you're great, Forty-six. I mean, Laticia," said Blue Tie.

"Tatiana," she corrected.

"Dude," interjected Yellow Tie.

"Hang on, dude, I'm making progress here."

"Dude," said Yellow Tie again.

"Would you please excuse me while I confer with my associate for a moment?" Blue Tie asked Tatiana.

"There's number thirteen, we're wasting our time with this forty-six business," whispered Yellow Tie.

"But isn't thirteen bad luck?"

"With those legs, I think not, my friend."

"Dude, you're right, where is she?"

As the two ties headed off in the direction of number thirteen, Tatiana walked over to Sam and grabbed her arm. Sam handed Tatiana her purse.

"This is a nightmare," said Tatiana.

"Tell me about it."

Tatiana waved to Kate and Dylan—hobbling behind Kate with drink and cane in hand—as they were making their way back from the crowded bar in the middle of the outdoor party. Kate balanced three fruity-looking drinks in her hands, all of which were garnished with little umbrellas and minuscule neon-colored plastic animals perched on the glass rims.

As Kate passed out the drinks, she looked up at the party entrance.

"Well, well, well. Look what the cat dragged in," she said.

Sam was in midsip when she looked over to see Matt Sullivan entering the party. She choked and spit back into her cup.

"T.G., Sam: Totally Gross!" said Kate.

Matt Sullivan gave nods to Blue Tie and Yellow Tie but didn't actually stop to talk to them. Instead, he headed straight for the bar.

"Is that him?" asked Tatiana.

"It sure is," said Kate. "Oh my god, I am so excited he's here!"

Sam was frozen. At that moment, as Matt Sullivan walked past her in the distance, she felt a desperation and a loneliness she had never felt before. Of all the magazine parties in all of the world, why did he have to walk into hers?

"How do I look?" asked Kate.

"You look HOT! Go get him, sexy," said Dylan. "Oh, do you want to borrow my cane?"

"That's very sweet of you, D, but no," Kate said. "Sammy, come with me. You can reintroduce us."

"Oh, Kate, you know, I'm not really—"

"What else are you going to do? Keep spitting into your cup? It's a party, Cuz, one must mingle."

"She's right, Sam," said Tatiana. "Wallflowers are totally 1991."

Kate grabbed Sam's arm and pulled her toward the bar where Matt Sullivan was waiting for his drink.

"I have no idea where she gets those dates from," Kate said. "She's so chronological. Always has been. Oh, Sammy! Put your drink down, quick! It has to look like we just got here and need drinks, otherwise it'll look like we just went to the bar to talk to him."

"But that's what we're doing."

"You are so literal!"

Sam set her drink down on a dragon's empty tray. She didn't want it in the first place. She didn't want much of anything right now aside from a new life, or maybe wings to fly back to Northampton, and/or a thorough brainwashing so that she wouldn't remember that any of this had ever happened. Kate nudged Sam as they peered at Matt Sullivan from behind two tall scantily clad human toothpicks (i.e., models).

"Okay, you go first," she said. "Just get next to him and act surprised when you see him."

The beads of sweat were accumulating on Sam's nose, and she was sure she was about to faint from anxiety. But she did as she was told and sidled up to the bar with Kate behind her, pushing her along.

"Stop pushing me."

"Stop moving so damn slow then!"

"Okay!"

"Okay!"

Matt Sullivan turned around to see what all the hissing was about.

"Sam? I almost didn't recognize you. What a nice surprise. I didn't know you were coming to this," he said.

Nobody did earnest like Matt Sullivan. Sam *loathed* earnest. He leaned in and tentatively kissed Sam on the cheek. Kate leaned over Sam's shoulder toward him.

"I brought her. Being the good cousin that I am."

"Kate, right? So, we meet again. What brings you to this . . . unique function?"

"Well, I have to make sure my little cousin has a good time while she's in our fair city."

Kate squeezed Sam. Sam thought she might just vomit.

"So, are you involved in *Magazine*?" Matt asked Kate. "You certainly look like you could be on the list."

"Ah, yes, well, they asked me, but I had my publicist tell them I couldn't do the photo shoot due to demanding midterms, you know how it is."

Matt Sullivan laughed, clearly amused. But Sam couldn't believe what she was seeing and hearing. Was her cousin really flirting with the only guy with whom she had ever been madly in like?

"Also, my best friend is Tatiana Ford. She's on the list. Why are you here?"

"A friend of mine works at *Magazine*," he said as he glanced at Sam, who was chewing on her lip in an attempt not to cry, sweat, fall, or any combination thereof. "You look great, Sam. Enjoying your first Hollywood party?"

Matt Sullivan had never used this tone with Sam before. It was as if he was talking to a small child. Sam wondered if he was going to offer her a Shirley Temple.

"Oh, it's not her first party!" Kate answered. "I've had her under my tutelage for a few weeks now. This is old hat for her."

Sam just loved it when people talked about her like she wasn't there. Especially when one of those people was Matt Sullivan. But he did say she looked great. Did he say that to all the girls?

"Listen, good seeing you both, but I should go find my friend."

"Okay," said Kate. "Oh, and Matt, give me a call some-time."

Matt looked at Sam, but she looked away. This was going to get ugly. Sam could tell Matt was trying to gage her reaction. As if it was a dare, and he was taking it, he whipped out his cell phone.

"Okay, sure. What's your number?"

Sam cringed. Kate looked at her. Didn't Sam say she had already given Kate's number to Matt?

"I thought that Sam . . ."

Matt Sullivan stood there with his drink and cell phone in hand, ready to type in Kate's number. Kate just gave it to him. She'd take it up with Sam later. Kate politely said good-bye and started walking away from the bar, assuming that Sam was right behind her. But as Sam turned to follow her, she felt a familiar hand grab hers. She turned around to look directly at Matt Sullivan.

"Sam, I'm sorry about yesterday. I didn't realize . . . and then when I saw you and Ross together, I . . ."

Sam had never heard Matt Sullivan fumble for words.

"But nothing is going on with us," said Sam. "I was just upset, he was there, and then you walked in. . . ."

"I know." He squeezed her hand. "Let me make it up to you."

"Matt, I don't understand you. Why are you like this?"

"Like what?"

"Sam! Are you coming or what?" Kate yelled from the periphery of the crowded bar area.

"I gotta go," said Sam.

She took her hand from Matt Sullivan's grasp and walked toward Kate, who had one hand on her hip and looked pretty pissed off.

"Um, Sam, what was that about?" asked Kate. "I thought you gave him my phone number?"

"No, I . . . I told you I put it in his in-box. Maybe he didn't see it."

Sam hated lying, and that seemed to be all she was doing recently.

"Something's going on here, Sam. You don't want me dating someone you work with? Are you embarrassed by me or something?"

"It's just weird, Kate. I mean, I like to keep my work life and my family life separate."

"Well, maybe you should have thought about that before you let Norman get you an internship and give you room and board for the summer."

"Yeah, maybe."

"Ugh, I am so over your passive-aggressive sphinx-y innocence. SNOK, Sam. Totally and utterly SNOK."

Kate turned on her high heel and made a beeline for Dylan and Tatiana, who were still standing underneath the faux Chinese pagoda. Sam looked over to see Kate venting and gesticulating wildly to the girls. They all looked over at Sam at the same time. It was safe to say they were talking about her and her "SNOK" behavior. She turned away from the girls to look back at the bar, and it seemed that Matt Sullivan had disappeared into a sea of people, models, and dragons. Sam felt more lost, alone, and confused than ever.

"Dumpling?" asked a dragon.

"No thanks," answered Sam.

"You all right, sweetheart?"

"Not really. I wish I could just disappear. Want to trade costumes?"

"Honey, it's about a hundred degrees in here. Trust me, you're the lucky one."

But Sam didn't feel so lucky anymore. She took another look at Kate laughing with Dylan and Tatiana, and quietly slipped out the back entrance of the party. She walked outside, where people were still lined up to get in. She could see the white stretch Hummer parked up the block, but she knew she couldn't walk one more step in Kate's shoes. She kicked them off, grabbed them both in one hand, and started walking barefoot.

"Sam!"

She turned around to see Matt Sullivan walking toward her.

"Sam, wait!"

She kept walking as she heard him catching up to her. She breathed deeply, fighting off the involuntary Matt Sullivan-induced goose bumps.

"Where are you going?"

"Home."

"Barefoot?"

"I'll be fine."

"Wait."

Matt Sullivan walked in front of Sam and stopped. He looked over his shoulder at her.

"Hop on," he said. "Don't worry. I won't drop you."

"Aren't we a little old for piggyback rides?" she asked.

"You tell me, eighteen."

Sam smiled in spite of herself. She slowly put her arms around Matt Sullivan's neck with her shoes still dangling from one hand. She hopped onto his back and wrapped her legs around his waist. He held on to her bare legs, and he effortlessly walked up the block, carrying Sam on his back. She nestled her head between his neck and his shoulder. But just as she got comfortable there, the ride was over, and Matt Sullivan gently placed her down on the cold pavement again. Sam fixed her dress and looked up at him.

"Sullivan! Come on!" yelled Matt's friend from the entrance of the party. Matt waved to him.

"I'll call you tomorrow," he said to Sam.

"It is tomorrow."

"Then I'll call you today. I promise."

He took her hand in his and he kissed her on the lips. It was undeniable: Matt Sullivan had a way of disappearing from and then reappearing into Sam's life. It never failed to leave her confused, excited, angry, and worst of all, wanting more. He released her hand and walked back to the party to meet his friend who was waiting for him with his mai tai.

Sam watched as Matt Sullivan disappeared once again. She looked up at the large white Hummer, and she sighed as she stepped into it, hoping she would make it home before it turned into a pumpkin.

CHAPTER TWENTY-FOUR

GRIFFIN MILL: *Can we talk about something other than Hollywood for a change? We're educated people.* —THE PLAYER

When Sam awoke the following morning, she was just as exhausted and confused as she had been when she had fallen asleep the night before. She looked over at Kate, who was, as usual, still asleep. Sam hadn't even heard her cousin come in from the *Magazine* party the night before. She had no idea how she should act toward Kate now. She couldn't tell her that Matt Sullivan was actually Doe and what had happened between them. Besides, it was too late. Matt had already had his effect on Kate. And Kate was a total piranha when she set her sights on something—or someone— she wanted.

Sam looked at the alarm clock: 10 A.M. Would Matt Sullivan call as promised? And if so, when? She fought the thought out of her mind, because Ross would arrive soon to take her to the Getty. Sam's mother was thrilled when Sam told her that she would finally be going.

Sam took a quick shower and dressed in all her own black clothes fished out from her overstuffed, yet recently untouched, single bottom drawer. Wearing all black on a summer day in Los Angeles was almost unheard of, but it made Sam feel more comfortable to be back in her own dark armor. She went downstairs to the kitchen to make breakfast and wait for Ross, but before she could grab some kind of tasteless, calorie-less carbless excuse for food, the phone rang.

The phone system at Uncle Norman's house was almost as complicated as the one at Authentic Pictures. There were six lines and an intercom for each room, and the front gate rang to one of the phone lines. Kate always unplugged the phone in their room at night, as she hated being woken up in the morning. But the line that was ringing was the front gate. Sam didn't remember how to open the gate from the phone, so she went outside, walked to the end of the driveway, opened the gate manually, and climbed into Ross's decrepit truck. She also didn't want him to turn off the ignition, as she knew it would probably be a production to get it started again.

"Where's the funeral?" he asked.

Sam glared at him.

"I'm just kidding. Jeez. Rough night?" he asked.

"Nah. I'm just over this whole Hollywood scene, you know?"

"Uh-huh. I was never under it, so no, I wouldn't know."

"Ha-ha."

"You ready for some culture?" asked Ross in a terrible British accent.

"I was born ready."

"That's my girl."

The two made their way in the truck along Sunset Boulevard, which twisted and turned through Westwood, Bel Air, and into Brentwood to the Getty. They parked in the underground structure and took the cable car up to the museum. As they slowly pulled up the hill, Sam craned her neck over the 405 Freeway to see all of Los Angeles. Ross nudged her as they came over the final plateau and the structure of the Getty museum came into sight. It was large, white, and imposing. But it was beautiful and grand, and Sam felt a rush of happiness and contentment to be there. She had been so completely immersed in Hollywood (and Matt Sullivan), that just the notion of seeing and appreciating something other than movies (and Matt Sullivan) was enough to make Sam forget about Kate (and Matt Sullivan), and the superficial Hollywood world that now lay beneath her.

Ross and Sam spent the most time looking at the paintings in the Impressionist wing. Sam was charmed by Monet's *Sunrise*, which was one of her father's favorite paintings. At some point, lost in her own world, Sam lost track of Ross. She walked through several rooms before she found him standing quietly in front of Van Gogh's painting *Irises*. Sam had always loved the painting, which depicted a richly colored field of irises. She stood next to Ross and stared at the painting with him.

"Do you know why he painted one iris a different color from all the others?" Ross asked.

"No. Why?"

"Because he was lonely."

Ross pushed his glasses up the bridge of his nose and remained fixated on the painting. Perhaps she and Ross had more in common than she thought? They were both loners. But Sam assumed that Ross was content this way. He didn't try to fit in. And while she had never made an effort to fit in during high school, here in Los Angeles she had. She had to admit, she was *still* trying to fit in.

Sam and Ross walked leisurely around the gallery and through the manicured gardens. In typical Sam fashion, she tripped and almost fell over the wooden Japanese bridge into the shallow stream below before Ross caught her arm and steadied her.

"I worry so much about you! I really do!" he said. "No one should ever leave you alone."

"I know, I know, I'm accident prone. It's a problem."

"What do you do if someone isn't there to catch you?"

"I fall," she said. "Don't worry, Ross. I always get back up."

Sam continued walking. Ross watched her for a moment and then jogged to catch up.

They sat on a stone bench in the garden and talked about what they saw in the museum, about books that they loved, and about movies they had seen. Ross was one of the smartest people Sam had ever met. He was a walking encyclopedia of film, and as far as Sam could tell, he had seen every movie, read every book about movies, and read every script ever written. What's more, he had an uncanny ability to remember everything about what he had read, not to mention a photographic memory. But Ross had not been a straight-A student in high school the way Sam had been. In fact, he admitted that he was not much of a student at all. What he learned and what he knew, he had taught and read himself. Sam talked about some of her favorite classic novels, which Ross hadn't read. Ross talked about his favorite classic films, which Sam hadn't seen. And at that moment, Sam felt closer to Ross than anyone else and appreciative that he had taken her to this special place, and that he was, well, Ross. As far as Sam could tell, he never pretended to be anything or anyone other than who he was. And he made no apologies for it either. Sam had a lot of respect for that. She'd always considered herself that way, but now, she had to reconsider. She was dressing differently, eating differently, even talking differently. And while it was fun to step outside of herself for a little while, it was good to start living in her own clothes, her own imagination, and her own independent thoughts once again. They hadn't broached the topic of work at all, but Sam decided to tell him about her movie idea.

"I think it's great!" said Ross. "So, who's the perfect guy?"

"Well, that's the thing. I thought I might have found him. But now I'm not so sure he exists at all. He's like this myth, you know? He's this myth that every girl grows up believing she can find for real. But really, he's Bigfoot: you always hear that someone has seen him, or heard him, or even found an imprint of his Bigfoot-step, but he never *actually* materializes. I do know one thing: at the very least, he would be a man of his word."

"Uh-huh," said Ross, mentally taking notes. "Well, if you want any help, or if you want me to read what you have, I'd be honored."

"Thanks. I'd like that. Matt is reading it now. Or, he said he would."

"Wait, what? You gave it to Matt? What did I tell you about him?"

"I know, he's the devil. But I think you may be wrong about him. He's not so bad."

"Well, don't tell me I didn't warn you. Watch your back with that guy."

Sam laughed. It was sweet that Ross was so protective of her. She put her arm around his shoulders and gave him a friendly squeeze.

"Don't worry, Ross, I'll be fine. I'm a big girl."

"If you dance with the devil, the devil don't change. . . ."

"The devil changes you . . . I know, Ross. Sometimes you're so dramatic."

"I'm just saying. . . ."

Sam took her arm back and stared out over the gardens. She thought about calling Uncle Norman's house to see if Matt Sullivan had called yet, as he had promised he would.

"We should go," said Ross. "I told my mom we would be at the house by five. Remember, I've warned you, they're weird. Just take them with a grain of salt."

"I will, Ross, I will. I'm looking forward to it."

"Don't say you weren't warned."

"I wouldn't dare."

CHAPTER TWENTY-FIVE

GARY: *This isn't my car. This isn't my suit. Those weren't even my friends.*

HILLY: *Why are you telling me this?*

GARY: *Because I want you to like me for what I am.* —WEIRD SCIENCE

Sam and Ross pulled up to a low gray-stucco house with a white picket fence. The street was quiet and lined with houses that looked almost identical to Ross's. There were no imposing gates, and there was no tall shrubbery. It was so normal, Sam was in shock. Had she become that accustomed to the extravagance of Beverly Hills?

As Ross used his entire body to park his truck (so much for power steering), Sam took the time to observe her new surroundings. There was something quite comforting about being away from all the glitz and glamour of Hollywood. She looked at the house to her right. There was a red rosebush and yellow flowers lining the narrow walkway to the front door.

Sam jumped as a teenage female face popped up in one of the small rectangular windows lining the narrow glass frame of the front door. Sam smiled. The face disappeared and was immediately replaced by a grown-up female face.

"Home, sweet home," said Ross. "Wait, don't go any- where."

He hopped out of the car and ran around to Sam's side. He extended his right arm with a welcoming flourish as he pulled on her door . . . which didn't budge. He tried the whole sequence again. No luck. Ross knocked on the closed window and yelled to Sam.

"Try unlocking it!"

The front door of the house opened to reveal Ross's parents and his little sister, who all stood in the doorway, watching.

"Welcome!" yelled Ross's mom.

Ross was still struggling with the car door. He glared at his family over his shoulder. Sam waved from inside the old truck.

"It *is* unlocked!" Sam yelled.

"Try again," yelled Ross.

"Why don't you kids come on inside?" shouted Ross's mom.

"One second, Mom!"

"I'll just climb out the driver's side," yelled Sam.

"What?" Ross yelled.

"The mini quiches are getting cold!" Ross's mom yelled.

Sam rolled down her window.

"I'll just climb out the driver's side," she said.

"Okay. Good idea."

Sam grabbed her bag and climbed over the stick shift and parking brake into the driver's seat. She lost her balance and fell against the horn, which blared like a dying sheep. It might as well have been an air raid siren; neighbors came around front from their backyards and from inside their homes and looked out their windows to see what caused the commotion.

"I'm fine! Sorry," said Sam.

She finally stepped out of the truck as Ross came around to her side to help her down.

"Sorry," said Ross.

"Hi, kids!" shouted Ross's mom.

"She's a little overzealous," Ross whispered to Sam. "She doesn't get out much."

Sam laughed as they walked up the path to the front door to greet Ross's family. Ross's mom, Mrs. Gordon—or Paula, as she insisted on being called—a plump woman with red cheeks, long curly blond hair, and pale blue eyes, threw herself on Sam with a big hug.

"It is such a pleasure to *finally* meet you!" said Paula. "I just can't tell you how excited we are. Ross has said the nicest things about you—"

"Uh, Mom," interrupted Ross's sister.

Ross's sister looked like a younger, thinner, female version of Ross, with the same dirty-blond hair and blue eyes.

"Hold on, Meredith, I'll introduce you in a moment," said Paula. "She's very impatient."

"But, Mom," said Meredith.

"One moment!" said Paula. "Sam, it's not every day that Ross brings home a *friend*! You know, he doesn't really like anyone. I don't know where he gets it from."

"MOM!"

"What, Meredith, what is it?!"

Meredith pointed toward the street. They all turned. Slowly but surely, the truck was moving. Sam must have dislodged the parking brake as she struggled to get out! Ross ran off after the truck.

"Crap!" said Ross.

"Ross! Language!" said Paula.

"Sorry, Ross!" Sam said.

The truck was picking up speed and heading directly for his father's new red Hyundai parked on the street. Ross grabbed onto the driver's side door handle of the truck, fumbling with the keys. Ross's dad, Mr. Gordon, froze.

"Not my new car!"

The truck was gaining speed. Ten feet to impact.

"Hurry up, Ross!" yelled Paula.

Five feet.

"He is SO not going to make it," said Meredith, laughing.

Three feet. Sam covered her eyes.

"My car!" said Mr. Gordon.

Ross got the door open, and just as the truck was about to crash, he yanked the parking brake and it lurched to a stop. It was just barely grazing his father's car. Everyone gave a huge sigh of relief. Ross caught his breath as he leaned over with his hands on his knees. He looked up and smiled, wiping his brow.

"Close one!" he said.

Sam uncovered one eye and looked at Meredith.

"Is it over?" Sam asked.

A grinding noise came from the truck. The parking brake gave way, and it gave a final lurch into the fender of his father's car.

"*Now*, it's over," said Meredith.

The damage to the car was negligible to everyone except Bob Gordon. It was just a little dent in the fender, but Ross's father seemed heartbroken nonetheless. He clearly loved that car, but he helped his son move the truck back to its original spot without too much complaining. They put wooden wedges in front of the wheels so that it wouldn't move again.

In the meantime, Paula brought the mini quiches out to the front yard and served them to everyone, including the many curious neighbors, who had watched the whole episode. Sam apologized profusely, but they reassured her that this happened all the time. She felt horribly, but as Dylan might say, the quiches were DELICIOUS! And Ross's family was warm and welcoming.

"Mr. Gordon, I am so sorry about your car," said Sam. "Is there anything I can do? Anything at all?"

"You can call me Bob," he said.

"Oh, okay," said Sam. She was accustomed to calling her parents' friends Mr. and Mrs., so she was a little uncomfortable. It went against all her instincts.

"And I assume you've met my loudmouth kid sister?" asked Ross.

"Ross, when are you going to stop saying that?" Meredith said. "I happen to be thirteen years old. ThirTEEN! *Helloooo?* Teen! Therefore, I am not a 'kid' anymore. I mean, I have boobs!"

"She gets them from me," said Paula.

"Well, she doesn't get them from me!" said Bob.

"Guys! Could we change topics please?" asked Ross.

"She's so pretty," Paula whispered loudly to Ross.

Sam was embarrassed and wanted to say "I'm right *here*!" but she didn't. Anyway, as weird as they were, it was nice to be around an actual family again, and one that clearly loved one another so much. They all stood outside the front door in silence.

"Let's go inside," said Paula and Ross at the same time.

"You guys are such weirdos," said Meredith. "Sorry about them, they're like totally socially challenged."

Sam followed the Gordon family into the house. Inside, the walls were paneled in rich dark wood, and the carpeting was a thick plush blue—it may not have been as aesthetically pleasing, but it was certainly more inviting than the prickly sisal carpeting at Uncle Norman's. Sam was surprised to see monkeys everywhere. Monkey paintings, monkey sculptures, monkey potpourri holders—even the couch was upholstered in a lime-green-and-red-circus-themed pattern featuring monkeys wearing red beanies. Set out neatly on the glass coffee table with iron legs that resembled trees (with monkeys clinging to them) were bowls of chips and popcorn. Carbs. *Hello, my old friend*, thought Sam. She hadn't come into contact with anything involving yeast or flour in too long. It was a relief. Ross and Sam sat down on the monkey couch while Meredith plopped down on the carpet across from them. Paula disappeared into the kitchen, and Bob went to the backyard to start the barbecue.

"I should have warned you about the monkeys," said Ross.

"They're cute," replied Sam. Okay, they were a little creepy, but cute. Kind of.

"Bob and I just love monkeys," said Paula, walking back from the kitchen with four glasses of iced tea. "They're good luck!"

There weren't just monkey pictures everywhere. Gordon family pictures also lined the walls. Front and center were shots of the family at the Grand Canyon—Ross with a book in hand and Meredith rolling her eyes at the camera. There was a picture of Ross winning a spelling bee, Meredith dressed up as Catwoman for Halloween, Ross in a football uniform sitting on the bench.

Ross got up from the couch to bring the burgers out to Bob. On his way to the kitchen, he flicked Meredith's ear with his fingers.

"You're such a dork!" she yelled. "He's a dork," she repeated.

While Meredith returned to intently inspecting her hair for split ends and upon finding them, splitting the hairs farther, Bob and Ross were outside grilling hamburgers. Paula, on the other hand, was inside grilling Sam. She wanted to know everything—where Sam grew up, what her parents were like, what she studied, and what she thought of Los Angeles.

"Give her a break, would you?" Ross returned to the living room with two fresh glasses of iced tea.

"I thought you were getting me one?" asked Meredith.

"Only have two hands, sorry. Too bad, so sad."

"You are *soooo* immature!" said Meredith.

"I'll get you one," said Paula. "I have to finish getting dinner ready anyway."

"May I help?" asked Sam.

"Oh no, dear. You're sweet to offer. You two just stay here and . . . enjoy each other. Meredith, come help me please. Let's leave the kids alone, shall we?"

"This sucks!" said Meredith.

"Merry! Language!"

"Sorry."

Meredith got up and followed her mother into the kitchen. Sam was a little perplexed by the warm—yet decidedly bizarre—way they were treating her, but she chose to simply enjoy it rather than question it further.

Minutes later, at the dinner table, Ross had to tell his parents to stop asking Sam questions long enough so that she could get a mouthful of food. He called it the Gordon Inquisition. Too bad for him, they then used that opportunity to tell embarrassing stories about Ross from his childhood.

"Rossy was always a finicky eater," said Paula.

"Mom!" said Ross.

"Finicky? Paula, the boy ate matches, for God's sake," said Bob.

"Oh, Bob. He only ate matches when he was anxious!"

"You ate matches?" Sam asked.

"Some kids play with matches," said Bob. "Our kid ate them."

"Dad!"

"Son, it's true. We were concerned."

"And he wonders why he has a sensitive stomach!" said Paula.

"Okay guys, that's—"

"Well, you do," said Paula. "He does," she repeated to Sam.

"He eats the entire apple, core and all," Meredith volunteered.

"Thank you, Meredith. I don't believe anyone asked you," Ross said. "Sam, I have no idea what they're talking about. Lies, all lies."

"He swallows his gum!" cried Meredith.

"You swallow your gum?" asked Sam.

"No. Sometimes. Yes."

"Tell her what you did with your contact lenses!" said Meredith.

"But you wear glasses," said Sam.

"Yes, I do wear glasses. Now. Because I drank my contact lenses."

"You *drank* your contact lenses?"

"More than once!" said Meredith.

"But how—"

"I put them in a glass of water, and . . . what? I was thirsty! They're *invisible*!"

Sam was laughing so hard she thought the potato salad might come out through her nose. Ross couldn't help but laugh at himself.

After the warm apple pie dessert (definitely not on the Kate Rose diet plan), Sam offered to bring the dishes into the kitchen and insisted that Paula stay seated. Paula then insisted that Meredith help Sam.

"Again? This totally sucks," Meredith whined. "I mean, sorry, this totally stinks!"

As the two girls placed the dishes in the sink, Sam looked

out the kitchen window at the backyard, which had an old-fashioned charcoal barbecue and a plastic yellow and red jungle gym. Meredith noticed Sam looking out the window.

"My mother refuses to get rid of that piece of junk jungle gym. I haven't used it in forever. It's her way of denying the fact that I'm pretty much a grown-up now."

Sam laughed. *Ah, to be thirteen again*, she thought. Although it was only five years ago, to Sam it seemed like thirteen was a world away, and you certainly couldn't pay her to go back to high school.

"And my dad refuses to get rid of the old barbecue," Meredith continued. "He loves it. It's rusty, and so I think it's probably poisonous, but I guess everyone in this family has, like, separation anxiety or something."

"I understand that," said Sam.

"Can I ask you something?" asked Meredith.

"Sure."

"You seem pretty cool."

"Um, thanks."

"And you're like pretty and everything."

"Thanks again?"

"So, like, what are you doing with my brother? He is such a weirdo."

"What do you mean? Ross is great! I don't have siblings, so I think you're lucky to have a big brother. Plus, I would be totally lost without him at work."

"No, but I mean, why would you want to be his *girlfriend*? He's never even had one before."

Ross had told his family that Sam was his girlfriend? So that's why they were so excited to meet her! Before Sam even had time to process the information, Paula came into the kitchen, carrying the last of the dishes.

"What are you girls chatting about in here?"

"None of your beeswax," said Meredith.

She left for the dining room, leaving Sam, trapped, in the kitchen with Paula.

"Sam," Paula said. "I just want to reiterate how glad I am to have met you. I must be honest and say that I have never seen Ross so happy, at least not since he won the state finals with his debate team. But that was an entirely different kind of euphoria. I'm sure you've noticed he's so . . . cynical for a nineteen-year-old. I have no idea where he gets it. But since he met you, he's like a different person."

"Thanks," Sam muttered. "I mean, glad I can . . . help."

Paula put her arm around Sam's shoulders and kissed her on the cheek. While Sam actually needed a good hug, she couldn't help feeling surprised and conflicted, not to mention embarrassed. What exactly had he told them?

Back at the table, Ross smiled at Sam. She looked away.

CHAPTER TWENTY-SIX

AARON ALTMAN: *I grant you everything. But give me this:*
he personifies everything that you've been fighting against.
And I'm in love with you. How do you like that? I buried the lead.
—BROADCAST NEWS

"Sam, is something wrong?" asked Ross.

They were back in Ross's truck on the 405 Freeway heading toward Beverly Hills and Uncle Norman's.

"You didn't say anything through all of dessert," Ross went on. "Did my mom say something to upset you?"

"No."

"Did Meredith?"

"No, Ross, it's fine. Let's just drop it, okay?"

Ross looked over at Sam. She rolled down her window. As the wind blew her hair away from her face, she self-consciously tucked a lock behind her right ear. She could feel Ross looking at her.

"Did I do something wrong?" he asked.

Sam couldn't hold it in any longer.

"Aside from telling your entire family that I'm your girl-friend?"

"Sam, I can explain."

"Ross, don't bother. I mean, how could you put me in that position? Your family was so wonderful to me, and then I find out they think I'm something—someone—I'm not? I'm having a tough enough time out here remembering who I am, and now . . . I mean, what was I supposed to say?"

"I'm sorry, Sam. They just assumed, because I always talk about you—"

"It doesn't matter anymore. You let them believe it, what-ever it was. And now you made me a liar too. Ross, I just don't think of you like that, in that way."

"But maybe . . . I mean, we have so much fun together. And you're so unlike other girls. Sam, you're special. I just thought—"

"Well, you thought wrong, okay? I've got to be honest, Ross, not that you afforded me or your family that courtesy. The thing is, I'm in love with someone else."

There, she said it.

Ross looked like he had just been punched in the stomach. He stared straight ahead. Sam stared out the window. She couldn't believe what she had just said. Was it even true?

"What, you're in love with *Matt Sullivan*?"

Ross was only joking, but Sam tensed up. She looked over

at him, then, unable to hold his gaze, she looked guiltily out the window again.

"You don't know him," she said.

"And you do?! Sam, you don't have to be with me, but come on, Matt Sullivan? That guy is the worst! He'll just use you, and hurt you. He's dishonest. He's manipulative. He's not smart. He's completely self-involved. *And* he's an ineffective assistant!"

Ross hit the steering wheel in frustration. Sam remained silent. She didn't want to believe what Ross was saying.

Sam had lost her last ally and her only other friend. Kate was mad at her and obsessed with the only boy Sam had ever really liked or loved or hated or whatever it was she felt for Matt Sullivan at this point. Maybe once she talked to Matt, it would all be clear. Surely, Matt would have called and left a message for her at Uncle Norman's house by now. Would it be too late to call him back by the time she got home?

Sam and Ross drove the rest of the way back to Beverly Hills in silence. When they arrived at Uncle Norman's, they could barely look at each other.

"I'll see you tomorrow," said Sam.

"Yeah. See ya."

But Sam still couldn't get her car door open. Ross took off his seat belt and stepped out of the truck to let her out the driver's side. He offered to help her down, but she climbed out on her own. Once they were on level ground, they stood face-to-face.

"So, bye," said Sam.

Ross raised his hand as she ran into the house. Before closing the front door behind her, Sam watched as Ross got back in his truck and laboriously maneuvered it out of the driveway.

When Sam entered the house, Uncle Norman was reading in the living room.

"Sammy! Where's the funeral?"

"Hi, Uncle Norman."

"Everything okay? You look like you just lost your best friend."

"I'm okay. Did anyone call for me, by any chance?"

"Well, I spoke to your dad earlier, but otherwise no."

"Are you sure? I mean you were probably out at some point, right?"

"Well, I went to play golf this morning. But there were no messages when I got home. Were you expecting to hear from someone?"

"Yeah, kind of."

"Well, it's only ten-thirty, you never know. Is your friend a night owl?"

"I don't know. Maybe. Is Kate here?"

"No, Kate is sleeping over at Dylan's house, so you're on your own tonight. Well, I hope your friend doesn't call too late. I'm going to sleep."

Norman got up from the couch, gave Sam a hug, and then continued up the stairs to his bedroom. Sam checked the answering machine in the kitchen: nothing. She grabbed a bottle of Evian out of the fridge and went upstairs to her room. Manuela was off on Sundays, and Kate had left the room in a total mess, so Sam cleared a path through the strewn clothes and shoes, and fell onto her bed. She stared up at the ceiling.

He wouldn't just *not* call, right? After all, he promised. You don't just give a girl a romantic piggyback ride and then not call! And Sam's treatment . . . had he read it? Sam had always been in a hurry to grow up, but if this was any indication of what adulthood was going to be like, she decided that maybe high school wasn't so tough after all.

CHAPTER TWENTY-SEVEN

MARC ANTONY: *This was the most unkindest cut of all.*
—SHAKESPEARE, *Julius Caesar* (III,ii,187)

Sam was dreading going back to Authentic Pictures on Monday morning. Once again, Matt Sullivan had disappointed her. And she knew she had set herself up for it this time. It didn't help that she slept through the snooze on her alarm clock that morning, making her twenty minutes late to work.

Sam didn't see Ross's truck parked in the lot behind the building when she arrived, but Alexandra's car was there already. Sam entered the office through the back door, and upon entering the copy room, she found Alexandra looking through her desk! Sam knew she didn't care for her, but rifling through her desk took the dislike to a whole other level. Sam cleared her throat loudly.

"Oh, Sam. Good morning," said Alexandra.

"Did you find what you were looking for?" asked Sam.

"Um. No. Paper clips?"

Sam walked over to her and picked up the box of paper clips that was on the desk right in front of her face.

"Thanks. Oh, and BTW, Ross called—his truck broke down on the 405. He's not going to be in for a while. And Matt has a dentist appointment this morning. I told him I'd watch his phones, but Rob really needs me, so you'll have to sit in for Matt."

"But . . . I don't know how to roll calls."

"You'll learn. You're a smart girl, aren't you, Sam? I mean, what would *Dickens* do in this situation?"

The D-witch in training was even more evil than the D-witches themselves. Sam had never rolled calls before, although she had watched Matt rolling with Lawrence.

On Sam's way to Matt's desk, Ellen walked in, toting her Gucci dog carrier with Princess Cujo inside, already barking. Rebecca arrived moments later and gave Ellen a one-armed hug. Princess Cujo almost bit Rebecca's finger off when she reached in the bag to tap her on the head. It was just another dog-eat-D-witch day in Hollywood.

Sam took a deep breath as she stood over Matt Sullivan's desk, which was a mess as usual. Multicolored Post-it notes lined his cubicle walls and computer frame, and papers were scattered everywhere. Luckily, Amy had just walked in, and she came over to help. First, Amy pulled up Lawrence's calendar for

Sam on Matt's computer. Turns out, Lawrence had an appointment with his therapist that morning, so he wouldn't be calling in for another thirty minutes or so. Sam hoped that might give Ross enough time to get back, but it was unlikely, given the truck's track record.

Amy gave Sam a crash course in rolling calls. Amy explained that rolling calls was simply connecting Lawrence with another call, and then listening in on the conversation. It became tricky, however, when other calls came in while he was in the middle of a call, and she would have to put Lawrence (who expected his assistant to hear everything and be available to him the moment he got off the call) on hold. Add an ill-fitting headset, a sticky mute button, and pressure to the equation, and it could be a recipe for disaster. Amy showed Sam Lawrence's call sheet, which illustrated to whom he owed calls, and from whom he was waiting to hear back. From her adjacent cubicle, Alexandra watched Amy trying to show Sam the basics and snickered at them while simultaneously staring at Rob, who was flexing his muscles and looking at his reflection in his office mirror.

"Amy, we really need you over here," said Ellen.

"Yeah, we have stuff we need you to do?" said Rebecca.

Princess Cujo yapped.

As Amy apologized and left Sam's side, Lawrence's phone rang. Sam put on the headset, adjusted the mouthpiece—pausing briefly to appreciate/lament that Matt Sullivan's mouthpiece was just inches from her own mouth, and then to realize how monumentally pathetic she had become—took a deep breath and picked up the call.

"Lawrence Miller's office," said Sam.

"Who is this?"

There was loud street noise in the background.

"This is Sam, may I ask who is calling?"

"It's Lawrence. Where's Matt?"

"He had a dentist's appointment this morning. I thought you had your shr—I mean, I thought you had an appointment."

"My shrink is not on my side. Everyone is now officially against me. So I will no longer be seeing him. I refuse to pay someone to make my life more difficult. I have you people for that."

Sam heard Lawrence's car door slam. The street noise was replaced by the sound of his BMW's ignition, followed by the clear and soothing sound of waves.

"I hate this ambient music! It always makes me have to go to the bathroom!" he yelled as the sound of the waves faded. "Enough chitchat. Who do I owe? And do I have a meeting? What time is the *Stealing Mars* premier tonight?"

"The screening is in Westwood at seven-thirty, the party will follow. And you have a meeting at Warner Brothers, but not until eleven A.M."

"I'll head over now. I need directions. In the meantime, connect me to Steve Press."

Sam scoured the call sheet but could find no one with that name.

"Um, he's not on your call sheet, Mr. Miller."

"Um, he's the president of production at one of the major studios, Samantha? And call me Lawrence. Mr. Miller makes me feel like my father. I hate my father."

"Okay."

Lawrence huffed into his earpiece. Sam put him on hold and desperately flipped through the *Creative Directory*, which had all the names and numbers of anyone who was anyone (or assisting anyone) in the film industry. With Lawrence on hold on the first line, Sam dialed Steve's office, spoke to his assistant, who got Steve on the phone, and then connected them.

"Alexandra," Sam called.

Alexandra pretended she didn't hear her.

"Alexandra!"

Alexandra looked up and around as if she could hear that someone was trying to get her attention but didn't know where the voice was coming from.

"Does *anyone* know how to get to Warner Brothers?" Sam shouted.

The phone rang again. She had taken her headset off and hadn't been listening to Lawrence's conversation. She put Lawrence and Steve's line on hold.

"Lawrence Miller's office."

"Samantha. Have they heard of a mute button where

you're from? Or are you doing this just to make my life more miserable?"

"I'm sorry, Mr. Miller, it won't happen again, I promise."

"Get Steve back on for me. And for God's sake, use the mute button."

Sam got Steve back on the phone.

"Mr. Miller, you're on with Mr. Press."

Sam went to put her headset on mute, only she pressed the "release" button by accident. Both men were cut off.

"No!" she yelled.

Sam put her hands over her eyes, as if that would erase what had just happened. She heard a giggle from behind her. Alexandra was watching her while pretending to read a script with her feet up on her desk. The phone rang again. Sam cringed as she picked up the phone.

"Lawrence Miller's office?"

"Did God put you on this earth for the sole purpose of destroying me? Just tell me one thing, I am about to get on the freeway from Santa Monica to get to the valley. What do I take, north or south? I always forget."

Sam hadn't even driven on the freeway yet, nor did she have a great sense of direction. She put Lawrence on mute and made a final attempt to get Alexandra's attention.

"Alexandra, please help me, which way on the freeway from Santa Monica to the valley?"

"South."

"Thank you, you are such a lifesaver."

Maybe Alexandra wasn't so bad after all.

"South," Sam told Lawrence with confidence.

"Fine, I'll call you once I get on the freeway."

Lawrence hung up. Sam breathed a brief sigh of relief. She tried to straighten up Matt's desk and get organized before Lawrence called back again. This time, she was determined to be ready for him, mute button and all. She was about to go to MapQuest to find exact directions but got sidetracked when she opened Matt's e-mail account by accident. She peeked at his out-box—she was only human, after all. The last e-mail sent was to Lawrence, entitled "*Weird Science* for Girls treatment." When Sam opened it, she saw her treatment word for word, with a note from Matt asking Lawrence to take a look at it. Her name was nowhere to be found on the treatment or in the e-mail. Was Matt Sullivan trying to pass off her idea as his own?

The phone rang again. Sam knew it would be Lawrence, but she wasn't sure she could get the words out.

"Lawrence Miller's office."

"I'm going the wrong way!" he screamed. "I asked you one simple question, just one—"

"But I was told you should go south."

"I said north," said Alexandra.

"No, you did not!" yelled Sam.

She was still staring in awe at Matt Sullivan's computer and the e-mail he had sent to Lawrence. Was he just using her all along?

"Samantha, if I ever find my way out of this freeway hell, you are fired! Did you hear me? Fired!"

But Sam wasn't listening anymore. In a daze, she took off her headset while Lawrence continued yelling. She went into the copy room, got her belongings, and left Authentic Pictures without so much as a good-bye to anyone. She knew Lawrence would call the D-witches himself and tell them what happened. His version, anyway.

Hollywood had won: Samantha Rose was going home.

CHAPTER TWENTY-EIGHT

ANDIE WALSH: *I just want to let them know that they didn't break me.* —PRETTY IN PINK

As Sam drove back to Uncle Norman's house, she thought about how she might explain to her parents why she was coming home two weeks early. She wondered if Jean would still hire her to work at Fine Vintage like she had in past summers. She thought about summer nights alone in her bedroom, reading all her favorite authors and eating her mother's minestrone. The thought was certainly comforting, but surprisingly, it now left Sam feeling a bit empty. She wasn't so sure she would be satisfied by that anymore. She liked having friends her age. She liked being independent. And while many of the executives at Authentic tried to make her feel trivial and insignificant, she had enjoyed the aspects of film development in which she was involved, and she was intrigued by the world of Hollywood, even by the uncertain future it offered her. But how could she stay now? She was convinced that Kate and Ross both hated her, and Matt Sullivan had stolen her idea, her hard work, and her heart. And anyway, she didn't have much of a choice—she had been fired.

Sam drove through Beverly Hills, past the Coffee Bean on Beverly Drive, where they now knew her name and her complicated CBIB drink by heart. She pulled up to Uncle Norman's house to find the driveway empty. Sam let herself in with her house key and heard the vacuum going upstairs. She followed the noise to the guest room, where she found Manuela sitting on the end of Kate's bed with the vacuum running next to her, as she watched her Spanish soap opera. She jumped when Sam entered the room.

"Sorry, Manuela. I didn't mean to scare you."

"*¿Samita, no estas trabajando hoy día?*"

"*No trabaje*, Manuela."

"*¿Mañana?*"

"I go today . . . *Yo voy?*"

"*¿Dónde?*"

"Home."

Manuela understood that word and turned off the vacuum.

"I help you," she said.

"You speak English?" asked Sam.

"Sure."

"Why didn't you say anything before?"

Manuela shrugged and went downstairs to get Sam's wash

for her to pack as Sam started gathering her things. She looked at the single drawer that Kate had given her the first day she arrived. It seemed like years ago that she had unpacked into it. She folded the designer jeans and sexy tops that Kate had bought for her, even though she couldn't imagine where she would wear them back in Northampton. In gathering her cosmetics, she came upon Kate's gooey suntan lotion. She unscrewed the cap and smelled it. It reminded her of the freedom she'd felt, the naive optimism she'd had, and her first attempt at upping her chill factor. She put the lotion back on the shelf and continued packing until all that was left of Sam's was the black crochet top that Kate had borrowed the night they went out with Tatiana and Dylan for the first time. She laid it out on Kate's bed to leave for her and picked up the phone to call a cab.

"This had better be good."

Sam turned around to see Kate standing in the doorway with one of her fuchsia velour sweatpants legs pulled up over her knee. Sam put the phone down.

"So? Manuela got me out of my waxing appointment. She said it was an emergency. Have you ever walked around with only one leg waxed, Sam? It's VERY disorienting."

"I'm sorry. I didn't realize she was calling you. I was going to leave you a note."

"Where are you going?"

"I'm going home. I'm . . . I'm really sorry, Kate . . . for the way I've acted. I never gave Matt Sullivan your phone number. I lied to you."

Kate walked into the room and sat down on Sam's bed.

"Is that why you're going home, Cuz? That's crazy. I am totally over him. I talked to him again after you left the party that night, and he was, like, a total snooze. And his pores were, like, really big. Anyway, then I met another boy. He was one of the dragons. He's a struggling actor, and he's adorable. I wanted to tell you, but we kept missing each other over the weekend. And last night, I had to drive Dylan and her dog, Springsteen, to the animal emergency room. She thought he had a tumor."

"Oh my God, is he okay?"

"Yeah, it was actually his belly button."

"Wow."

"Yeah."

Sam laughed to herself. And here she thought Kate and the girls hated her. She was really going to miss them. She sat down on the bed next to Kate.

"So, what else is it, Sammy? Doe?"

"Kate, Matt Sullivan is Doe. Doe is Matt Sullivan. Surprise!"

Kate jumped up and pointed at Sam.

"I knew it! I totally knew it! But you didn't say anything, so I wasn't sure. You little devil! His pores really weren't that big, I just have, like, *really* good vision. And he wasn't that boring, I mean, he wasn't *not* boring, but I'm sure he's cool."

"He's not."

"He's not not boring?"

"No, he's not so cool."

"What happened?"

"I think he stole my idea."

Kate sat down and listened while Sam told her the whole story. Kate was outraged.

"That's it! I'm calling Norman."

"No, Kate, please, let's not involve him."

"He's a lawyer, Sammy. He can tell us how to approach this whole situation. And he can tell us how to take this guy down."

Kate loved a good fight even more than she loved carbs.

"But I'm not so sure I want to do that to him," said Sam. "I mean, we're talking about ruining someone's career here."

"What? After all this, you still like the guy?"

"Like you didn't still have feelings for Colby even after the losing-your-virginity debacle/disaster/disappointment?"

"That's a low blow, Sammy. But I guess you're right: I still wanted him to like me as much as I liked him. What girl doesn't want that? Ugh, why are we all such masochists?"

"I don't know. I've never been like this before. I can't stand it."

"I know. Sometimes, I truly loathe boys. But you know what makes it a whole lot easier?" asked Kate.

"No, what?"

"Revenge! Grab your treatment, Sammy. Let's get a CBIB and discuss our next move."

Kate smiled that mischievous smile that Sam had come to both love and fear. Kate put her arm around Sam, who leaned her head on Kate's shoulder. Sam looked over at her packed bag and single empty drawer.

"But my suitcase . . ."

"Cuz, you can unpack later. Besides, I could really use that extra drawer."

"Not on your life!" said Sam.

The girls climbed into Kate's convertible. On their descent through the hills, Sam saw a figure running slowly and laboriously toward them, but he wasn't in jogging clothes. As they got closer, Sam told Kate to slow down. She looked carefully at the boy in the khaki pants and plaid short-sleeved, button-down shirt trudging up the hill. He was sweating profusely and completely winded.

"Ross?"

"Sam," he said. "Sam (*wheeze*), Amy told me (*wheeze*) . . . you left (*wheeze*) . . . and (*wheeze*) . . . Matt stole your . . . I (*wheeze*) saw his computer. . . ."

"Spit it out, would you?" said Kate.

"Don't go!" blurted Ross.

"But Ross—" Sam started.

"I love y—, your idea. You can't leave! You can't let them beat you. We have to fight."

Ross leaned with his hands on his knees trying desperately and dramatically to catch his breath.

"We're just going to The Coffee Bean," said Kate.

"Oh," said Ross.

"I'm not leaving, Ross. I'm going to fight."

"Well, all right then," he said.

"Hop in," said Kate. "You're an accomplice now."

Ross climbed in the back, still dripping with sweat.

"Where's your truck anyway?" asked Sam.

"It didn't make it up the hill. It's on the side of the road."

"Ross . . ."

"I know, I gotta get a new car. One battle at a time, Sammy, one battle at a time."

The girls looked at each other, and Kate put the gas pedal to the floor. This was war.

CHAPTER TWENTY-NINE

All is not lost; th' unconquerable will,
And study of revenge, immortal hate,
And courage never to submit or yield.
—MILTON, *Paradise Lost*

Armed with frothy CBIBs and low-carb biscotti, Kate, Sam, and Ross walked into the swanky law offices of Rose, Abate, Lee, Leshko, Lederman, Berman, Hirsch, Oppenheim, Underwood, Fritz, Boyer, Brewster, Pearl, Sachs, Switzenbaum, Schuon, Ruckdeschel, Rodigari, Goldspink & Associates. The office was on the top floor of a highrise in Century City. Tinted floor-to-ceiling windows revealed breathtaking views of Santa Monica, endless white beaches, and the blue-green ocean. Kate, still in her matching velour sweat suit with only one leg waxed, walked purposefully up to the front desk.

"Kate Rose and colleagues to see Norman Rose. It's an emergency."

"Hold on please," replied the receptionist.

Kate, Sam, and Ross leaned on the black marble desk, their eyes trained intently on the woman behind it. Ross took a long final slurp of his drink. It made a loud sucking noise. The receptionist looked up at him, annoyed.

"Sorry," he said.

"Mr. Rose will be with you in a moment. You can take a seat," she said.

As they made their way to the forest green couches, Alice Walker, Norman's assistant, entered the lobby. While Alice and Kate had spoken often over the phone, they had never met in person. Alice was a petite woman, but she had a commanding voice and walked quickly with purpose. She oozed efficiency.

"Kate?"

"Hi, Alice, nice to finally meet you," said Kate. "Is he ready for us?"

"Yes, but he has a conference call in five minutes, so you're going to have to make it quick. Sorry."

"What a surprise. We just need a brief consultation with legal counsel."

"Okay, follow me then."

On the right side of the hall was each attorney's office. Across the hall from each office was the cubicle for their assistant. R, A, L, L, L, B, H, O, U, F, B, B, P, S, S, S, R, R, G, & Assoc. was the most respected entertainment law firm in Los Angeles. The office operated like an expensive European sports car: powerful yet silent and smooth. Kate carried herself as if she were wearing an Armani suit, even though she was still in her velour "leisure wear." Sam and Ross both felt underdressed and out of place in the immaculate and hushed surroundings. Alice led them to the corner office, where Norman was just getting off a phone call. He pointed at them to sit down on the couch and chairs across from his desk. It was warm in his office, and Sam could feel beads of sweat accumulating on the tip of her nose again. *Oh God, please let the air go on soon*, she thought.

Sam and Ross sat on the plush couch while Kate walked around inspecting the office. She hadn't been there since she was a little girl, and it had been renovated several times since then.

Kate was surprised to see framed photos on Norman's desk and on the walls of his office: Kate at nine years old at summer camp, Kate at thirteen standing with Norman after a school play carrying a dozen roses, Kate at her sweet sixteen party wearing a tiara, and Kate in her cap and gown graduating from high school. She had no idea he even had these photos, let alone that he cared enough to have them framed and displayed, jeopardizing the minimalist aesthetic for which he was constantly striving.

"I have to jump, my meeting just walked in," Norman said into his headset, "but I promise you, I'll get in to it. *Ciao*."

He threw his headset onto his desk. His suit jacket was on the back of his chair and his tie was loosened.

"Hi, honey," he said to Kate. He got up from behind his desk and awkwardly went over to Kate to give her a hug. He then leaned on the edge of his desk. Kate fell into the chair next to Sam.

"Hi, Norman. Nice pictures. I didn't know you—"

"Cared?"

"Yeah."

Father and daughter stared at each other. The gloves were on, as usual.

"Hi, Sam," said Norman.

"Hi, Uncle Norman. This is my friend Ross Gordon. He works with me at Authentic. Or, I *used* to work with him at Authentic."

"Hi, Ross. What do you mean, 'used to'?"

"I got fired today."

"But you're not getting paid!"

"I know."

"That's the least of our worries, Norman," said Kate. "Please, have a seat. We are here to seek legal counsel. For several issues."

"Okay, how can I help?" he asked, an amused smile on his face.

"Lawrence's assistant, one Matt Sullivan," Kate began.

"I've spoken to him," interrupted Norman. "Nice enough kid. Ineffective assistant, though."

Ross elbowed Sam and mouthed, "See?"

Sam put her finger to her lips and shushed him. Kate continued by telling Norman the whole story as Sam had told it to her. Between what Kate had learned from watching Court TV and what she had discovered on the Internet when they surfed the Web on the computer at The Coffee Bean, she confidently threw around terms like "copyright infringement" and pointed out that Matt e-mailing Sam's treatment to outside parties was "wrongful dissemination of material in order to benefit financially." Norman sat back in his chair, listened intently, and halfway through Kate's filibuster, broke into a smile.

"What? Why are you smiling? Are you laughing at me?"

"No, I'm just proud. I haven't seen you this passionate about something since you discovered boys."

"Thanks. But you're changing the subject."

"You're right. I'm sorry," said Norman.

Alice knocked and opened the door a crack.

"Mr. Rose, I have your conference call holding."

"Alice, tell them we have to reschedule. My daughter needs me."

Alice looked flabbergasted, but she ducked out and closed the door quietly behind her. Kate stared after her in awe. Her father never canceled conference calls for her. But then again, she had never really asked him to.

"So, what should we do?" asked Kate. "Sue his ass, right?"

"The problem here, kids, is that there's nothing really to sue for. There are no damages per se—"

"But he stole my treatment!" Sam said.

"I know that, Sammy, but it's not like he stole it, made it into a film, and reaped financial benefits from it. There is nothing to sue for at this point."

"But what about copyright infringement? Wrongful dissemination of material?" asked Kate. She wanted to get her money's worth out of her new fancy terminology.

"Sammy, he may have tried to pass off your idea as his own, and I understand you're hurt, but the goal is to stay out of court. And considering Lawrence is my client, there is certainly a conflict here and I have to think about his interests as well. Sammy, I can get you your job back. Lawrence can be temperamental, but believe it or not, at the end of the day, he's not a bad guy. Why don't you leave a copy of the treatment with me? I'd like to read it. But in the meantime, I think you need to confront this Matt Sullivan on your own, tell him what you saw, and hear what he has to say."

"So, no court?" asked Kate.

"No court," said Norman.

"Damn!" said Kate. "I could have testified. I would make a great witness."

"Frankly, I think you would make a great lawyer," said Norman. "Sam, Ross, would you give us a moment?"

"Yes, of course," said Sam.

Sam and Ross stood up. Sam left Norman a copy of her

treatment, and she and Ross exited his office. Norman sat down in the chair next to Kate.

"Kate, first of all, I want to thank you for taking such good care of your cousin, for involving her in your life and looking after her. It really means a lot to me."

"Are you seeing a new therapist?" Kate asked.

"No, I'm just trying to tell you that I know it's been a tough couple of years where our relationship is concerned, but I love you. And I wish you'd let me. I'm willing to work at it if you are."

These were the words Kate had been hoping to hear since she was fifteen.

"In the meantime," Norman continued, "and I don't want to push you into this, I just want to offer it to you as an idea. I know you've been bored this summer, and all your friends are doing other things. You seem to be interested in the law, in spite of me. Why don't you intern here for the rest of the summer? We could see each other every day. You could see if being a lawyer is a profession you might want to explore."

Kate had never thought about being a lawyer. That was always Norman's thing. Sure, she loved Court TV and she loved arguing, but Kate had never had an actual *job* before. Was he really suggesting they spend more time together? Did he really believe in her? Kate, a lawyer? She kind of loved the idea.

"Okay, yeah. That sounds cool. So, you'd be, like, my boss?" Kate tried to sound blasé.

"I'd be, like, your father."

"Oh. That's cool."

"I think we're supposed to hug now."

"Thanks, Dad."

"It's a business doing pleasure with you," he said.

"Ha-ha," said Kate.

Kate and her father hugged in the middle of his office. Kate then slipped outside to join Sam and Ross in the reception area.

"Everything okay?" asked Sam. "Is he mad?"

"No. He hired me."

"What?" asked Ross.

"I'm going to be a lawyer!"

"That's great, Cuz!" said Sam. "But you might want to get that other leg waxed first."

"Such a good point," said Kate. "Now let's go kick some Matt Sullivan ass!"

CHAPTER THIRTY

*She felt the loss of Willoughby's character yet more heavily
than she had felt the loss of his heart.*
—JANE AUSTEN, *Sense and Sensibility*

By the time that Kate, Sam, and Ross got to Authentic Pictures, all the executives had already left, and only the assistants remained. Lawrence never actually came into the office that day (probably too emotionally exhausted from the morning's precarious therapy and freeway incidents). Not to mention that he had to primp before the *Stealing Mars* premier that evening.

"Okay, so this is the plan," Kate said. "Sammy, you confront and distract Matt in the conference room. Ross, you sneak onto Matt's computer and print out the e-mail that he got from Sam and the one he sent out to Lawrence. I'll distract the headband-wearing-D-witch-in-training. Got it?"

"Got it," said Ross and Sam.

"Okay, break!" said Kate.

Sam couldn't believe she had to accuse Matt Sullivan of stealing her idea. How and why did it have to come to this? She took a deep breath and entered the office, which silenced when she walked in.

"What are *you* doing back?" asked Alexandra.

"I don't believe it's any of your business," Sam retorted.

Alexandra's mouth dropped open, and she huffed loudly.

"Hey!" said Amy. "I thought we lost you!"

"Nah, can't get rid of me that easily," replied Sam.

Sam walked over to Matt Sullivan's desk. He looked up as she reached his cubicle.

"Sam! Hi . . . I was going to call you. I'm so sorry to hear what happened this morning."

"Yeah, I kind of want to talk to you about that. Can we go into the conference room?"

"Sure. Is everything okay?"

Sam didn't answer. Matt Sullivan followed her into the conference room. She sat down, facing the glass wall of the room so that she could see out to the office. Everything seemed to be going according to plan: Kate was distracting Alexandra by attempting to snoop around Rob's office; Alexandra was in a complete tizzy as Kate started playing with Rob's barbells. Meanwhile, Ross had sneaked over to Matt's computer.

Matt Sullivan sat down across from Sam. She hated him with every ounce of her being. She hated that she had been naive enough to trust him. She hated that he lied to her so blatantly. She hated that she had so eagerly bought into the Matt Sullivan mystique. And most of all, she hated that part of herself that still truly believed there had to be some explanation for his behavior. After everything that had happened, she still wanted to believe the best of him. But right now, she had to stay strong, stern, and thick-skinned.

"So, you know I had to fill in for you this morning?"

"Yeah, Lawrence told me. He mentioned something about wrong directions and mute buttons and firing you. I didn't really listen. I just talked him down and told him he was crazy to fire you. I told him how great I think you are, how smart you are, and how hard you've worked."

"Thanks," Sam said.

Wait, why was she thanking him? Where was this conversation going? And how was he suddenly steering it? Sam looked out across the office at Ross and Kate. Kate looked over at her and gave her the thumbs-up sign, while Ross was nervously hunched over Matt's computer.

"I mean, thanks for putting in a good word for me, Matt, but—"

"Always, Sam. You know, I'm your biggest fan."

If Matt Sullivan was her biggest fan, Sam was terrified to meet her worst enemy. And if he was really her biggest fan, why did he try to steal all her hard work? And more importantly, why didn't he love her?

"So, was there something else?" Matt asked.

Sam's head was spinning. *Focus*, she thought to herself, *focus*.

"Yes, there is."

"Hit me," he said.

She kind of wanted to, but she took a deep breath and dove right in.

"So, when I was at your desk this morning, I accidentally saw your e-mail account. I'm really not a snoop or anything, and it's not like I was looking for anything, I was just trying to find directions for Lawrence. And I saw my treatment. And that you e-mailed it to Lawrence as your idea."

"Are you kidding?" he asked. He leaned forward and looked her straight in the eye. "I don't know what you're talking about! I can't believe you would think I would ever do that. I never even got your treatment. I thought you forgot to e-mail it to me."

"But, Matt, I saw it with my own eyes," said Sam. "I saw that you e-mailed it word for word to Lawrence as your idea."

"Sam, I don't know what to say. You must have seen wrong. I would never do that. Especially not to you. I mean, I got an A in ethics at Harvard. I don't go stealing anyone's ideas."

"But Ross saw it too," she said.

"Sam, you know, Ross is a little sweet on you, in case you hadn't noticed. Plus, he's a 'yes' man. And he feels threatened by me. He was probably just saying that he saw what you saw because he'd like to see me fired. If you don't believe me, you can check my e-mail account, and check Lawrence's. I can take you into his office right now. I mean, do you really think I would do something so underhanded? Risk my career? Risk our relationship?"

They had a relationship? Matt Sullivan looked sincere and concerned, even hurt by Sam's suspicions. Plus, he did have a point about Ross. Ross did hate him and would have loved to see him "burn."

"Well, no, and that's why I was so surprised. And hurt. And after everything with you and me. . . ."

"Sam, I think you're a really special girl. And I've meant everything I've said. I would never want to hurt you. I believe in you, I really do."

Sam felt sick. Had she been seeing things? Was Ross lying?

"Sam, I talked to Lawrence, and he took back what he said about firing you. I hope you'll continue working here for the rest of the summer. Besides, I'm getting promoted to a creative executive, so I'll have more freedom to really mentor you."

"Promoted? That's great. I mean, congratulations. I mean, thank you, I guess."

"I'm glad you talked to me about this, and that we cleared everything up. So we're cool?"

Matt Sullivan pushed his chair away from the table.

"Yeah, I guess."

As Matt and Sam stood up, Ross crept away from Matt's computer and slipped into the copy room before Alexandra could notice. Kate saw Ross making his move, so she dropped

Rob's barbells and left Rob's office before Alexandra had a full-on conniption.

"By the way, love the headband," Kate said.

Alexandra touched her head self-consciously. She closed the door to Rob's office and locked it with the key she kept on a bright orange lanyard around her neck. Matt Sullivan went back to his cubicle, and Sam walked across the office to the copy room where Ross and Kate met her.

"So?" asked Kate.

"He denied it. He denied everything," said Sam.

"He's even smoother than I thought. Thank God we have the evidence," said Kate.

Both Kate and Sam looked at Ross. Ross went pale and shook his head at the girls.

"What?" asked Kate.

"I couldn't find anything. He must have erased it all. There was no record of any e-mail from Sam, or of the e-mail he sent to Lawrence."

"You're kidding me!" said Kate. "What about Lawrence's e-mail account?"

"I checked that too. No record. Matt must have erased every trace of it."

"I cannot believe this!" said Kate.

"We have a record of Sam sending it to him, but there's no way of confirming if he received it or not," said Ross.

"Maybe he didn't do it?" asked Sam.

"WHAT?" asked Kate and Ross in unison.

"Maybe I saw wrong . . . I was so upset and distracted. Ross, are you sure you saw it?"

"Wait, now you think *I'm* the one who's lying?"

"Well, you do hate Matt," said Sam.

"Time-out, everyone," said Kate. "Let's not go pointing fingers at one another. Let's think about this. Ross, you are sure, beyond a shadow of a doubt, that you saw the same e-mail that Sam saw this morning on Matt's computer?"

"Yes, beyond a shadow of a doubt. Yes." He nodded emphatically.

"Is there anyone else who could have had access to his account?" asked Kate.

"Not really. I mean, the only other person who was here this morning before me was . . ."

"Alexandra," they all said.

"Okay, but what would be her motivation?" asked Sam.

"That she hates you, and wants you fired because she's in love with Rob and she thinks he likes you more than her, and she's threatened by you because you're smarter than she is and she's aligned with the D-witches?" said Ross. "Just a guess."

"Don't bother sugarcoating it for me, Ross, really, I'll be fine."

"This from the girl who just basically called me a liar."

"I never called you a liar!"

"Cut it!" yelled Kate. "Hypothetically, Alexandra could

have forwarded that e-mail to Lawrence from Matt's computer, knowing full well that because he was supposed to see his shrink in the morning, he wouldn't be in to receive it, and that Matt would be out and Sam would see it."

"Yes, but how did she know my truck would break down?" asked Ross.

Sam looked at him and rolled her eyes. It was a pretty good bet that Ross's truck would break down.

"Okay, that's easy, but how did she know I would be late and Sam would have to take over?" asked Ross.

"She could have done it all at the last minute, and then erased all the evidence after Ross saw it but before Matt did," said Kate.

"Wait, but how would she know about my treatment in the first place? And is she really even that smart?" asked Sam.

"She's cunning, not smart," said Ross. "There's a big difference."

"But how can we know for sure?" asked Sam.

The three stood in silence. Unless someone confessed, which was highly unlikely, there was no way of knowing if Matt Sullivan had really attempted to steal Sam's treatment or not.

"He's getting promoted," Sam said.

"WHAT?!" asked Ross.

"Yeah, Sammy, you just buried the lead right there," said Kate.

"He's going to be a creative executive. He says he wants to mentor me," said Sam.

"I'll bet he does," said Ross.

"So, there's nothing we can do?" asked Sam.

They looked at each other, stumped.

"There's one thing we can do," said Ross.

Kate and Sam turned to him expectantly.

"We can still show your treatment to Lawrence."

"But he hates me," said Sam.

"Sam, one thing you'll learn about Hollywood is that people hate you only until they realize you can offer them something of value."

Kate, Ross, and Sam jumped as Matt Sullivan walked into the copy room.

"Am I interrupting?"

"No," said Ross.

"I'm heading out to the premier now. Ross, get Lawrence's phones if they ring, would you?"

"Sure," said Ross.

"Okay, see you guys later."

Matt Sullivan walked out of the copy room just as the phone rang.

"Lawrence Miller's office," said Ross.

"Ross, it's Lawrence. Is Sam still there?"

"Yeah, she's right here."

"Put me on with her."

Ross put Lawrence on hold and looked at Sam.

"It's Lawrence. He wants to talk to you."

"What? Why?"

"Sam, just take the phone."

Sam cringed, took the phone (careful to hold it far enough from her ear in case Lawrence started yelling), and nodded at Ross. He took the call off hold.

"Hello?"

"Samantha. First of all, I wanted to say that what happened this morning was . . . unfortunate. But I'm a forgiving man, and so, you're not fired."

"Oh, thanks," said Sam. She rolled her eyes at Ross and Kate, who looked at her eagerly.

"I'm going to be honest, Samantha, you were not my favorite person. It's not completely your fault. I have trust issues. That's what my therapist says anyway. Of course, I fired him. That aside, your Uncle Norman sent me your treatment."

Sam covered the phone and whispered to Kate and Ross.

"Uncle Norman sent him my treatment!"

"What did he think?" asked Kate.

"*Shhhh!*" said Ross.

"Surprisingly, I think you have a great idea. A little heady, perhaps, but we can always dumb it down later. Now I can't make any promises about your idea, but I'd like you to write this for me on spec, and to keep interning for me."

Sam had learned over the last few weeks that writing something on spec meant that you wrote it for free, with the assumption that you sell it when it's finished and the person who develops it with you is attached as the producer of the project.

"Are you kidding?" asked Sam.

"I don't kid," said Lawrence. "I'm kidding."

Sam didn't know if she should laugh. Was Lawrence actually making a joke? Sam laughed nervously, hedging her bets.

"So, I'm promoting Matt to be my creative executive. He's very smart, ambitious, and well liked, and I'm hoping he'll be a better executive than he is as an assistant. And I'm promoting Ross to be my assistant. So, what do you think?"

"You're getting promoted!" she whispered to Ross.

"I am?" he asked.

Sam's head was swimming. Lawrence actually liked her idea? She would get to develop her own screenplay? But she only had two more weeks of her internship, and then she was supposed to start her freshman year at Smith.

"But I'm supposed to go back to Massachusetts for college in the fall," she said.

"Well, there are colleges in Los Angeles."

"Do you think my internship could count as a class?"

"Samantha, do I sound like a guidance counselor to you?"

College in California? What would Sam's parents say? It was one thing to move into the dorms across the street, it was another thing entirely to move into the dorms across the country.

"Thank you Mr. . . . I mean, Lawrence. I really appreciate it. Do you mind if I take a couple days to think about everything?"

"Take your time," he said. "Listen, why don't you and Ross come to the premier tonight? I'm feeling generous."

"We'd love that. Thanks," said Sam.

"Great. Put Ross back on."

"Okay, bye."

She handed the phone back to Ross.

"Yes, Lawrence. Okay, thanks," said Ross. And with that, he hung up.

"So?" asked Sam.

"Looks like I'm Lawrence's new assistant . . . yeah, I'll burn."

Sam laughed. Kate jumped up and hugged her cousin.

"This is so great! I can't believe it! So, Sammy, are you going to stay? You could live with us! The east wing of the house is nearly done, and we could each have our own room. You could have more than one drawer!"

"But you're going back to Michigan," said Sam. "Aren't you?"

"Oh, yeah. I forgot that part. It's so cold in Michigan."

"Well, nothing is for sure yet, but I'm thinking about it. Oh, and Lawrence invited us to the premier of *Stealing Mars*, you know, his movie starring Ashley Hatcher about the first baseball game in space."

"Sounds like a shoo-in for an Oscar," said Kate. "Well, what are we waiting for, Cuz? We have to go change!"

The girls hugged, grabbed their bags, and ran out of the copy room.

"Come on, Ross!" yelled Sam over her shoulder as the girls rushed out the back door of the office.

CHAPTER THIRTY-ONE

VERONICA SAWYER: *You know what I want?*
Cool guys like you out of my life. —HEATHERS

By the time Sam, Kate, and Ross got back to Uncle Norman's house and changed for the premier, the movie had already started. Kate reassured Sam and Ross that they could just show up at the after party without anyone noticing that they hadn't actually seen the movie. She reminded them to just say they loved it. That's what everyone said anyway.

Kate and Sam changed quickly in their room. Sam dug into her packed suitcase and pulled out her favorite vintage dress and pumps—she hadn't worn them since she arrived in Los Angeles. She borrowed Kate's fitted, white silk jacket that she loved. Sam did her own makeup, using some of her own and some of Kate's liquid blush and super-duper mascara. She looked at her reflection in the mirror. She smiled. She saw herself, now a combination of old and new Sam. And it *totally* worked.

Kate put on one of her own designer dresses with her own stilettos but borrowed some of Sam's vintage costume jewelry.

"Are you sure you don't want to wear my stilettos, Sammy? They look so great on you," said Kate.

"I think I want to walk in my own shoes tonight, Kate. But thank you."

"Are you sure?"

"Kate . . ."

"Okay, okay, I get it. You're you. I'm me."

"BCF?" asked Sam.

"Huh?"

"Best Cousins Forever?"

"Always."

They hugged and then pulled back to look at each other.

"You look great," said Sam.

"No, you look great," said Kate.

"No, you!"

"No, you!"

"No . . ."

"I'm sure you both look great . . . can we go?" asked Ross.

He was waiting in the hallway, outside the guest room. When Sam opened the door, his eyes widened.

"Wow," he said. "You look . . ."

"Great?" suggested Kate.

"Beautiful," he said.

Sam blushed. Ross was wearing a pair of jeans and one of Uncle Norman's blue dress shirts that Kate had fished out of his enormous closet. The shirt brought out the blue in Ross's eyes, and as he pushed his glasses up his nose, Sam imagined him accidentally swallowing his contact lenses and giggled at how cute and sweet he really was.

"You don't look too bad yourself," said Sam.

"Okay, mutual admiration society meeting adjourned for now. Let's go. We don't want to miss the first inning of the party!" said Kate.

She grabbed her jacket, took Sam's hand, and guided them all out of the guest room, down the stairs, outside, and into her car.

Kate valeted at the baseball diamond in Westwood where the premier party was taking place. Kate, Sam, and Ross walked past the red carpet, past the reporters and the ever-present paparazzi, and into the party. In keeping with the baseball-game-in-space theme, there were stands on the periphery of the baseball diamond that offered hot dogs, beer, and orange cocktails made with Tang. Women in scantily clad space-age pseudobaseball uniforms were distributing boxes of Cracker Jacks, bags of peanuts, ice cream Dippin' Dots, and sushi (the Hollywood premier staple hors d'oeuvres served regardless of the genre or theme of film). The crowd at the party was just as bizarre and eclectic as the menu; it was a combination of suits, starlets, space cadets, and everything in between. Sam, now more accustomed to the Hollywood nightlife, was highly amused by the premier party but not at all surprised.

After quickly scanning the crowd, Kate spotted Uncle Norman standing with Lawrence by third base. Kate led Sam and Ross over to them. Norman reintroduced Lawrence to Kate, but Lawrence was focused on Sam.

"Well, well, Samantha. My little screenwriter, how are you?"

"Great, Lawrence. Thanks for inviting us. Excellent party."

"It's miserable. I hate these things. How did you like the movie?"

Sam looked at Kate and Ross nervously. She had learned not to disparage Lawrence's movies after her first disastrous staff meeting. And Kate had told her to say she had seen it. But Sam didn't want to lie anymore. So, she didn't. Instead, she got creative.

"Lawrence, it's really . . . *out of this world.*"

Kate let out a laugh and covered her mouth. She pretended to start coughing to mask her giggles. Sam patted her back (okay, she whacked her) until Kate had controlled herself. Both girls smiled at Lawrence innocently.

"My thoughts exactly. Norman, girls, always a pleasure."

And with that, Lawrence walked away.

"You almost blew it, you freak!" said Sam.

"I know, I'm sorry. Who knew you were so punny?" asked Kate.

"Well, at least I didn't lie! The movie takes place on Mars, right? That's about as out of this world as it gets!"

"Dad, can you believe what a clever niece you have?"

"Actually, I can. Sammy, Lawrence told me the good news. I'm so proud of you. Have you told your parents yet? Your father is going to kill me."

"I haven't had a chance. But I really want to thank you, Uncle Norman. Thank you for all your help, and for passing along my treatment, and for getting me this internship, for everything. I really appreciate it."

"My pleasure, Samantha," he said. "So, Miss Kate Rose, don't be late for work tomorrow morning. I hear the boss is a real stick-in-the-mud."

"Ha-ha," said Kate. "I won't, Dad."

Norman kissed both girls on the head before walking away to find Step Molly.

"Kate! Sam!"

Dylan ran up to the girls. She was dragging a wiry young guy behind her by the hand. He looked a little stunned and out of his element. Dylan's hand-carved cane was gone, her silk sling was nowhere in sight, and she wasn't coughing or hyper-ventilating. Dylan actually looked . . . healthy!

"This is Ben. He's a *healer*!" said Dylan.

"I'm premed," Ben explained.

"We met in the emergency room last night. He *healed* me. Isn't he great?"

"I gave her a Tylenol."

As everyone said hello to one another, Tatiana arrived with an immaculately manicured man in a suit.

"Holler!" Tatiana called.

Sam could have sworn she knew that man with Tatiana from somewhere. But from where?

"Ladies!" she said. "So, guess who just got the lead in a huge studio film?"

The girls all let out squeals and screams as they hugged and congratulated Tatiana. Sam noticed Ross and Ben take a step back from her excited and rowdy group of girls. The boys looked at the group, and then at each other.

"Hey, man," said Ross.

"Hey," said Ben.

They nodded at each other while Sam turned back to the girls to form a group hug. Tatiana's date cleared his throat in her ear, and she removed herself from Kate, Dylan, and Sam's embrace.

"Oh, sorry! Everyone, this is my agent, Michael," said Tatiana.

"Hello, girls. You must be very proud of your friend."

"We're *always* proud of her!" said Kate.

But Agent Michael had already turned away to receive a call on his cell phone. And that's when it hit Sam: it was Mr. Cell

Phone from her plane ride to Los Angeles! Clearly, her vomiting on him had made no impact whatsoever on his terrible cell phone etiquette. Sam turned away from him, just hoping he wouldn't figure out how they knew each other.

"Hey, don't I know you from somewhere?" Agent Michael asked Sam.

"No, I don't think so," said Sam.

This was enough for Agent Michael, who walked off to greet another group of people.

"Tots, he seems so nice!" said Dylan.

"Oh, he's totally full of it," said Tatiana. "But he's a damn good agent."

"A toast!" said Kate. "To Tatiana being the next 'It' girl, to Dylan not being sick or injured, to Sammy staying in LA to be a writer, and to me becoming a lawyer!"

But just as the girls were clinking glasses, Matt Sullivan entered the circle.

"What are *you* doing here?" asked Kate.

"Hi, Kate. How are you?" he asked.

"I'm great. Come on, girls," she said.

Kate grabbed Sam's arm and started to lead her away.

"Sam, can I talk to you for a minute?" he asked. "Please."

Sam looked at Kate and winked confidently. Kate hesitantly let go of her cousin's hand. Sam nodded to Matt Sullivan, who looked at the ground as he led her past home base behind the batting cage. He leaned on the chain-link fence, hooking his right hand into the wiring. He looked up and took a deep breath. Sam thought about her moments with him in the office supplies cage. But instead of butterflies in her stomach and goose bumps on her arms, Sam now felt a deep sense of numbness. She saw Matt Sullivan differently now. She saw herself differently.

"Lawrence told me about your treatment. Congratulations, Sam, you deserve it."

"Thanks."

"Sam, I have a confession to make: I lied to you. I did e-mail your treatment to Lawrence without telling him it was your idea . . . but I only did that because I knew he wouldn't look at it if I told him you wrote it."

"So, you looked me directly in the eye this afternoon and you lied to me? What else did you lie about, Matt? Us? Was that all just some game to you? Was it some messed-up Hollywood rite of passage I had to go through to become an official intern?"

"No. Sam, I'm trying to be honest now. That was the only thing I lied about."

"The A in ethics?"

Matt Sullivan opened his mouth as if to instinctively deny it, but instead, he looked down at the ground. He kicked some dirt with his sneaker.

"C plus."

"You got a C in *ethics*?"

"Plus."

"Why are you telling me all this now, Matt?"

"Because I feel really guilty about everything, and my therapist said I needed to be honest with you in order to clear my conscience."

"So was he telling you to lie to me the last six weeks?"

"No, Sam . . . it's not like that. My spiritual advisor told me that I needed your forgiveness, otherwise I would have bad karma. Or chi. Or something."

"Well, maybe you should think about getting your own opinion for once." Sam started to walk away but stopped in her tracks. She couldn't help herself. She turned around and looked him in the eye. "I *really* liked you, Matt. Do you know that?"

Matt Sullivan was silent. Sam shook her head and smiled.

"Why would you? You don't think about anyone but yourself."

She walked away from Matt Sullivan, who remained seated on the bench in the dugout, alone.

"Sammy! Come dance with us," yelled Kate.

Kate had been watching Sam and Matt from the crowded dance floor. Tatiana was dancing with her, and Dylan was on her stomach trying to do the "Centipede" while Ben clapped along.

"Come on, Sammy!" said Dylan.

"D, break-dancing is so 1984!" said Tatiana. "I LOVE it!"

Sam smiled. For the first time in her life, she really fit in. Who would ever have thought it would be in Hollywood? Sam waved to the girls and headed over to the dance floor. Her vintage pumps were sinking deeper and deeper into the damp soil of the baseball field with each new step, and she almost fell when an arm caught hers.

"Careful," said Ross.

Sam looked up at him. He extended his arm out toward her.

"Shall we?" he asked.

"Don't mind if we do," she said.

Sam linked her arm through his, and they walked toward the dance floor. Once there, Ross clumsily attempted to spin Sam away from him and reel her back in to him. She laughed and gave him a hug. She thought for a moment about the smooth Matt Sullivan who had reeled her in so effortlessly on their very first night together. But now she looked over at her friends who danced around her, and she realized then and there that she just didn't need him anymore.

"So, Sammy, tell us," said Kate. "Are you going to be a writer or are you going to be a D-girl?"

"I don't know yet," said Sam. "Right now, I'm just . . . a girl in development."

Sam breathed in the crisp night air and smiled. She was sure about one thing: this was a whole new ball game.